Arthur D. Hall

Cuba

its past, present, and future

Arthur D. Hall

Cuba
its past, present, and future

ISBN/EAN: 9783337378790

Printed in Europe, USA, Canada, Australia, Japan

Cover: Foto ©Andreas Hilbeck / pixelio.de

More available books at **www.hansebooks.com**

CUBA

IT'S PAST, PRESENT, AND FUTURE

BY

A. D. HALL.

NEW YORK
STREET & SMITH, Publishers
81 Fulton Street

CONTENTS.

CUBA

ITS PAST, PRESENT, AND FUTURE

CHAPTER I.

DISCOVERY AND EARLY HISTORY.

''The goodliest land that eye ever saw, the sweetest thing in the world.''

Such was Columbus' opinion of Cuba, just after he first beheld it, and, after the lapse of four hundred years, the words, making due allowance for the hyperbole of enthusiasm, still hold good. And this, too, in spite of all the trials and tribulations which the fair ''Pearl of the Antilles'' has been forced to undergo at the hands of her greedy and inhuman masters.

The eyes of all the world are now upon this indescribably beautiful and fertile country. Like Andromeda, she has been shuddering and gasping in the power of a monster, but at last a Perseus has come to her rescue. Somewhat tardily perhaps the United States, united now in every meaning of the word, has from pure philanthropy embraced her cause—the United States whose watchword, with a sturdy hatred of the oppressor, has ever been and always will be ''freedom.'' The star of hope, symbolized by the lone star upon the Cuban flag, and so long concealed by gloomy, threatening clouds, is now shining clear and bright; and all civilization is waiting with happy confidence for the day, God willing not far distant, when "Cuba Libre" shall be not only an article of creed, but an established fact.

The island of Cuba, the largest and richest of the West Indian Islands, and up to the present the most important of Spain's colonial possessions, not so vast as they once were but still of no inconsiderable value, was discovered by Columbus during his first voyage to the far west.

For many centuries, even back to the time of Solomon, the chief object of explorers had been a discovery of a passage to India and the fabulous wealth of the East. In the thirteenth century, Marco Polo, the famous Venetian explorer, went far beyond any of his predecessors and succeeded in reaching Pekin. He also heard of another empire which was called Zipangri, the same that we now know as Japan. When he returned and published what we are sorry to say was none too veracious an account, Polo being only too ready to draw upon his imagination, other nations. were fired by emulation.

The Portuguese were the first to achieve any positive result. Early in the fifteenth century, inspired by an able and enterprising sovereign, they doubled Cape Non, discovered Madeira, occupied the Azores and reached the Senegal and the Cape Verde Islands. In 1486, Bartholomew Diaz sighted the Cape of Good Hope, which some ten years later Vasco da Gama, the most famous of all Portuguese explorers, rounded, and then proceeded some distance toward India.

It was after hearing the wonderful tales of these explorers that Columbus became inspired with the idea of sailing westward on the unknown waters, expecting thus to reach India. After untold discouragements, and finally by the generosity of Queen Isabella, who was brought to believe in his conjectures, he set sail from Palos, August 3, 1492, with three small vessels manned by about ninety sailors. The following 12th of October he first sighted the western hemisphere, which, however, he thought to be Asia, and by the way, lived and died in that belief. This land was one of the Bahama Islands, called by the natives Guanahani, but christened by Columbus as San Salvador. It is now known as Cat Island.

The 28th of the same month Columbus discovered Cuba, entering the mouth of a river in what he believed to be that "great land," of which he had heard so much.

From the very beginning, it was as it has existed to the present day—the Spaniards looked for gold and were determined to exploit their new possessions to the very last peseta that could be wrung from them.

The island was first called Juana, in honor of Prince John, son of Ferdinand and Isabella; but, after Ferdinand's death, it received the name of Fernandina. Subsequently, it was designated, after Spain's patron saint, Santiago, and still later Ave Maria, in honor of the Virgin.

Finally it received its present name, the one originally bestowed upon it by the natives. Cuba means "the place of gold," and Spain has constantly kept this in mind, both theoretically and practically.

At first, however, the answers received in Cuba in reply to the questions of her discoverers as to the existence of gold were not satisfactory. It seemed as if this ne plus ultra to the Spaniards was to be found in a neighboring and larger island, which has been known by the various names of Hayti, Hispaniola and Santo Domingo. The prospect of enrichment here was so inviting that the first settlement of Spain in the New World was made in Hayti.

The aborigines seem to have made no resistance to the coming among them of a new race of people. They were apparently peaceful and kindly, dwelling in a state of happy tranquillity among themselves.

Their character is best demonstrated by an extract from a letter written by Columbus to their Catholic majesties, Ferdinand and Isabella:

"The king having been informed of our misfortune expressed great grief for our loss and immediately sent aboard all the people in the place in many large canoes; we soon unloaded the ship of everything that was upon deck, as the king gave us great assistance; he himself, with his brothers and relations, took all possible care that everything should be properly done, both aboard and on shore. And, from time to time, he sent some of his relations weeping, to beg of me not to be dejected, for he would give me all that he had. I can assure your highnesses that so much care would not have been taken in securing our effects in any part of Spain, as all our property was put toegther in one place near his palace, until the houses which he wanted to prepare for the custody of it were emptied. He immediately placed a guard of armed men, who watched during the whole night, and those on shore lamented as if they had been much interested in our loss. The people are so affectionate, so tractable and so peaceable, that I swear to your highnesses that there is not a better race of men nor a better country in the world. They love their neighbor as themselves, their conversation is the sweetest and mildest in the world, cheerful and always accompanied by a smile. And although it is true that they go naked, yet your highnesses may be assured that they have many very commendable customs; the king is served with great state, and his behavior is so decent that it is pleasant to see him, as it is likewise the wonderful memory which these people have, and their desire of knowing everything which leads them to inquire into its causes and effects."

Strange and far from pleasant reading this in the light of future events. By so-called savages the invading Spaniards were treated with the utmost kindness and courtesy, while many generations later the descendants of these same Spaniards, on this same island, visited nothing but cruelty and oppression upon those unfortunates who after all were of their own flesh and blood.

As has been said, the first settlement of the Spaniards was made on the island of Hayti. But the dreams of enormous revenue were not realized, in spite of the fact

that the natives were men, women and children reduced
to slavery, and all the work that was possible, without
regard to any of the dictates of humanity, was exacted
from them. In spite of the fact, did we say? No, rather
because of it. For, owing to the hardships inflicted
upon them, the native population, which originally was
considerably over a million, was reduced to some fifty
thousand, and it was therefore impossible to extract
from the earth the riches it contained. Thus, does un-
bridled greed ever overleap itself.

After its discovery, Cuba was twice visited by Columbus, in April, 1494, and again in 1502, but these
visits do not seem to have been productive of any particular results.

It was not until 1511 that the Spaniards thought it
worth while to colonize Cuba, and only then because
they believed that they had exhausted the resources of
Hayti, in other words, that that particular orange had
been sucked dry.

Therefore they sent a band of three hundred men under Diego Velasquez, who had accompanied Columbus
on his second voyage, to make a settlement on the
island.

Velasquez and his companions found the natives
peaceful and happy, ruled over by nine independent
chiefs. They met with but little resistance, and that
little was easily overcome. Soon the weak and guileless
Indians were completely subjugated.

There was one instance which it is well worth while
to relate here as showing the Spanish character, which

centuries have not changed, and which is as cruel and bloodthirsty to-day as it was then.

There was one native chief, a refugee from Hayti, named Hatuey, who had had previous dealings with the Spaniards, and knew what was to be expected from them. He had strongly opposed their invasion, was captured, and sentenced to be burned alive at the stake. As the flames curled about him, a Franciscan monk held up a crucifix before him, urging him to abjure the impotent gods of his ancestors and embrace Christianity.

Hatury, knowing well that his conversion would not save him from a horrible death, and remembering all the atrocities he had seen committed, asked where Heaven was and if there were many Spaniards there.

"A great many of them," answered the monk.

"Then," cried Hatury, "I will not go to a place where I may meet one of that accursed race. I prefer to go elsewhere."

Hatury's death ended all rebellion, if struggling for one's rights can be rebellion, and the iron hand of tyranny, whose grasp has never since been relaxed, closed firmly upon the beautiful island.

Three hundred of the natives were given as slaves to each Spaniard, but, as in Hayti, it was found that they were not strong enough for the enormous tasks their masters would have imposed upon them. So negro slaves were imported from the mother country, and their descendants remained in the bonds of serfdom for centuries.

The first permanent settlement was made at Santiago de Cuba, on the Southeastern coast, the scene of Admiral Sampson's recent brilliant achievements, and this was for a long time the capital of the colony. Then came Trinidad, and in 1515 a town was started called San Cristoval de la Habana, which name was transferred four years later to the present capital, the first named place being rechristened Batabana.

The natives were treated with the utmost cruelty, so cruelly, in fact, that they were practically exterminated. Only a comparatively few years after the settlement of the island there were scarcely any of them left. The result of this short sighted policy on the part of Spain was that agriculture declined to an enormous extent, and Cuba became virtually a pastoral country.

In 1537, the king appointed as captain-general Hernando de Soto, the picturesque adventurer, who was afterwards famous as the discoverer of the Mississippi and for his romantic search for the fountain of eternal youth.

All powers, both civil and military, were vested in the captain-general, the title bestowed upon the governors, although many of them were civilians.

Shortly after this appointment, Havana was reduced to ashes by a French privateer, and De Soto built for the city's protection the Castillo de la Fuerza, a fortress which still exists. But this precaution proved ineffectual, as in 1554, the city which had gained considerably in importance, as it had now become the capital, was again attacked and partially destroyed by the French.

Two other fortresses were then constructed, the Punta and the Morro.

The discovery of Mexico and other countries drew away from the island the majority of its working population, and the government passed a law imposing the penalty of death upon all who left it.

Spain also imposed the heaviest trade restrictions upon Cuba. It was exploited in every direction for the benefit of the mother country and to the exclusion of every one else. All foreigners, and even Spaniards not natives of Castile, were prohibited from trading with the island or settling in it.

The consequence was that the increase of population was slow, the introduction of negroes, whose labor was most essential for prosperity, was gradual, and the progress and growth of the island were almost stopped.

Moreover, Spain was ruler of the greater part of the Atlantic, and a most despotic ruler she proved herself to be. Numerous tales are told of the atrocities committed upon navigators, especially those of England.

When Cromwell, who caused many liberal ideas to be introduced into England, tried to induce Spain to abolish the Inquisition and to allow the free navigation of the Atlantic, the Spanish ambassador replied:

"For my master to relinquish those prerogatives would be the same as to put out both his eyes."

One instance of Spain's cruelty, for which, however, she suffered a well-merited retribution, may be related here. In 1564, a party of French Huguenots settled in Florida near the mouth of the river St. John. A certain

Menendez, who was sailing under orders to "gibbet and behead all Protestants in those regions," fell upon the colonists and massacred all he could find. Some of the settlers, who happened to be away at the time, shortly afterward fell into the hands of Menendez, who hanged them all, placing this inscription above their heads: "Not as Frenchmen, but as heretics." In 1567, however, a French expedition surprised a body of Spaniards who had undertaken to found St. Augustine, and in their turn hanged these settlers, "Not as Spaniards, but as murderers."

Hampered and oppressed as they were, deprived of a free and convenient market for the produce of the soil by reason of the monopolies imposed by the mother country, it is not strange that the Cubans had recourse to smuggling, and this was especially the case after the British conquest of Jamaica in 1655. So universal did the practice become, that when Captain-General Valdez arrived, he found that nearly all the Havanese were guilty of the crime of illicit trading, the punishment of which was death. At the suggestion of Valdez, a ship was freighted with presents for the king, and sent to Spain with a petition for pardon, which was finally granted.

But the whole of Europe was against Spain in her arrogant assumption of the suzerainty of the New World. Especially were her pretensions condemned and resisted by the English, French, Portuguese and Dutch, all of whom were engaged in colonizing different portions of America. Then arose a body of men, who were productive of most important results. These were known as buccaneers, and were practically a band of piratical adventurers of different nationalities, united in their opposition to Spain.

Hayti, as has already been intimated, had been almost depopulated by the oppressive colonial policy of Spain. The island had become the home of immense herds of wild cattle, and it was the custom of the smugglers to stop there to provision their ships.

The natives, which were still left, had learned to be skilled in preserving the meat by means of fire and smoke, and they called their kilns "boucans." The smugglers, besides obtaining what they desired for their own use of this preserved meat, established an extensive illicit trade in it. Hence, they obtained the name of buccaneers.

Spanish monopolies were the pest of every port in the New World, and mariners of the western waters were filled with a detestation, quite natural, of everything Spanish.

Gradually, the ranks of the buccaneers were recruited. They were given assistance and encouragement, direct and indirect, by other nations, even in some cases being furnished with letters-of-marque and reprisal as privateers.

The commerce of Spain had been gradually dwindling since the defeat of the so-called Invincible Armada, and the buccaneers commenced now to seize the returning treasure ships and to plunder the seaboard cities of Cuba and other Spanish possessions.

Even Havana itself was not spared by them.

The buccaneers, indefensible though many of their actions were, had a great influence upon the power and colonial tactics of Spain.

Beyond this, they opened the eyes of the world to the rottenness of the whole system of Spanish government and commerce in America, and undoubtedly did much to build up the West Indian possessions of England, France and Holland.

It is curious to note here the career of one of their most famous leaders, an Englishman named Morgan. He was barbarous in the extreme and returned from many expeditions laden · with spoil. But, finally, he went to Jamaica, turned respectable and was made deputy-governor of the island. He died, by favor of Charles II., the ''gallant'' Sir Henry Morgan.

But in 1697, the European powers generally condemned the buccaneers.

In spite of the lessons they had received, and the universal protest of other nations, the Spaniards, obstinate then as ever, refused to change their policy. They persisted in closing the magnificent harbors of Cuba to the commerce of the rest of the world, and that, too, when Spain could not begin to use the products of the island. Still she could not and would not allow one bit of gold to slip from between her fingers. She has always held on with eager greed to all that she could lay her hands on. It is certainly food for the unrestrained laughter of gods and men that she has recently been sneering at the United States as a nation of traders and money grubbers.

CHAPTER II.

THE BRITISH OCCUPATION—SPAIN'S GRATITUDE.

In the early years of the eighteenth century, Cuba was more or less at peace, that is so far as Spain, a degenerate mother of a far more honorable daughter, would allow her to be at peace, and she increased in population, and, to a certain extent, in material prosperity.

But in 1717, a revolt broke out, a revolt which was thoroughly justified.

Spain felt that the agricultural wealth of the island was increasing, and she desired for herself practically the whole of the advantages which accrued from it.

Therefore, she demanded a royal monopoly of the tobacco trade.   This demand was strenuously and bitterly opposed by the Cubans.

The Captain-General, Raja, was obliged to flee, but finally the trouble was ended, and Spain, by might far rather than by right, had her way.   The monopoly was established.

But the oppressive government led to another uprising in 1723, which again was quickly quelled.   Twelve of the leaders were hanged by Guazo, who was at that time the captain-general.

Twice, therefore, did the one who was in the wrong conquer, simply from the possession of superior force.

It is said that the mills of God grind slowly, but

they grind exceeding small. And in the light of recent events, this seems to be, and in fact, so far as human intelligence can determine, it is true.

Richard Le Gallienne, to-day, toward the end of the nineteenth century, speaks in clarion tones, as follows:

> "Spain is an ancient dragon,
>   That too long hath curled
> Its coils of blood and darkness
>   About the new-born world.
>
> Think of the Inquisition
>   Think of the Netherlands!
> Yea! think of all Spain's bloody deeds
>   In many times and lands.
>
> And let no feeble pity
>   Your sacred arms restrain;
> This is God's mighty moment
>   To make an end of Spain."

About this time, that is, from 1724 to 1747, Cuba, chiefly, if not almost entirely, at Havana, became a ship building centre, of course, once more, at least for a time, to the advantage of Spain. In all, there were constructed some one hundred and twenty-five vessels, carrying amongst them four thousand guns. These ships comprised six ships of the line, twenty-one of seventy to eighty guns each, twenty-six of fifty to sixty guns, fourteen frigates of thirty to forty guns and fifty-eight smaller vessels.

But then Spain became jealous—imagine a parent jealous of the success of its child!—and the ship-building industry was peremptorily stopped. During the present century, in Cuba only the machinery of one steamer, the Saqua, has been constructed, and two ships, one a war steamer and one a merchant steamer, have been built at Havana.

What a commentary on the dominating and destructive policy—self-destructive policy, too—of Spain!

In 1739, there arose in England a popular excitement for a war against Spain. One of the chief incidents which led to this was an episode which caused Thomas Carlyle to call the strife that followed "The War of Jenkins' Ear."

The English had persisted in maintaining a trade with Cuba in spite of Spain's prohibition.

A certain Captain Jenkins, who was in command of an English merchantman, was captured by a Spanish cruiser. His ship was subjected to search, and he himself, according to his own declaration, put to the torture. The Spaniards, however, could find little or nothing of which to convict him, and, irritated at this they committed a most foolish act, a deed of childish vengeance. They cut off one of his ears and told him to take it back to England and show it to the king.

Jenkins preserved his mutilated ear in a bottle of spirits, and, in due course of time, appeared himself before the House of Commons and exhibited it to that body.

The excitement ensuing upon the proof of this outrage to a British subject beggars description.

Walpole was at that time prime minister, and, although essentially a man of peace, he found it impossible to stem the tide, and public sentiment compelled him to declare war against Spain.

This war, however, was productive of but little result one way or the other.

But before long another struggle ensued, which was far more reaching in its consequences.

In 1756, what is known in history as the Seven Years War, broke out. This seems to have been a mere struggle for territory, and, besides a duel between France and England, involved Austria, with its allies, France, Russia and the German princes against the new kingdom of Prussia.

This naturally led to an alliance between England and Prussia.

Towards the end of the war, early in 1762, hostilities were declared against Spain.

An English fleet and army, under Lord Albemarle, were sent to Cuba. The former consisted of more than two hundred vessels of all classes, and the latter of fourteen thousand and forty-one men.

The opposing Spanish force numbered twenty-seven thousand six hundred and ten men.

With the English, were a large number of Americans, some of whom figured later more or less prominently in the war of the Revolution. Israel Putnam, the hero of the breakneck ride at Horseneck, and General Lyman, under whom Putnam eventually served, were among these, as was also Lawrence Washington, a brother of "The Father of His Country."

By the way, the American loss in Cuba during this campaign was heavy. Very few, either officers or men, ever returned home. Most of those who were spared by the Spanish bullets succumbed to the rigors of the tropical climate, to which they were unaccustomed and ill-prepared for.

May this experience of our forefathers in the last century not be repeated in the persons of our brothers of the present!

The defense of Havana was excessively obstinate, and the Cuban volunteers covered themselves with glory.

But, in spite of the superior force of the Spanish, the English were finally successful.

Taking all things into consideration, it was a wonderful feat of arms, one of which only the Anglo-Saxon race is capable.

Nevertheless, it was only after a prolonged struggle that the victory was complete.

At last, on the 30th of July, Morro Castle surrendered, and about two weeks afterward, the city of Havana capitulated.

The spoil divided among the captors amounted to about four million seven hundred thousand dollars.

The English remained in possession of Cuba for something like six months, and during that time instituted many important and far-reaching reforms, so much so in fact that when the Spaniards regained possession, they found it very difficult to re-establish their former restrictive and tyrannous system.

For instance, the sanitary condition of Havana, which was atrocious even in those comparatively primitive days of hygiene, was vastly improved. All over the island, roads were opened. During the time of the English occupation, over nine hundred loaded vessels entered the port of Havana, more than in all the previous entries since the discovery.

The commerce of the island improved to a remarkable extent, and for the first time the sugar industry began to be productive.

If the British had remained in possession of Cuba, it is probable that that unhappy island would have been spared much of its misery and would have been as contented, prosperous and loyal as Canada is to-day.

It really seemed as if an era of prosperity had begun, when by the treaty of Paris, in February, 1763, most of the conquests made during the Seven Years' War were restored to their original owners, and among them unfortunately in the light of both past and future events, Cuba to the misrule of the Spaniards.

England, however, was eminently the gainer by this treaty, as she received from France all the territory formerly claimed by the latter east of the Mississippi, together with Prince Edward's Island, Cape Breton, St. Vincent, Dominica, Minorca and Tobago. In return for Cuba, Spain ceded to England Florida, while the Spanish government received Louisiana from France. On the other hand, Martinique, Guadeloupe, Pondicherry and Goree were returned to France.

It was impossible for the Spanish to undo in a day all the good that the English rule, short though it was, had accomplished.

Moreover, it was more than fortunate for Cuba that there followed not long after two governors of more than ordinary ability and humanity, both of whom had her interests at heart, and they caused a period of unwonted prosperity, most grateful to the Cubans, to follow.

The first of these governors, or to give them their rightful title, captain-generals, was Luis de Las Casas, who was appointed in 1790.

Now, for the first time in her history, Cuba really made rapid progress in commercial prosperity as well as in public improvements. Las Casas developed all branches of industry, allowed the establishment of newspapers, and gave his aid to the patriotic societies.

He also introduced the culture of indigo, removed as far as his powers permitted the old trammels, which an iniquitous system had placed upon trade, and made noble efforts to bring about the emancipation of the enslaved Indian natives.

His attitude toward the newly established republic of the United States was most generous, and this helped largely to develop the industry of the island.

By his judicious administration, the tranquillity of Cuba remained undisturbed during the time of the rebellion in Hayti, and this in face of the fact that strenuous efforts were made by the French, to form a conspiracy and bring about an uprising among the free people of color in Cuba.

Another thing that will redound forever to the credit of Las Casas and which should make his memory beloved by all Americans—it was through his efforts that the body of Columbus was removed from Hayti where it had been entombed and deposited in its present resting-place in the Cathedral of Havana.

In 1796, Las Casas was succeeded by another just and philanthropic governor, the Count of Santa Clara. The latter greatly improved the fortifications which then guarded the island and constructed a large number of others, among them the Bateria de Santa Clara, just outside Havana, and named in his honor.

It was undoubtedly due in a very great measure to the kindly policies of these two noble and far seeing men that Cuba at that time became confirmed in her allegiance to the mother country; and had they been followed by men of equal calibre of both mind and heart, it is more than probable that the history of Cuba would have been devoid of stirring events. For, as the old saying has it: "Happy nations have no history."

In 1795 a number of French emigrants arrived from San Domingo, and proved a valuable acquisition.

In 1802, a disastrous fire occurred in a suburb of Havana, called Jesu Maria, and over eleven thousand four hundred people were rendered destitute and homeless.

About this time, the star of Napoleon Bonaparte, the greatest of heroes or the greatest of adventurers, according to the point of view, was in the ascendant. Almost without exception there was not a country in Europe that had not felt the weight of his heavy hand, and, to all intents and purposes, he was the master of the continent.

Spain was by no means to escape his greed for conquest and power.

Her country was overrun and ravaged by his victorious armies. Her reigning family was driven away. Napoleon deposed the descendant of a long line of Bourbons, Ferdinand VII., and placed his own brother, Joseph Bonaparte, upon the throne.

Then the attitude and the action of Cuba were superb. Her loyalty was unwavering. Every member of the provincial council declared his fidelity to the old dynasty, and took an oath to defend and preserve the island for its legitimate sovereign.

More than this—the Cubans followed this declaration up by deeds, which ever speak louder than mere words. They made numerous voluntary subscriptions, they published vehement pamphlets, and they sent their sons to fight and shed their blood for the agonized mother country.

For this, Cuba received the title of ''The Ever Faithful Isle,'' by which it has been known ever since.

A very pretty compliment truly! But let us see in what other and more substantial ways was Cuba's magnificent fidelity rewarded.

The answer is as brief as it is true. In no way whatever.

Many promises were made at the time by the Provisional Government at Seville, chief among them being that all Spanish subjects everywhere should have equal rights. But not one of these promises was ever kept.

On the contrary, it was not long before the oppression became greater than ever. There were deprivation of political, civil and religious liberty, an exclusion of the islanders from all public offices, and a heavy and iniquitous taxation to maintain the standing army and navy.

Clothed as they were with the powers of an Oriental despot, most of the captain-generals from Spain covered themselves with infamy, the office as a rule having been sought (and this was distinctly realized by the Spanish government) only as an end and means to acquire a personal fortune.

To realize the practically absolute authority given to the captain-generals, it is only necessary to read the royal decree promulgated after Joseph Bonaparte had been deposed and the Bourbon king, Ferdinand, restored to the throne.

A portion of this amazing document is as follows:

''His majesty, the king our Lord, desiring to obviate the inconveniences that might, in extraordinary cases, result from a division of command, and from the interferences and prerogatives of the respective officers: for the important end of preserving in that precious island his legitimate sovereign authority and the public tranquility, through proper means, has resolved, in accordance with the opinion of his council of ministers, to give to your excellency the fullest authority, bestowing upon you all the powers which by the royal ordinances are granted to the governors of besieged cities. In consequence of this his majesty gives to your excellency the most ample and unbounded power, not only to send away from the island any persons in office, whatever their occupation, rank, class or condition, whose continuance therein your excellency may deem injurious, or whose conduct, public or private, may alarm you, replacing them with persons faithful to his majesty, and deserving of all the confidence of your excellency; but also to suspend the execution of any order whatsoever, or any general provision made concerning any branch of the administration as your excellency may think most suitable to the royal service."

For over one hundred and seventy years these orders have received little or no change, and they still remain practically the supreme law of Cuba.

This was the way that magnanimous, grateful, chivalrous Spain began to reward "The Ever Faithful Isle" for its unparalleled loyalty and devotion.

And Heaven save the mark! this was only the beginning.

"That precious island," says the royal decree. Precious! There was never a truer word spoken. For Spain has always loved Cuba with a fanatical, gloating passion, as the fox loves the goose, as Midas loved gold, and as in in the case of Midas, this love has eventually led to her destruction.

CHAPTER III.

CUBA'S EARLY STRUGGLES FOR LIBERTY.

It was in 1813 that the Bonapartist regime came to an end in Spain, and Ferdinand VII. reascended the throne. In the very beginning he paid no attention to the Constitution; he dissolved the Cortes and did his best to make his monarchy an absolute one.

Again, as has been said, Cuba felt the yoke of his despotism, all previous promises, when the aid of the island was to his advantage, being as completely ignored as if they had never been made.

In Spanish America, revolutionary movements had been begun some three years before, and after stubborn warfare, Buenos Ayres, Venezuela and Peru finally succeeded in obtaining complete independence from Spanish authority.

From all these countries, swarms of Spanish loyalists made their way to Cuba, and were ordered to be maintained at the expense of the island.

Spain also desired to make of Cuba a military station, whence she could direct operations in her efforts to reconquer the new republic. This plan was vehemently opposed by the Cubans.

Discontent rapidly fomented and increased throughout the island. Numerous secret political societies were formed, and there arose two great opposing factions, the one insisting that the liberal constitution granted by the Provisional Government of Seville at the time the Bourbon king was deposed should be the fundamental law of Cuba, while the other proclaimed its partisanship of rigid colonial control.

In 1821, Hayti declared its independence of Spain, and in the same year Florida passed into the possession of the United States.

Both these events increased the feeling of unrest and discontent in Cuba, and this was further augmented by the establishment of a permanent military commission, which took cognizance of even ordinary offences, but particularly of all offenses against disloyalty.

An attempt at revolution, the purpose being the estab-lishment of a republic, was made in 1823 by the "Soles de Bolivar" association. It was arranged that uprisings should take place simultaneously in several of the Cuban cities, but the plans became known to the government and the intended revolution was nipped in the bud, all the leaders being arrested and imprisoned the very day on which it had been arranged to declare independ-ence.

In 1826 Cuban refugees in Mexico and in some of the South American republics planned an invasion of Cuba to be led by Simon Bolivar, the great liberator of Co-lombia, but it came to nothing, owing to the impossi-bility of securing adequate support both of men and money.

A year or two later these same men attempted another uprising in the interests of greater privileges and freedom.   A secret society, known as the "Black Eagle" was organized, with headquarters at Mexico, but with a branch office and recruiting stations in the United States.

This invasion, however, also proved abortive, owing chiefly to the determined opposition displayed by the slave-holders both in the United States and Cuba. The ringleaders were captured and severely punished by the Spanish authorities.

The struggles for freedom had attracted the attention of the people of the United States and were viewed by them with ever-increasing interest and sympathy.

After the acquisition of Florida, the future of the is-land of Cuba became of more or less importance to the people of the United States and has remained so to the present day. As President Cleveland said in his message of December, 1896:   "It is so near to us as to be hardly separated from our own territory." The truth of this is apparent when it is remembered that the straits of Florida can be crossed by steamer in five hours.

It began to be feared that Cuba might fall into the hands of England or France and the governments of those countries as well as that of Spain were informed that such a disposition of it would never be consented to.   Its position at the entrance of the gulf of Mexico could not be disregarded.   The American government declared its willingness that it should remain a Spanish colony, but stated it would never permit it to become the colony of another country.

In 1825 Spain made a proposition that, in consideration of certain commercial concessions the United States should guarantee to her the possession of Cuba; but this proposition was declined on the ground that such a thing would be contrary to the established policy of the United States.

One of the most important consequences of Spain's efforts to regain possession of the South American republics, the independence of which had been recognized by the United States, was the formulation of what has since been known as the "Monroe Doctrine." In his message of December 2, 1823, President Monroe promulgated the policy of neither entangling ourselves in the broils of Europe, nor suffering the powers of the old world to interfere with the affairs of the new. He further declared that any attempt on the part of the European powers "to extend their system to any portion of this hemisphere" would be regarded by the United States as "dangerous to our peace and safety," and would accordingly be opposed.

Although since then there has been more or less friction with England over the Monroe doctrine, at that time she greatly aided in its becoming established as a feature of international law, and strengthened the position of the United States, by her recognition of the South American republics.

The Spanish slave code, by which the slave trade, which had formerly been a monopoly, was made free, had given a great stimulus to the importation of slaves. It was almost brought to an end, however, by the energetic efforts of Captain-General Valdez. But the increased consumption of sugar in Great Britain, owing to reduction of duty and the placing of foreign and British sugars on the same basis gave a new stimulus to the traffic; and, in their own pecuniary interest, ever more prominent with them than any question of humanity, the Spanish relaxed their efforts, and the slave trade attained greater dimensions than ever before.

In 1844 there occurred an uprising which was more serious than any which had preceded it. The slaves on the sugar plantations in the neighborhood of Matanzas were suspected of being about to revolt. There was no real proof of this, and in order to obtain evidence a large number of slaves were tortured. It was evident that Spain was still ready, if in her opinion occasion required it, to have recourse to the barbarities of the old Inquisitorial days. By evidence manufactured by such outrageous methods, one thousand three hundred and forty-six persons were tried and convicted, of whom seventy-eight were shot, and the others punished with more or less severity. Of those declared guilty, fourteen were white, one thousand two hundred and forty-two free colored persons, and fifty-nine slaves.

The project of annexation to the United States was first mooted in 1848, after the proclamation of the French republic. The people of the slave States, in view of the increasing population and the anti-slavery feeling of the North and West were beginning to feel alarmed as to the safety of the "peculiar institution," and there was a strong sentiment among them in favor of annexing Cuba and dividing it up into slave states. President

Polk, therefore, authorized the American minister at Madrid to offer one hundred million dollars for Cuba; but the proposition was rejected in the most peremptory manner. A similar proposal was made ten years afterward in the Senate, but after a debate it was withdrawn.

The next conspiracy, rebellion or revolution (it has been called by all these names according to the point of view and the sympathies of those speaking or writing of it) broke out in 1848. It was headed by Narciso Lopez, who was a native of Venezuela, but who had served in the Spanish army, and had attained therein the rank of major-general.

This was of considerable more importance than any of the outbreaks that had preceded it.

The first attempt of Lopez at an insurrectionary movement was made in the centre of the island. It proved to be unsuccessful, but Lopez, with many of his adherents, managed to escape and reached New York, where there were a large number of his sympathizers.

Lopez represented the majority of the Cuban population as dissatisfied with Spanish rule, and eager for revolt and annexation to the United States.

In 1849, with a party small in numbers, he attempted to return to Cuba, but the United States authorities prevented him accomplishing his purpose.

He was undaunted by failure, however, and the following year, he succeeded in effecting another organization and sailed from New Orleans on the steamer Pampero, with a force which has been variously estimated at from three to six hundred men, the latter probably being nearer the truth.

The second in command was W. S. Crittenden, a gallant young Kentuckian, who was a graduate of West Point, and who had earned his title of colonel in the Mexican war.

They landed at Morillo in the Vuelta Abajo. Here the forces were divided; one hundred and thirty under Crittenden remained to guard the supplies, while Lopez with the rest pushed on into the interior.

There had been no disguise in the United States as to the object of this expedition. Details in regard to it had been freely and recklessly published, and there is a lesson to be learned even from this comparatively trivial attempt to obtain freedom as to a proper censorship of the press in time of warfare.

The Spanish government was fully informed beforehand as to all the little army's probable movements. The consequence was that Lopez was surrounded and his whole force captured by the Spanish.

The expected uprising of the Cuban people, by the way, had not taken place.

Hearing no news of his superior officer, Crittenden at first made a desperate attempt to escape by sea, but, being frustrated in this, he took refuge in the woods.

At last he and his little force, now reduced to fifty men, were forced to capitulate.

The United States Consul was asked to interfere in the case of Crittenden, but refused to do so. It was said at the time that there were two reasons for this: First, there was no doubt whatever as to the nature of the expedition, and secondly, the consul, who does not appear to have been particularly brave, was alarmed for his personal safety.

The trial, if trial it can be called, and condemnation followed with the utmost, almost criminal, celerity.

In batches of six, Crittenden and his fifty brave surviving comrades were shot beneath the walls of the fortress of Alara.

When the Spaniards ordered Crittenden, as was the custom, to kneel with his back to the firing party, the heroic young Kentuckian responded:

"No! I will stand facing them! I kneel only to my God!"

It is stated that the bodies of the victims were mutilated in a horrible manner.

There was no inconsiderable number of Cubans who sympathized with Lopez, but, held as they were under a stern leash, they did not dare to intercede for him.

He was garroted at Havana, being refused the honorable death of a soldier. Some others of his comrades were shot, but most of them were transported for life.

The sad fate of Crittenden aroused the greatest indignation and bitterness in the United States, but the tenets of international law forbade anything to be done in the case.

During the administration of President Pierce, there occurred an incident which threatened at one time to lead to hostilities, and which was one of the first of the many incidents that have embittered the United States against Spain as regards its administration of Cuba.

This was the firing on the American steamer, Black Warrior, by a Spanish man-of-war.

The Black Warrior was a steamer owned in New York, and plying regularly between that city and Mobile. It was her custom both on her outward and homeward bound trips to touch always at Havana. The custom laws were then very stringent, and she ought each time to have exhibited a manifest of her cargo. But still this was totally unnecessary, as no portion of her cargo was ever put off at Havana.

She was therefore entered and cleared under the technical term of "in ballast." This was done nearly thirty times with full knowledge and consent of the Spanish revenue officers; and, moreover the proceeding was in accordance with a general order of the Cuban authorities.

But in February, 1850, the steamer was stopped and fired upon in the harbor of Havana. The charge brought against her was that she had an undeclared cargo on board. This cargo was confiscated, and a fine of twice its value imposed. The commander of the vessel, Captain Bullock, refused to pay the fine, and declared that the whole proceeding was "violent, wrongful and in bad faith."

But, obtaining no redress, he hauled down his colors, and, carrying them away with him, left the vessel as a Spanish capture. With his crew and passengers, he made his way to New York, and reported the facts to the owners.

The latter preferred a claim for indemnity of three hundred thousand dollars. After a tedious delay of five years, this sum was paid, and so the matter ended.

The affair of the Black Warrior was one of the cases that led to the celebrated Ostend Conference.

This conference was held in 1854 at Ostend and Aix-la-Chapelle by Messrs. Buchanan, Mason and Soule, United States ministers at London, Paris and Madrid, and resulted in what is known as the Ostend manifesto.

The principal points of this manifesto were as follows:

"The United States ought if possible to purchase Cuba with as little delay as possible.

"The probability is great that the government and Cortes of Spain will prove willing to sell it because this would essentially promote the highest and best interests of the Spanish people.

"The Union can never enjoy repose nor possess reliable securities as long as Cuba is not embraced within its boundaries.

"The intercourse which its proximity to our coast begets and encourages between them (the inhabitants of Cuba) and the citizens of the United States has, in the progress of time, so united their interests and blended their fortunes that they now look upon each other as if they were one people and had but one destiny.

"The system of immigration and labor lately organized within the limits of the island, and the tyranny and oppression which characterize its immediate rulers, threaten an insurrection at every moment which may result in direful consequences to the American people.

"Cuba has thus become to us an unceasing danger, and a permanent cause for anxiety and alarm.

"Should Spain reject the present golden opportunity for developing her resources and removing her financial embarrassments, it may never come again.

"Extreme oppression, it is now universally admitted, justifies any people in endeavoring to free themselves from the yoke of their oppressors. The sufferings which the corrupt, arbitrary and unrelenting local administration necessarily entails upon the inhabitants of Cuba cannot fail to stimulate and keep alive that spirit of resistance and revolution against Spain which has of late years been so often manifested. In this condition of affairs it is vain to expect that the sympathies of the people of the United States will not be warmly enlisted in favor of their oppressed neighbors.

"The United States has never acquired a foot of territory except by fair purchase, or, as in the case of Texas, upon the free and voluntary application of the people of that independent State, who desired to blend their destinies with our own.

"It is certain that, should the Cubans themselves organize an insurrection against the Spanish government, no human power could, in our opinion, prevent the people and government of the United States from taking part in such a civil war in support of their neighbors and friends."

We have quoted thus largely from the Ostend manifesto, because it seems to us, with one exception, to be so pertinent to the present status of affairs.

The one exception is: We no longer desire the annexation of Cuba. The present war is a holy war. It has been entered into wholly and entirely from motives of philanthropy, to give to a suffering and downtrodden people the blessings of freedom which we ourselves enjoy.

Moreover, the manifesto clearly shows that the causes of Cuban uprising are of no recent date; and that, before the United States rose in its wrath, it was patient and long-suffering.

Although the Senate debated the questions raised by the manifesto for a long time, nothing resulted from the deliberations.

Questions of extraordinary moment were arising in our own country, from which terrible results were to ensue, and for the time being, indeed for years to come, everything else sank into insignificance.

Meantime, the question of independence was still being agitated in Cuba.

General Jose de la Concha, in anticipation of a rising of the Creole population threatened to turn the island into an African dependency. He formed and drilled black troops, armed the native born Spaniards and disarmed the Cubans. Everything was got in readiness for a desperate defense. The Cuban junta in New York had enlisted a large body of men and had made ready for an invasion. Under the circumstances, however, the attempt was postponed. Pinto and Estrames, Cubans taken with arms in their hands, were executed, while a hundred others were either condemned to the galleys or deported. General de la Concha's foresight and vigilance unquestionably prevented a revolution, and for his services he was created Marquis of Havana.

Then ensued a period of comparative quiet, but the party of independence was only awaiting an opportunity to strike.

Long before this, Spain had entered upon the downward path. ''A whale stranded upon the coast of Europe,'' some one designated her. She had been accumulating a debt against her, a debt which can never be repaid.

And she has no one to blame for her wretched feeble, exhausted condition but herself—her own obstinacy, selfishness and perversity.

Truly, Spain has changed but little, and that only in certain outward aspects, since the time of Torquemada and the Inquisition. She is the one nation of Europe that civilization does not seem to have reached.

The magnificent legacy left her by her famous son, Christopher Columbus, has been gradually dissipated; the last beautiful jewel in the crown of her colonial possessions, the ''Pearl of the Antilles'' is about to be wrested from her.

Her case is indeed a pitiable one, and yet sympathy is arrested when we remember that her reward to Columbus for his magnificent achievements was to cover his reputation with obloquy and load his person with chains.

CHAPTER IV.

THE TEN YEARS' WAR.

For about fourteen years after 1854, the outbreaks in Cuba were infrequent, and of little or no moment. To all intents and purposes, the island was in a state of tranquility.

In September, 1868, a revolution broke out in the mother country, the result of which was that Queen Isabella was deposed from the throne and forced to flee the country.

This time Cuba did not proclaim her loyalty to the Bourbon dynasty, as she had done some sixty years before. She had learned her lesson. She knew now how Spanish sovereigns rewarded loyalty, and the fall of Isabella, instead of inspiring the Cubans with sympathy, caused them to rush into a revolution, an action which, paradoxical as it may seem, was somewhat precipitate, although long contemplated.

All Cuba had been eagerly looking forward to the inauguration of political reforms, or to an attempt to shake off the pressing yoke of Spain. At first it was thought that the new government would ameliorate the condition of Cuba, and so change affairs that the island might remain contentedly connected with a country of which she had so long formed a part.

But these hopes were soon dissipated, and the advanced party of Cuba at once matured their plans for the liberation of the island from the military despotism of Spain.

A declaration of Cuban independence was issued at Manzanillo in October, 1868, by Carlos Manuel de Cespedes, a lawyer of Bayamo.

This declaration began as follows:

"As Spain has many a time promised us Cubans to respect our rights, without having fulfilled her promises; as she continues to tax us heavily, and by so doing is likely to destroy our wealth; as we are in danger of losing our property, our lives and our honor under further Spanish dominion, therefore, etc., etc."

Thus was inaugurated what was destined to prove the most protracted and successful attempt at Cuban freedom, up to that time.

It is certain that the grievances of the islanders were many, and this was even recongized to a certain extent in Spain itself.

In a speech delivered by one of the Cuban deputies to the Cortes in 1866 occurs this passage:

"I foresee a catastrophe near at hand, in case Spain persists in remaining deaf to the just reclamations of the Cubans. Look at the old colonies of the American continent. All have ended in conquering their independence. Let Spain not forget the lesson; let the government be just to the colonies that remain. Thus she will consolidate her dominion over people who only aspire to be good sons of a worthy mother, but who are not willing to live as slaves under the sceptre of a tyrant."

In 1868 the annual revenue exacted from Cuba by Spain was in the neighborhood of twenty-six million dollars; and plans were in progress by which even this great revenue was to be largely increased. Not one penny of this was applied to Cuba's advantage. On the contrary, it was expended in a manner which was simply maddening to the Cubans.

The officials of the island, be it understood, were invariably Spaniards. The captain-general received a salary of fifty thousand dollars a year; at this time, this sum was twice as much as that paid to the President of the United States. The provincial governors obtained twelve thousand dollars each, while the Archbishop of Santiago de Cuba and the Bishop of Havana were paid eighteen thousand dollars apiece. In addition to these large salaries, there were perquisites which probably amounted to as much again.

Even the lowest offices were filled by friends of Spanish politicians. These officials had no sympathy with Cuba, and cared nothing for her welfare, save in so far as they were enabled to fill their own pockets.

The stealing in the custom houses was enormous. It has been estimated at over fifty per cent of the gross receipts. Every possible penny was forced from the native planters under the guise of taxes and also by the most flagrant blackmail.

By a system of differential duties, Spain still managed to retain a monopoly of the trade to Cuba while the colonists were forced to pay the highest possible rates for all they received from the mother country

The rates of postage were absurdly outrageous. For instance there was an extra charge for delivery. When a native Cuban received a prepaid letter at his own door, he was obliged to pay thirty-seven and a half cents additional postage.

The taxes on flour were so high that wheaten bread ceased to be an article of ordinary diet. The annual consumption of bread in Spain was four hundred pounds for each person, while in Cuba, it was only fifty-three pounds, nine ounces. In fact, all the necessaries of life were burdened with most iniquitous taxation.

Then again there was the interest on the national debt. While the Spaniards paid three dollars and twenty-three cents per capita, six dollars and thirty-nine cents, nearly double, was exacted from the Cubans.

All these were the chief causes of the revolution which began in 1868, and many of them still existed a few years ago and led to the last revolution. By the way, there is but little chance but that it will prove the last, bringing as its consequence, what has been struggled for so long—the freedom of Cuba.

The standard of revolt in the Ten Years War, as has been stated, was raised by Carlos Manuel de Cespedes. He was well known as an able lawyer and a wealthy planter. In the very beginning, he was unfortunately forced to take action before he had intended to do so, by reason of news of the projected outbreak reaching the authorities in Havana.

A letter carrier, who from his actions gave rise to suspicions, was detained at Cespedes' sugar plantation,

La Demajagua, and it was found that he was the bearer of an order for the arrest of the conspirators.

With this information, immediate action became necessary. Cespedes deemed it expedient to strike at once, and with only two hundred poorly equipped men, he commenced the campaign at Yara.

This place was defended by a Spanish force too strong for the insurgents. But Cespedes was not long in attracting to himself a most respectable following.

At the end of a few weeks he found himself at the head of fifteen thousand men. The little army, however, was anything but well provided with arms and ammunition. Among them were many of Cespedes' former slaves whom the general promptly liberated.

Attacks were made on Las Tunas, Cauto Embarcardero, Jiguana, La Guisa, El Datil and Santa Rita, in almost every case victory remaining with the insurgents.

On the 15th of October it was decided to attack Bayamo, an important town of ten thousand inhabitants. On the 18th the town was captured. The governor, with a small body of men, shut himself up in the fort, but a few days after was forced to capitulate.

For the relief of Bayamo, a Spanish force under Colonel Quiros, numbering, besides cavalry and artillery, about eight hundred infantry, started out from Santiago de Cuba, but was defeated and driven back to Santiago with heavy losses.

The Spanish general, Count Valmaseda, was sent from Havana into the insurrectionary district, but was attacked and forced to return, leaving his dead on the field.

Afterwards Valmaseda, who had increased his force to four thousand men, marched on Bayamo. He received a severe check at Saladillo, but eventually succeeded in crossing the Cauto. The Cubans saw the hopelessness of defending the place against such superior numbers, and, rather than have it fall into the hands of the enemy, burned the city.

In December, General Quesada, who afterward played a most prominent part in the war, landed a cargo of arms and took command of the army at Camarguey.

Before the close of the year, Spain, realizing how desperate was to be the struggle, had under arms nearly forty thousand troops which had been sent from Europe, besides twelve thousand guerillas recruited on the island and some forty thousand volunteers organized for the defense of the cities. These latter were in many respects analogous to the National Guard of the United States. They were raised from Spanish immigrants, between whom and the native Cubans have always existed a bitter enmity and jealousy.

In the spring of 1869, the revolutionists drew up a constitution, which provided for a republican form of government, an elective president and vice-president, a cabinet and a single legislative chamber. It also made a declaration in favor of the immediate abolition of slavery. Cespedes was elected president and Francisco Aquilero vice-president.

It is said that at the beginning of the war, before being driven to reprisals, the Cubans behaved with all humanity. They took many Spanish prisoners of war, but paroled them. On the other hand, the Cuban prisoners were treated with the utmost treachery and cruelty. In all parts of the island, no Cuban taken a prisoner of war was spared; to a man they were shot on the spot as so many dogs.

Valmaseda, the Spanish general, in April, 1869, issued the following proclamation, which speaks for itself:

"Inhabitants of the country! The re-enforcements of troops that I have been waiting for have arrived; with them I shall give protection to the good, and punish promptly those that still remain in rebellion against the government of the metropolis.

"You know that I have pardoned those that have fought us with arms; that your wives, mothers and sisters have found in me the unexpected protection that you have refused them. You know, also, that many of those I have pardoned have turned against us again.

"Before such ingratitude, such villainy, it is not possible for me to be the man I have been; there is no longer a place for a falsified neutrality; he that is not for me is against me, and that my soldiers may know how to distinguish, you hear, the orders they carry:

1st. Every man, from the age of fifteen years, upward, found away from his habitation and not proving a justified motive therefor, will be shot.

2d. Every unoccupied habitation will be burned by the troops.

3d. Every habitation from which does not float a

white flag, as a signal that its occupants desire peace, will be reduced to ashes.

"Women that are not living at their own homes, or at the house of their relatives, will collect in the town of Jiguana or Bayamo, where maintenance will be provided. Those who do not present themselves will be conducted forcibly."

The second paragraph was flagrantly untrue. Those who had fought against the Spaniards had not been pardoned. On the contrary, they had been put to death. Fearful atrocities had been committed in Havana and elsewhere. To cite only a few instances: The shooting of men, women and children at the Villanuesa Theatre, at the Louvre, and at the sack of Aldama's house.

Valmaseda's proclamation raised a storm of protest from all civilized nations, and the Spaniards, stiff and unbending, never wavered, but the policy embodied in Valmaseda's proclamation remained their tactics until the end of the war.

The United States was especially roused and disgusted. Secretary Fish, in a letter to Mr. Hale, then Minister to Spain, protested "against the infamous proclamation of general, the Count of Valmaseda."

Even a Havanese paper is quoted as declaring that,

"Said proclamation does not even reach what is required by the necessities of war in the most civilized nations."

The revolutionists were victorious in almost every engagement for the first two years, although their losses were by no means inconsiderable.

It has even been acknowledged recently by a representative of Spain to the United States that the greater and better part of the Cubans were in sympathy with the insurrection. This opinion appeared in a statement made by Senor De Lome (whose reputation among Americans is now somewhat unsavory) in the New York Herald of February 23, 1896.

The Cubans were recognized as belligerents by Chili, Bolivia, Guatemala, Peru, Columbia and Mexico.

There were two important expeditions of assistance sent to the Cubans in the early part of the war. One was under the command of Rafael Quesada, and, in addition to men, brought arms and ammunition, of which the insurgents were sadly in need. The other was under General Thomas Jordan, a West Point graduate and an ex-officer in the Confederate service. By the way, the South, with its well-known chivalry, has always evinced warm sympathy for the unfortunate Cubans. To their glory be it spoken and remembered!

Quesada managed to reach the interior without resistance. But Jordan, with only one hundred and seventy-five men, but carrying arms and ammunition for two thousand six hundred men, besides several pieces of artillery, was attacked at Camalito and again at El Ramon; he succeeded in repulsing the enemy and reaching his destination.

Soon after, as General Quesada demanded extraordinary powers, he was deposed by the Cuban congress, and General Jordan was appointed commander-in-chief in his stead.

In August, 1870, the United States government off·
ered to Spain their good offices for a settlement of the
strife. Mr. Fish, who was then secretary of State, proposed terms for the cession of the island to the Cubans,
but the offer was declined. This is only one of the many
times when Spain, in her suicidal policy, has refused to
listen to reason.

About this time the volunteers expelled General
Dulce, and General de Rodas was sent from Spain to
replace him with a re-enforcement of thirty thousand
men.

General de Rodas, however, remained in command
only about six months, he in his turn being replaced by
Valmaseda, again at the dictation of the volunteers.

Speaking of these volunteers, who it will be remembered were recruited from Spanish immigrants and who
were peculiarly obnoxious to Cubans of all classes, it
will not be out of place to relate here an act of wanton
cruelty upon their part.

This took place in the autumn of 1871. One of the
volunteers had died, and his body had been placed in a
public tomb in Havana. Later it was discovered that
the tomb had been defaced, by some inscription placed
upon it, no more, no less. Suspicion fell upon the students of the university. The volunteers made a complaint and forty-three of the young students were arrested and tried for the misdemeanor. An officer of the
regular Spanish army volunteered to defend them, and
through his efforts, they were acquitted.

This verdict did not satisfy the volunteers, however.

They demanded and obtained from the captain-general, who was a man of weak character, the convening of another court-martial two-thirds of which was to be composed of volunteers. Was there ever such a burlesque of justice? The accusers and the judges were one and the same persons. Of course, there could be but one result. All the prisoners were found guilty and condemned, eight to be shot, and the others to imprisonment and hard labor.

The day after the court-martial (?) fifteen hundred volunteers turned out under arms and executed the eight boys.

This incident filled the whole of the United States with horror and indignation. The action was censured by the Spanish Cortes, but the matter ended there. No attempt whatever was made to punish the offenders.

The insurgents waged an active warfare until the spring of 1871. They had at that time a force of about fifty thousand men, but they were badly armed and poorly supplied with necessities of all sorts. The resources of the Spaniards were infinitely greater. About this time the Cuban soldiers who had been fighting in the district of Camaguey signified a desire to surrender and cease the conflict, provided their lives were spared. The proposition was accepted. Their commander, General Agramonte refused to yield, and he was left with only about thirty-five men who remained loyal to him. He formed a body of cavalry, and continued fighting for some two years longer, when he was killed on the field of battle.

In January, 1873, the Edinburg Review contained a very strong article on the condition of affairs in Cuba, in the course of which it said:

"It is well known that Spain governs Cuba with an iron and blood-stained hand. The former holds the latter deprived of political, civil and religious liberty. Hence the unfortunate Cubans being illegally prosecuted and sent into exile, or executed by military commissions in time of peace; hence their being kept from public meeting, and forbidden to speak or write on affairs of State; hence their remonstrances against the evils that afflict them being looked on as the proceedings of rebels, from the fact that they are bound to keep silence and obey; hence the never-ending plague of hungry officials from Spain, to devour the product of their industry and labor; hence their exclusion from public stations, and want of opportunity to fit themselves for the art of government; hence the restrictions to which public instruction with them is subjected, in order to keep them so ignorant as not to be able to know and enforce their rights in any shape or form whatever; hence the navy and the standing army, which are kept in their country at an enormous expenditure from their own wealth, to make them bend their knees and submit their necks to the iron yoke that disgraces them; hence the grinding taxation under which they labor, and which would make them all perish in misery but for the marvelous fertility of their soil."

In July, 1873, Pieltain, then captain-general, sent an envoy to President Cespedes to offer peace on condition that Cuba should remain a state of the Spanish republic, but this offer was declined.

In December of the same year, Cespedes was deposed by the Cuban Congress, and Salvador Cisneros elected in his place. The latter was a scion of the old Spanish nobility who renounced his titles and had his estates confiscated when he joined the revolution. He was and is distinguished for his patriotism, intelligence and nobility of character. It was his daughter, Evangelina Cisneros, who was rescued from the horrors of a Spanish dungeon by Americans, and brought to the United States.

After his retirement, Cespedes was found by the Spaniards, and put to death, according to their usual policy: "Slay and spare not."

The war dragged on, being more a guerrila warfare than anything else. The losses were heavy on both sides. There is no data from which to obtain the losses of the Cubans, but the records in the War Office at Madrid show the total deaths in the Spanish land forces for the ten years to have been over eighty thousand. Spain had sent to Cuba one hundred and forty-five thousand men, and her best generals, but while they kept the insurgents in check they were unable to subdue them. The condition of the island was deplorable, her trade had greatly decreased and her crops were ruined.

For years there had been a constant waste of men and money, with no perceptible gain on either side.

By 1878, both parties were heartily weary of the struggle and ready to compromise.

General Martinez de Campos was then in command of the Spanish forces, and he opened negotiations with the Cuban leader, Maximo Gomez, the same who was destined later to attain even more prominence. Gomez listened to what was proposed, and after certain deliberations, terms of peace were concluded in February, 1878, by the treaty of El Zanjon.

This treaty guaranteed Cuba representation in the Spanish Cortes, granted a free pardon to all who had taken part directly or indirectly, in the revolution, and permitted all those who wished to do so to leave the island.

At first glance these terms seem fair. But, as we shall see later, Spain in this case as in all others was true to herself, that is, false to every promise she made.

CHAPTER V.

THE VIRGINIUS EMBROGLIO.

There was one event of the ten years' war which deserves to be treated somewhat in detail, as the universal excitement in the United States caused by the affair for a time appeared to make a war between the United States and Spain inevitable. And the Cubans hoped that this occurrence would lead to the immediate expulsion of the Spaniards from Cuba.

The hopes thus raised, however, were doomed to meet with disappointment, as the diplomatic negotiations opened between the United States and Spain led to a peaceable settlement of the whole difficulty.

The trouble was this: On the 31st of October, 1873, the Virginius, a ship sailing under the American flag, was captured on the high seas, near Jamaica, by the Spanish steamer Tornado, on the ground that it intended to land men and arms in Cuba for the insurgent army.

The Virginius was a steamer which was built in England during the civil war, and was used as a blockade-runner. She was captured and brought to the Washington Navy Yard. There she was sold at auction. The purchaser was one John F. Patterson, who took an oath that he was a citizen of the United States. On the 26th of September, 1870, the Virginius was registered in the custom house of New York.

As all the requisities of the statute were fulfilled in her behalf, she cleared in the usual way for Curacoa, and sailed early in September for that port.

It was discovered a good many years after that Patterson was not the real owner of the vessel, but that, as a matter of fact, the money for her purchase had been furnished by Cuban sympathizers, and that she was virtually controlled by them.

From the day of her clearance in New York, she certainly did not return within the territorial jurisdiction of the United States.

Nevertheless, she preserved her American papers, and whenever she entered foreign ports, she made it a practice to put forth a claim to American nationality, which claim was always recognized by the authorities in those ports.

There is no evidence whatever to show that she committed any overt act, or did anything that was contrary to international law.

She cleared from Kingston, Jámaica, on the 23rd of October, 1873, for Costa Rica.

As President Grant said in his message to Congress, January 5th, 1874, she was under the flag of the United States, and she would appear to have had, as against all powers except the United States, the right to fly that flag and to claim its protection as enjoyed by all regularly documented vessels registered as part of our commercial marine.

Still quoting President Grant, no state of war existed conferring upon a maritime power the right to molest and detain upon the high seas a documented vessel, and it could not be pretended that the Virginius had placed herself without the pale of all law by acts of piracy against the human race. (And yet this very thing is what the Spaniards, without rhyme or reason, did claim. Ever since they have been claiming what was false, as for instance their reports of the victories (!) in the American-Spanish war. By so doing they have made themselves the laughing-stock of nations, for, although they never hesitate to lie, they do not know how to lie with a semblance of truth, which might be, far be it from us to say would be, a saving grace).

If the papers of the Virginius were irregular or fraudulent, and frankly they probably were, the offense was one against the laws of the United States, justifiable only in their tribunals. However, to return to facts, on the morning of the 31st of October, the Virginius was seen cruising near the coast of Cuba. She was chased by the Spanish man-of-war Tornado, captured, and brought into the harbor of Santiago de Cuba on the following day.

One hundred and fifty-five persons were on board, many of whom bore Spanish names. This was made a great point of by the Spanish authorities, although as a matter of fact it proved nothing.

This action was not only in violation of international law, but it was in direct contravention of the provisions of the treaty of 1795.

Mr. E. G. Schmitt was at that time the American vice-consul at Santiago, and he lost no time in demanding that he should be allowed to see the prisoners, in order to obtain from them information which should enable him to protect those who might be American citizens, and also whatever rights the ship should chance to have.

Mr. Schmitt was treated with the utmost discourtesy by the authorities, who practically told him that they would admit of no interference on his part, and insisted that all on board the Virginius were pirates and would be dealt with as such.

And indeed they were.

The Virginius was brought into Santiago late in the afternoon of the first of November, and a court-martial was convened the next morning to try the prisoners.

Within a week fifty-three men had received the semblance of a trial and had been shot.

Meanwhile England, who even her worst enemies cannot deny, is always on the side of humanity, intervened.

Reports of the barbarous proceedings had reached Jamaica, and H. M. S. Niobe, under the command of Sir Lambton Lorraine, was dispatched to Santiago with instructions to stop the massacre.

The Niobe arrived at Santiago on the eighth, and Lorraine threatened to bombard the town unless the executions were immediately stopped.

This threat evidently frightened the bloodthirsty governor, for no more shooting took place.

It was a noble act on the part of Sir Lambton Lorraine, and the American public appreciated it. On his way home to England, he stopped in New York. It was proposed to tender him a public reception, but this Sir Lambton declined. But by way of telling what a "brick" he was considered, a silver brick from Nevada was presented to him, upon the face of which was inscribed: "Blood is thicker than water. Santiago de Cuba, November, 1873. To Sir Lambton Lorraine, from the Comstock Mines, Virginia City, Nevada, U. S. A."

President Grant, through General Daniel E. Sickles, who then represented the United States at Madrid, directed that a demand should be made upon Spain for the restoration of the Virginius, for the return of the survivors to the protection of the United States, for a salute to the flag, and for the punishment of the offending parties.

When the news of the massacre reached Washington, the Secretary of State telegraphed Minister Sickles:

"Accounts have been received from Havana of the execution of the captain and thirty-six of the crew and eighteen others. If true, General Sickles will protest against the act as brutal and barbarous, and ample reparation will be demanded."

Minister Sickles replied:

"President Castelar received these observations with his usual kindness, and told me confidentially that at seven o'clock in the morning, as soon as he read the telegram from Cuba, and without reference to any international question, for that indeed had not occurred to him, he at once sent a message to the captain-general, admonishing him that the death penalty must not be imposed upon any non-combatant, without the previous approval of the Cortes, nor upon any person taken in arms against the government without the sanction of the executive."

About that time, a writer of some celebrity, who was also a war correspondent, named Ralph Keeler, mysteriously disappeared. Although it was never proven, there is little doubt but that he was assassinated by the Spaniards.

Then, as now, there was an intense hatred in the Spanish breast against every citizen of the United States.

As Murat Halstead expresses it, there seemed to be a blood madness in the air.

Mr. Halstead, by the way, tells an anecdote of a madman, who seized a rifle with sabre attached and assaulted a young man who had asked him an innocent question. He knocked him down and stabbed him to death with a bayonet, sticking it through him a score of times as he cried:

"Cable my country that I have killed a rebel!"

The murderer was adjudged insane. Further comment is unnecessary.

To return to the controversy over the Virginius between the United States and Spain.

General Sickles, as he had been instructed, made a solemn protest against the barbarities perpetrated at Santiago.

The Spanish Minister of State replied in a rather ill-humored way, and amongst other things, he said that the protest of America was rejected with serene energy.

This somewhat ridiculous expression gave General Sickles a chance to rejoin, which he did, as follows:

"And if at last under the good auspices of Senor Carvajal, with the aid of that serenity that is unmoved by slaughter, and that energy that rejects the voice of humanity, which even the humblest may utter and the most powerful cannot hush, this government is successful in restoring order and peace and liberty where hitherto, and now, all is tumult and conflict and despotism, the fame of the achievement, not confined to Spain, will reach the continents beyond the seas and gladden the hearts of millions who believe that the new world discovered by Columbus is the home of freemen and not that of slaves."

About this time, Spain asked the good offices of England as an intervener, but to his glory be it spoken and to the nation which he represented, Lord Granville declined, "unless on the basis of ample reparation made to the United States."

Spain continued to dilly-dally and evade the question of her responsibility.

On the 25th of November Mr. Fish telegraphed to Minister Sickles:

"If no accommodation is reached by the close of to-morrow, leave. If a proposition is submitted, you will refer it to Washington, and defer action."

This was just after Minister Sickles had informed the authorities at Washington that Lord Granville regarded the reparation demanded as just and moderate.

On the 26th, however, just as the American minister

was preparing to ask for his passports, close the legation and leave Spain, he received a note from Senor Carvajal which conceded in part the demands of the United States.

This proposition was virtually that the Virginius and the survivors should be given up, but the salute was to be dispensed with, in case Spain satisfied the United States within a certain time that the Virginius had no right to carry the flag.

After considerable correspondence an arrangement was finally arrived at, Spain further agreeing to proceed against those who had offended the sovereignty of the United States, or who had violated their treaty rights.

In his message, President Grant says:

"The surrender of the vessel and the survivors to the jurisdiction of the tribunals of the United States was an admission of the principles upon which our demand had been founded. I therefore had no hesitation in agreeing to the arrangement which was moderate and just, and calculated to cement the good relations which have so long existed between Spain and the United States."

The following words, spoken by Secretary Fish to Admiral Polo, in an interview during the progress of the negotiations, are worthy to be quoted:

"I decline to submit to arbitration the question of an indignity to the flag. I am willing to submit all questions which are properly subjects of reference."

On the 16th of December the Virginius, with the American flag flying, was delivered to the United States at Bahia Honda.

The vessel was unseaworthy. Her engines were out of

order and she was leaking badly. On the passage to New York she encountered a severe storm, and, in spite of the efforts of her officers and men, she sank off Cape Fear. The survivors of the massacre were surrendered at Santiago de Cuba on the 18th, and reached New York in safety.

About eighty thousand dollars were paid by Spain as compensation to the families of the American and British victims who perished at Santiago. But no punishment was ever visited upon the governor who ordered the executions. There was a tremendous amount of feeling aroused in the United States over the Virginius affair, and the government was severely criticized and censured for not avenging the inhuman butcheries and the insults to the flag.

But it must be remembered that the government had a very hard task to deal with. There was little or no doubt but that the Virginius, at the time of her capture was intended for an unlawful enterprise, in spite of Captain Fry's words in a letter to his wife just before his execution:

"There is to be a fearful sacrifice of life from the Virginius, and, as I think, a needless one, as the poor people are unconscious of crime and even of their fate up to now. I hope God will forgive me, if I am to blame for it."

The clamor of the American people for revenge was fiery in its intensity, but the government did not yield to it, in which it was right. There has been more than one time in our history when if public opinion had been allowed to rule, the results would have been fatal; and the very men who were most abused, in the light of future events, have been praised for their wisdom and moderation.

Murat Halstead sums up the whole matter in a clear and just manner. He says in his admirable book, "The Story of Cuba:"

"It is not, we must say, a correct use of words to say that the United States was degraded by the Virginius incident. In proportion as nations are great and dignified, they must at least obey their own laws and treaties. When Grant was President of the United States and Castelar was President of Spain, there was a reckless adventure and shocking massacre, but we were not degraded because we did not indulge in a policy of vengeance."

CHAPTER VI.

AGAIN SPAIN'S PERFIDY.

Before proceeding further, it is necessary to call attention to one very important matter which was the direct result of the Ten Years' War. If the insurgents accomplished nothing else, they may well be proud of this achievement.

Their own freedom they failed to obtain, but they were the cause of freedom being bestowed upon others.

We refer to the manumission of the slaves.

The Spanish slave code, promulgated in 1789, is admitted everywhere to have been very humane in its character. So much so that when Trinidad came into the possession of the English, the anti-slavery party resisted successfully the attempt of the planters of that island to have the Spanish law replaced by the British.

Once again, however, were the words of Spain falsified by her deeds. Spanish diplomacy up to the present day has only been another name for lies. For, notwithstanding the mildness of the code, its provisions were constantly and glaringly violated.

In 1840, a writer, who had personal knowledge of the affairs of Cuba, declared that slavery in Cuba was more destructive to human life, more pernicious to society, degrading to the slave and debasing to the master, more fatal to health and happiness than in any other slaveholding country on the face of the habitable globe.

It was in Cuba that the slaves were subjected to the coarsest fare and the most exhausting and unremitting toil. A portion of their number was even absolutely destroyed every year by the slow torture of overwork and insufficient sleep and rest.

In 1792 the slave population of the island was estimated at eighty-four thousand; in 1817, one hundred and seventy-nine thousand; in 1827, two hundred and eighty-six thousand; in 1843, four hundred and thirty-six thousand; in 1867, three hundred and seventy-nine thousand, five hundred and twenty-three, and in 1873, five hundred thousand, or about one-third of the entire population.

In 1870, two years after the beginning of the war, in which the colored people, both free and slaves, took a prominent part, the Spanish legislature passed an act, providing that every slave who had then passed, or should thereafter pass, the age of sixty should be at once free, and that all yet unborn children of slaves should also be free. The latter, however, were to be maintained at the expense of the proprietors up to their eighteenth year, and during that time to be kept as apprentices at such work as was suitable to their age. Slavery was absolutely abolished in Cuba in 1886. Spain was therefore the last civilized country to cling to this vestige of barbarism, and she probably would not have abandoned it then had she not been impelled to by force and her self-interest.

After the treaty of El Zanjon, it was supposed by the Cubans, and rightly too, had they been dealing with an honorable opponent and not a trickster, that the condition of Cuba would be greatly improved.

The treaty, in the first place, guaranteed Cuba representation in the Cortes in Madrid. This was kept to the letter, but the spirit was abominably lacking.

The Peninsulars, that is, the Spaniards in Cuba, obtained complete control of the polls, and, by unparalleled frauds, always managed to elect a majority of the deputies. The deputies, purporting to come from Cuba, might just as well have been appointed by the Spanish crown.

In other and plainer words, Cuba had no representation whatever in the Cortes.

The cities of Cuba were hopelessly in debt and they were not able to provide money for any municipal services.

There were no funds to keep up the schools, and in consequence they were closed.

As for hospitals and asylums, they scarcely existed. There was only one asylum for the insane in all the island, and that was wretchedly managed. This asylum was in Havana. Elsewhere, the insane were confined in the cells of jails.

The public debt of Spain was something enormous, and Cuba was forced to pay a part of the interest on this which was out of all proportion.

Perez Castaneda spoke of this in the Spanish Cortes in the following terms:

"The debt of Cuba was created in 1864 by a simple issue of three million dollars, and it now amounts to the fabulous sum of one hundred and seventy-five million dollars. What originated the Cuban debt? The wars of Santo Domingo, of Peru and of Mexico. But are not these matters for the Peninsula? Certainly they are matters for the whole of Spain. Why must Cuba pay that debt?"

Again, Senor Robledo, in a debate at Madrid, after speaking of the fearful abuses existent in the government of Havana, said:

"I do not intend to read the whole of the report; but I must put the House in possession of one fact. To what do these defalcations amount? They amount to twenty-two million, eight hundred and eleven thousand, five hundred and sixteen dollars. Did not the government know this? What has been done?"

In 1895 it was alleged that the custom house frauds in Cuba, since the end of the Ten Years War, amounted to over one hundred millions of dollars. It is enough to make one hold one's breath in horror. And, remember well, there was absolutely no redress for the suffering Cubans by peaceful means.

One more quotation. Rafael de Eslara of Havana, when speaking of the misery of the island, thus summed up the situation:

"Granted the correctness of the points which I have just presented, it seems to be self-evident that a curse is pressing upon Cuba, condemning her to witness her own disintegration, and converting her into a prey for the operation of those swarms of vampires that are so cruelly devouring us, deaf to the voice of conscience, if

they have any; it will not be rash to venture the asser-
tion that Cuba is undone; there is no salvation possible."

Taxation on all sides was enormous, the two chief
products of the island, sugar and tobacco, suffering the
most. While other countries gave encouragement to
their colonies, Spain did everything she could to dis-
courage her well-beloved "Ever Faithful Isle."

The Cuban planter had to struggle along with a heavy
tax on his crop, an enormous duty on his machinery,
and an additional duty at the port of destination.

America once rose in wrath against unjust taxation,
but her grievances were as nothing in comparison with
those of—we had almost written—her sister republic.
May the inadvertency prove a prophecy!

To show how the products of Cuba, under this ghastly extortion have declined, we make the following
statement, based on the most reliable statistics.

In 1880 Cuba furnished twenty-five per cent. of all
the sugar of the world. In 1895 this had declined to
ten and a half per cent. In 1889, the export of cigars
rated at forty dollars per one thousand amounted to ten
millions, nineteen thousand and forty dollars. In 1894
it was five millions, three hundred and sixty-eight
thousand, four hundred dollars, a loss of nearly one-
half in five years.

Then besides all this, Cuba had to pay the high sal·
aries of the horde of Spanish officials, nothing of which
accrued to her advantage.

There can be no doubt but that the treaty of El Zanjon
was a cheat, and its administration a gigantic scandal.

Can any fair-minded person think then that the Cubans were wrong, when driven to the wall, oppressed beyond measure, goaded to madness by an inhuman master, they broke out once again into open revolt, determined this time to fight to the death or to obtain their freedom?

CHAPTER VII.

SOME CUBAN HEROES.

Although the natural resources of Cuba are remark-able, as will be demonstrated later, and more than suffi-cient for all her people, a large number of Cubans have, either of their own free will or by force become exiles.

Besides over forty thousand in the United States, there are a large number in the islands under British control, as well as throughout the West Indies and in the South American republics.

It is perfectly natural that these exiles should feel the deepest interest in their native land, and although Spain has complained frequently of being menaced from beyond her borders, what else could she expect after the way in which she treated these exiled sons of hers? Besides she has had no just cause for grievance, as the right for foreign countries to furnish asylums to political offenders has been recognized from time immemorial, and, unless some overt act be committed, there can be no responsibility on the part of such foreign countries.

Enough perhaps has been said to show that the Cubans had every reason to once again rise in revolt, but in order that there may be no doubt as to the justice of their cause, let us recapitulate:

Spain has invariably drawn from the island all that could be squeezed out of it.

In spite of her protests she has never done anything for Cuba, all her aim being to replenish her own exhausted treasury and to enrich the functionaries of the Spanish government.

While Cuba is a producing country, she has been refused the right to dispose of her produce to other countries except at ruinous rates, in spite of the fact that Spain herself could not begin to consume all that Cuba had to offer. The market of the island, by the way, from the very nature of things, is the United States, and not Spain.

The rules which limit importation have been most rigid. For instance, American flour cannot enter Cuba free of duty, while it enters as a free product into Spain.

Spain has governed Cuba with a most arbitrary hand. The island has had nothing whatever to say as to the management of its own affairs.

The Cubans have purposely been kept in a state of ignorance, the system of education amounting practically to nothing.

The Spaniards have never kept one promise made, but after each promise have increased their oppression and tyranny.

In 1894 Senor Sagasta laid before the Cortes a project for reform in Cuba; but the sense of this project was confused in the extreme; there was little hope that a reform planned with such little method could meet with any degree of successful realization. In fact there was little or no possibility that the abuses under which the island groaned would be removed.

At last patience ceased to be a virtue. The present rising in Cuba was begun toward the close of 1894. The leader was Jose Marti, a poet and orator, who was then in New York. He at the outset, was the very soul of the revolutionary movement, and he held in his hands the threads of the conspiracy.

He was a man of charming and captivating personality, strong in his own convictions and devoted body, heart and soul to the interests of his country.

He was the son of a Spanish colonel and when quite young was condemned, for what reason has never been known, to ten years imprisonment in Havana. Afterwards, he was sentenced to the galleys for life.

When the amnesty was declared, after the Ten Years War, he was given back his freedom, but his resentment still continued and he vowed his life to obtaining the liberty of Cuba.

He went first to Central America, and afterwards took up his residence in the United States.

Everywhere he preached what he considered a holy war. Here and there he gathered together contributions, which he sent to Cuba for the secret purchase of arms and ammunition. He met with many rebuffs and disappointments, but not for one moment did he doubt the justice of his cause or its ultimate success. He was not a visionary man, but there were those even among the ones he had won over by his impassioned words who looked upon him as the victim of hallucinations. That this was not true, the events of the past few years have fully proven.

Marti organized his first expedition in New York, and set sail for Cuba with three vessels, the Lagonda, the Amadis and the Baracoa, containing men and war materials. This expedition was stopped, however, by the United States authorities.

Later, Marti joined Gomez, Cromlet, Cebreco and the Maceo brothers, all of whom had fought in the Ten Years War, at Santo Domingo, which was Gomez' home.

Some description of these men, all of whom have done magnificent work for the freedom of their country, may not be out of place.

Maximo Gomez is about seventy-five years of age, and he may perhaps be termed the "Washington" of the fight for liberty. It will be remembered that he was a leader in the Ten Years War. He is a man of excellent judgment, and, in spite of his years, of marvelous mental and physical activity. No better man could the insurgents have selected as their general-in.chief.

Flor Cromlet was a guerilla of unquestioned valor, who lost his life early in the campaign, but his name will live in the annals of free and independent Cuba. His mother was a mulatto, but his father was a Spaniard.

The Maceo brothers have been particularly distinguished. They were born of colored parents, and were of the type of the mulatto. Both were men of indomitable courage. Antonio Maceo was born at Santiago de Cuba in 1848. At the beginning of the Ten Years War, he was a mule driver, and could neither read nor write. He was one of the first to enlist in the Cuban army, and soon showed his courage and intelligence. He was rapidly promoted to superior rank and became a terror to the Spanish army. Their one idea seemed to be to capture him, but apparently he possessed a charmed life. During his leisure moments, which it can be imagined were but few, he managed to learn to read and write. He was one of the last combatants to lay down his arms in the former war, and then only because he saw that further struggle would only end in loss of life without the winning of liberty.

He was exiled and then travelled through America, studying constantly and ever endeavoring to improve himself. Here was a poor, obscure, descendant of slaves who by sheer perseverance, of course coupled with natural ability, afterward held the armies of a great nation at bay.

Antonio Maceo was killed in Havana province in 1896, probably through the treachery of one of his followers, and his brother died, but not until both had accomplished wonderful deeds of valor. It is a pity that they could not have lived to see the results of their unselfish patriotism.

Another mulatto who has won fame in the cause of "Free Cuba" is Augustin Cebreco.

The "Marion of Cuba," as he was called, Nestor Aranguren, must not be forgotten. He was at the head of a little band of men, all members of the best Havana families and graduates of the university. He was very much like the "Swamp Fox" of our Revolution in the way he would undertake some daring raid, and then retreat into the long grass of the Manigua to rest his tired horses and recruit his men. One of his most famous exploits was the capture of a train at the very gates of Havana. Aranguren treated his captives most kindly, with one exception, and in this he was justified. A man named Barrios had often informed against the insurgents, and he was condemned to death. Of him, Aranguren said: "That Cuban must die. I must rid my country of such an unnatural son. Thank God, there are few such traitors!"

The rest were allowed to go free.

To one of the Spaniards who were on the train, Aranguren said:

"If Spain should grant a generous and liberal autonomy, peace is not only possible, but probable; but, if she should persevere in her false colors, she will not regain control of this island, until every true soldier of Cuba is dead, and that will take a long time."

The ill-fated Aranguren died at the age of twenty-four.

It was not until May, 1895, that Marti and the other leaders thought it wise to go to Cuba. When they reached there, they found that the insurgents had already commenced the rebellion and had even gained some ground.

At first the Spanish authorities looked upon the insurrection as a trivial matter, nothing more serious than a negro riot.

They believed that it would be speedily suppressed as Spain had then in the island an army of nineteen thousand men, besides the fifty thousand volunteers, who could be called on in case of need. But, to make all sure, seven thousand more soldiers were sent over from Spain.

In addition to this, many men, who afterward were among the leaders of the insurgent party expressed their unqualified disapproval of the movement. And in this, they were undoubtedly sincere, as they had not the slightest idea that it could succeed.

The general lack of sympathy and the universal criticism that met the little band of revolutionists unquestionably contributed much toward the relaxation of the vigilance of the government.

But the government was soon to be undeceived. The insurrection became a very serious matter indeed. The insurgents pursued very much the same tactics that they had followed in the Ten Years War, that is, they would seldom risk an open battle, and the Spaniards could gain but little ground against the guerilla methods of their opponents.

The Cubans were very badly equipped; in fact they had scarcely any war material whatever. They began by appropriating indiscriminately any fire arms wherever they could find them, from the repeating rifle to the shot gun with the ramrod. Many of them were armed only with revolvers, and the majority of them had simply the "machete," a knife about nineteen inches in length.

Recruits constantly came to their ranks, however, and it was not long before they numbered over six thousand.

A political crisis now took place in Spain, and the conservative party came into power. Premier Canovas then appointed as governor-general of Cuba, Martinez Campos, who had been so successful, by diplomacy rather than by anything else, in ending the Ten Years War.

He landed at Guantanamo, and before visiting Havana, he issued the most elaborate instructions to every department of the military service, which now had been largely reinforced.

In the early part of the war, a great misfortune befell the Cubans, and that was in the loss of their beloved leader, Jose Marti.

On the 18th of May, a part of the insurgent army camped upon the plains of Dos Rios, where they learned that the enemy was in the neighborhood, in safety, protected by a fort.

The insurgents numbered about seven hundred cavalrymen, under the command of Marti and Gomez.

The next morning they came upon the Spanish outpost. Gomez, who has always shown himself to be a prudent general, thought it would be wiser not to risk a battle, but to continue their route, as the object of the expedition was not skirmishing, but to attempt to penetrate into the Province of Puerto Principe.

But Jose Marti, in his fiery enthusiasm longed to fall upon the enemy; he declared that not to do so would be dishonor. Gomez yielded.

Marti was mounted upon a very spirited horse. He was told that it was unmanageable, but he would not listen to reason. Crying, ''Come on, my children!'' and

"Viva Cuba Libre," he dashed upon the Spanish, followed by his men.

Before this onslaught, the Spaniards retreated, but in good order. Gomez cried to his troops to rally, but Marti, dragged on by his horse which he was unable to control, disappeared among the ranks of the enemy. He received a bullet above the left eye, another in the throat, and several bayonet thrusts in the body.

Led by Gomez, who was heart broken at the fate of his old companion and friend, the insurgents charged upon the Spaniards, but it was of no avail. The latter retained possession of the corpse of the gallant soldier, whose only fault was a too reckless bravery.

And now it is a pleasure to be able to recount one noble act on the part of the Spaniards, perhaps the only one in the whole course of the war.

General Campos, who was a just and honorable man, ordered the body of the illustrious patriot to receive decent burial, and one of the Spanish officers even pronounced a sort of eulogy over the remains.

There was a report that Gomez had also been killed, but this was a mistake. About a month afterward he crossed the trocha and entered the province of Puerto Principe, more commonly known as the Camaguey.

The trocha, by the way, was an invention of Campos in the preceding war, and was found to be of great value. It was practically a line of forts extending across the island between the provinces of Puerto Principe and Santa Clara, and it was intended that the insurgents should not be allowed to cross this line. Other trochas were afterwards erected, but they have not proved of any extraordinary advantage in the present insurrection.

An assembly, composed of representatives of all the bands that were under arms, met and elected the officers of the revolutionary government.

Salvador Cisneros, otherwise known as the Marquis of Santa Lucia, was elected president, the same office he had filled during the Ten Years War.

The other officers were:

Vice-President, Bartolomeo Maso.

Secretary of State, Rafael Portuondo y Tamayo.

Secretary of War, Carlos Roloff.

Secretary of the Treasury, Severo Pina.

General-in-Chief, Maximo Gomez.

Lieutenant-General, Antonio Maceo.

Afterwards, at another election, as officers, according to the Cuban constitution, only serve two years, there were replaced by the following:

President, Bartolomeo Maso.

Vice-President, Mendez Capote.

Secretary of State, Andres Moreno de la Torres.

Secretary of War, Jose B. Alemon.

Secretary of the Treasury, Ernesto Fons Sterling.

Maximo Gomez still remained general-in-chief.

Gomez and Campos were now pitted once more against each other, as they had been in the previous war.

Both men issued orders to their respective commands.

Gomez ordered the Cubans to attack the small Spanish outposts, capture their arms if possible setting at liberty every man who should deliver them up; to cut all railway and telegraph lines; to keep on the defensive and retreat in groups, unless the Cubans were in a position to fight the enemy at great advantage; to destroy Spanish forts and other buildings where any resistance was made by the enemy; to destroy all sugar crops and mills, the owners of which refused to contribute to the Cuban war fund; and, finally to forbid the farmers to send any food to the cities unless upon the payment of certain taxes.

On his part, Campos issued the following commands:

Several regiments to protect the sugar estates; other detachments to be placed along the railroads, and on every train in motion; to attack always, unless the enemy's numbers were three to one; all rebels, except officers, who surrendered, to be allowed to go free and unmolested; convoys of provisions to be sent to such towns as needed them.

Everything was now in readiness for a fierce campaign, and one that threatened to be protracted. It was not long before operations commenced in earnest. '

CHAPTER VIII.

CUBAN TACTICS.

There was one incident which occurred in the early part of the disturbances which caused a certain amount of excitement in the United States, as it was thought that it would prove to be a repetition of the Virginius affair.

On the 8th of March, 1895, the ship Allianca was bound from Colon to New York. She was following the usual track of vessels near the Cuban shore. But, outside the three mile limit, she was fired upon by a Spanish gunboat. President Cleveland declared this to be an unwarrantable interference by Spain with passing American ships. Protest was promptly made by the United States against this act as not being justified by a state of war; nor permissible in respect of a vessel on the usual paths of commerce, nor tolerable in view of the wanton peril occasioned to innocent life and property. This act was disavowed by Spain, with full expression of regret, and with an assurance that there should not be again such just cause for complaint. The offending officer was deposed from his command. All this was eminently satisfactory, and the United States took no further action in the matter.

The chief battle of the campaign, while Campos still remained governor-general, was that fought at Bayamo, in July, 1895. Campos himself commanded in person, and for the first time the Spaniards, ever vain-glorious and self-confident, became aware of the mettle of the men arrayed against them.

The Spanish forces numbered some five thousand men, while the Cubans had not much more than half that number. It was the Spanish strategy, however, to divide their men into detachments, and the Cubans were quick to take advantage of this. The fight was a long and bloody affair, but finally the victory, although not pronounced, remained with the Cubans.

The Spanish forces were more or less demoralized, and their loses were heavy. Thirteen Spanish officers were killed, while the Cubans lost two colonels. The Cubans admitted that fifty of their number were killed or disabled, but they claimed that the loss of the Spaniards was over three hundred.

It is impossible to tell much from the Spanish accounts, as they were far from being complete and were highly colored. It has been the same way in the present war, as witness the laughable "one mule" report, with which all are familiar.

In this engagement, General Santocildes was killed. It is said that Santocildes sacrificed his own life to save that of his friend and superior, Campos.

There are two very different stories told of the attitude of Antonio Maceo toward Campos in this battle. One is to the effect that he did not know that Campos was commanding in person, but when he was told of it the following day, he said:

"Had I known it, I would have sacrificed five hundred more of my men, and I would have taken him dead or alive! Thus with one blow I would have ended the war."

The other is quite different, and has been very generally believed amongst the Cubans. It is to the effect that, during the fight, Maceo recognized Campos, and, pointing him out to his men, ordered them not to harm him, as he was a soldier who made war honorably.

Murat Halstead relates two incidents of the battle of Bayamo, which, however, he declares must be taken with a large grain of salt. One, which comes from an insurgent authority is as follows:

"Campos only saved himself by a ruse. Taking advantage of the Cubans' well-known respect for the wounded, he had himself placed in a covered stretcher, which they allowed to pass, without looking inside the cover. When outside of the Cuban lines he was obliged to walk on foot to Bayamo, through six miles of by-paths, under cover of the darkness, only accompanied by a colored guide."

The other tells that a son of Campos, who was a lieutenant, was captured, but released with a friendly message to his father, who of course, was expected to follow so admirable an example.

Whether these anecdotes are true or not, one thing is certain. After the battle, Maceo collected the wounded, whom the Spaniards left upon the field in their retreat, and treated them in the most humane manner possible. He wrote to Campos the following letter:

"To His Excellency, the General Martinez Campos:

"Dear Sir—Anxious to give careful and efficient attendance to the wounded Spanish soldiers that your troops left behind on the battle-field, I have ordered that they be lodged in the houses of the Cuban families that live nearest to the battle-ground, until you send for them.

"With my assurance that the forces you may send to escort them back will not meet any hostile demonstrations from my soldiers, I have the honor to be, sir,

"Yours respectfully,

"Antonio Maceo."

While Maceo was thus maneuvering in the eastern part of the island, the general-in-chief, Maximo Gomez, was fighting in Camaguey. The population in the provinces of Puerto Principe and Santiago de Cuba had risen almost to a man, and the movement was well under way in the province of Santa Clara.

Several encounters took place, the most important being the attack upon the little city of Cascorro, which Gomez succeeded in capturing. He found there a large quantity of arms and ammunition, of which the Cubans were greatly in need.

Gomez proved himself quite as magnanimous as Maceo. The wounded were all cared for to the best of his ability, and the prisoners were returned to the Spanish leaders. This example, however, seems to have been utterly lost upon the Spaniards.

The insurgent forces, under Gomez, were at this time divided into six portions, operating in the six provinces, and commanded by Antonio Maceo, Aguerre, Lacret, Carillo, Suarez and Jose Maceo. Suarez was afterwards cashiered for cowardice, and replaced by Garcia.

In August, 1895, Maceo joined his chief at a place called Jimaguaya, where Gomez had called to him a large proportion of the Cuban forces, which numbered at that time about thirty thousand.

And against these undisciplined soldiers was arrayed a regular army of over eighty-five thousand men, not counting the armed volunteers.

The odds were terribly against the Cubans, but Gomez and Maceo were confident of success.

It should be mentioned here that there were quite a number of women fighting under Maceo, and these women did heroic service. In fact, the Cuban women have given innumerable proofs of their devotion, body and soul, to the cause of "Cuba Libre."

Gomez' objective point was Havana, and between Jimaguaya and Havana, there were over fifty thousand Spanish soldiers.

When Gomez started, he had about twelve thousand men, which he divided into three columns. He was quite well aware that the fighting must be of the guerilla stamp. In fact, it was the only species of warfare possible.

He therefore instructed his lieutenants to have recourse to strategy, to foil the enemy at every point. The one object was to reach Havana.

"In the event of a forced battle," he said finally, "overthrow them! Pass over them and on to Havana!"

The march was begun, the instructions being followed to the letter. Actual combat was everywhere avoided. The Spanish papers constantly had reports like this: "After a few shots the rebels ran away." They did not understand that this was exactly Gomez' tactics, and he was succeeding, too.

Every day' the insurgents advanced further and further west. At the end of a fortnight they reached the trocha of Jaruco, which had been constructed in the centre of the island. This trocha was occupied by a large and important Spanish force.

Gomez ordered Maceo to make a feigned attack upon the northern portion of the trocha. The Spaniards rushed there in a body, and Gomez, who had counted upon this very thing, crossed the southern part, which was left unprotected, without striking a blow.

As soon as Maceo knew that Gomez had passed over in safety, he immediately disappeared with his men, and soon after managed to rejoin his chief.

It was a very clever ruse, and Campos, whose head-quarters were then in Santa Clara realized that he had been outgeneralled. He ordered a hurried march to Cienfuegos, and there took command.

The evasive movements of the insurgents continued, and again and again was Campos outflanked.

With but little difficulty the Cubans crossed two other trochas, and finally entered the Province of Matanzas, which Campos had felt positive could never be invaded; the Spaniards meanwhile constantly retreating, nearer and nearer to the capital.

At last, Campos determined to force an open conflict. He told his lieutenants where they were to meet him.

This was in December, 1895.

Campos lay in wait for Maceo's forces at a point between Coliseo and Lumidero.

It seemed at first as if the insurgents were caught in a trap, and would be forced to accept a battle in the open, which could not fail to be disastrous to them.

But a happy thought came to Maceo, and, in connection with this plan, he issued his orders.

Suddenly, the cane-fields which surrounded the camp of the Spaniards burst into flame, and on each side was a great blazing plain. Campos knew that he had once more been foiled, and he gave the order to retreat at once.

This battle, if battle it can be called, had important results. It enabled Gomez to reach Jovellanos, a city which commanded the railroad lines of Cardenas, Matanzas and Havana. These lines Gomez destroyed as well as every sugar plantation upon his route.

As to the destruction of the sugar fields and the reason therefor, we shall have something to say later on.

Campos, completely outwitted and vanquished in his attempts to stop the onward progress of the insurgents, now fell back upon Havana, which he reached Christmas Day.

His reception in the capital was anything but a pleasant one. The Spaniards there had clamored from the very beginning for revenge without mercy, and they looked upon the successive checks which the army had received as little less than criminal. They demanded of the governor-general the reason for his repeated defeats, and even threatened him personally.

There were three political parties in Cuba, the Conservatives, the Reformists and the Autonomists. Campos met the leaders of these parties in an interview, and asked for their opinions. The consultation was very unsatisfactory, and as a result Campos proposed his resignation to which the ministry made no objection.

Shortly after, his resignation was sent in and accepted. He sailed for Spain the 17th of January, his place being temporarily filled by General Sabas Marin.

In spite of Martinez Campos' failure to subdue the insurrection, nothing but the greatest sympathy and respect can be felt for him, at least out of Spain, where, speaking in a general manner, humanity has no place, and gratitude is an unknown quantity.

Campos' services to his country had been great, including, as they did, the pacification of Cuba in the Ten Years War, the quelling of a revolt in Spain itself, and the restoration and support of the Spanish monarchy. At an advanced age, when he should have been enjoying a well deserved rest, he was sent away to fight a difficult war, and to risk the tarnishing of his laurels as a military commander.

All praise to Martinez Campos for his pure patriotism, his unswerving rectitude, his magnanimity and his exalted ideas of honor! This praise even the enemies of his country cannot refuse to him.

CHAPTER IX.

WEYLER THE BUTCHER.

No greater contrast to Campos could possibly be imagined than his successor, General Valeriano Weyler, known, and with the utmost justice, throughout Cuba and the United States as "The Butcher."

During his official life in Cuba, he proved again and again the truth of his reputation for relentless cruelty.

There is no doubt that during former wars he committed the most atrocious crimes.

It is not claimed that he ever showed any brilliant qualifications as a military leader, and it was precisely because he lacked the characteristics of General Campos, that Spain appointed him governor-general, hoping that his severity (no, severity is too mild a word, his savage brutality) would accomplish what Campos had failed to do.

In the light of events following his appointment, events which filled the whole civilized world with indignation and horror, it has been pretended by Spain that her ministry specially instructed him to "moderate his ardor."

Moderate his ardor, indeed! Granted that he obeyed instructions, if, indeed such instructions ever existed, just think for a moment what would have happened if he had not!

It is very hard to write in a temperate vein when Weyler is the subject. But where is the case for the plaintiff? Where are their defenders, when Nero, Caligula or Judas is in question?

Let us now contemplate a pen picture of "The Butcher," painted by Mr. Elbert Rappleye, a very clever American newspaper correspondent:

"General Weyler is one of those men who creates a first impression, the first sight of whom can never be effaced from the mind, by whose presence the most careless observer is impressed instantly, and yet, taken altogether, he is a man in whom the elements of greatness are concealed under a cloak of impenetrable obscurity. Inferior physically, unsoldierly in bearing, exhibiting no trace of refined sensibilities nor pleasure in the gentle associations that others live for, or at least seek as diversions, he is nevertheless the embodiment of mental acuteness, crafty, unscrupulous, fearless and of indomitable perseverance.

"Campos was fat, good-natured, wise, philosophical, slow in his mental processes, clear in his judgment, emphatic in his opinions, outspoken and withal, lovable, humane, conservative, constructive, progressive, with but one object ever before him, the glorification of Spain as a motherland and a figure among peaceful, enlightened nations. Weyler is lean, diminutive, shriveled, ambitious for immortality, irrespective of its odor, a master of diplomacy, the slave of Spain for the glory of sitting at the right of her throne, unlovable, unloving, exalted."

After telling of how he was admitted to Weyler's presence, Mr. Rappleye continues his vivid description.

"And what a picture! A little man. An apparition of blacks—black eyes, black hair, black beard, dark— exceedingly dark—complexion; a plain black attire. He was alone and was standing facing the door I entered. He had taken a position in the very centre of the room, and seemed lost in its immense depths. His eyes, far apart, bright, alert and striking, took me in at a glance. His face seemed to run to chin, his lower jaw protruding far beyond any ordinary indication of firmness, persistence or will power. His forehead is neither high nor receding; neither is it that of a thoughtful or philosophic man. His ears are set far back; and what is called the region of intellect, in which are those mental attributes that might be defined as powers of observation, calculation, judgment and exe- cution, is strongly developed."

Mrs. Kate Masterson, another American journalist, was, we believe, the only one, except Mr. Rappelye, who obtained an interview with Weyler.

Among other things that he said, Mrs. Masterson re- ports the following:

"I have shut out the Spanish and Cuban papers from the field as well as the American. In the last war the correspondents created much jealousy by what they wrote. They praised one and rebuked the other. They are a nuisance."

"I have no time to pay attention to stories. Some of them are true and some of them are not."

"The Spanish columns attend to their prisoners just as well as any other country in times of war." An obviously false statement, by the way. "War is war. You cannot make it otherwise, try as you will."

True to a certain extent, General Weyler, but not from your point of view. There are certain humanitarian principles, of which you seem to be ignorant that can be practiced in time of war as well as in time of peace.

Weyler declared to Mrs. Masterson that women, if combatants, would be treated just the same as men. As a matter of fact, whether combatants or non-combatants, he treated them worse than men.

He sneered at the Cuban leaders, at Maceo for being a mulatto, and for having, as he asseverated, no military instruction. And at Gomez, whom he declared was not a brave soldier and had never distinguished himself in any way.

It has always been the policy of the Spaniards to belittle the Cubans, sneering at them as being generaled by negroes, half breeds and illiterate to a degree. Beyond the fact that this is contemptibly false, they do not stop to think how they are dishonoring their own troops which have made such little headway against them.

When the Spaniards have forced the insurgents to surrender in all the revolts that have taken place, it has been mainly through false representations and lying promises, promises that they knew, when they made them, were never intended to be carried out.

Weyler's character may perhaps be best understood

from his own following egotistical statement, which is well-authenticated:

"I care not for America, England, or any other country, but only for the treaties we have with them. They are the law. I know I am merciless, but mercy has no place in war. I know the reputation which has been built up for me. I care not what is said about me unless it is a lie so grave as to occasion alarm. I am not a politician. I am Weyler."

Contrast with these utterances, the words of Maximo Gomez, the grand old man of Cuba, in his instructions to his men:

"Do not risk your life unnecessarily. You have only one and can best serve your country by saving it. Dead men cannot fire guns. Keep your head cool, your machete warm, and we will yet free Cuba."

Gomez, by the way, at one time, served under Weyler, the former a captain, the latter as a colonel. The noble Cuban leader certainly did not obtain his views of modern warfare from his then superior officer.

When Weyler arrived in Cuba he had at his command at least one hundred and twenty thousand regulars, fifty thousand volunteers and a large naval coast guard. Rather a formidable force to subdue what has been characterized as a handful of bandits.

His policy from the beginning was one of extermination, and he made war upon those who were not in arms against Spain as well as those who were, upon women and children as well as upon men.

Although Weyler did not begin what may be called

active operations until November (he arrived in February), still he persecuted by every means in his power the pacificos, that is, those who did not take arms for or against either side.

He conceived what General Fitzhugh Lee calls "the brilliant idea" of ruining the farmers so that they should not be able to give any aid to the insurgents.

Read carefully the text of his famous reconcehtrado order, which brought misery, ruin and death to the peaceable inhabitants of the island:

"I, Don Valeriano Weyler y Nicolau, Marquis of Tenerife, Governor-General, Captain-General of this island and Commander-in-Chief of the Army, etc., etc., hereby order and command:

"₁. That all inhabitants of the country districts, or those who reside outside the lines of fortifications of the towns, shall within a delay of eight days enter the towns which are occupied by the troops. Any individual found outside the lines in the country at the expiration of this period shall be considered a rebel and shall be dealt with as such.

"2. The transport of food from the towns, and the carrying of food from one place to another by sea or by land, without the permission of the military authorities of the place of departure, is absolutely forbidden. Those who infringe upon the order will be tried and punished as aiders and abettors of the rebellion.

"3. The owners of cattle must drive their herds to the towns, or the immediate vicinity of the towns, for which purposes proper escorts will be given them.

"4. When the period of eight days, which shall be reckoned in each district from the day of the publication of this proclamation in the country town of the district, shall have expired, all insurgents who may present themselves will be placed under my orders for the purpose of designating a place in which they may reside. The furnishing of news concerning the enemy, which can be availed of with advantage, will serve as a recommendation to them; also, when the presentation is made with firearms in their possession, and when, and more especially, when the insurgents present themselves in numbers.   Valeriano Weyler."

Was there ever a more damnable—there is no other word for it—a more damnable proclamation issued?

And the result? Words can scarcely do justice to it. It was the death-sentence of thousands and thousands of innocent people, the large majority of whom were women and children.

The peasant farmers, with their families, were only allowed to bring with them what they could carry on their backs, when they were forced to leave all that they had in the world, and remove to the places of "concentration," where it was impossible for them to make a living.

Before leaving they saw their houses and crops burned, and their live stock, be it much or little, that they possessed, confiscated.

Starvation was before them, and starve they did. And let the reader bear this fact well in mind—these were non-combatants, women and children.

The deaths have occurred in ghastly numbers. More than two hundred thousand have perished from starvation and starvation alone, with no hand from the government stretched out to aid them. The record made by the butcher and the butcher's emissaries is without parallel in all history. No wonder that the United States held its breath in horror, before raising its mailed hand to strike forever the chains from this suffering people.

General Weyler did not care how deeply he should wade in blood, nor to what age or sex this blood belonged, so long as he should attain his ends.

Talk as you please about the atrocities of the Turks, but they pale before those of the Spaniards in Cuba; acts committed, too, not in secret, but openly and by public proclamation.

Read what Stephen Bonsal, who was an eye-witness, says in his book: "The Real Condition of Cuba To-day."

"In the western provinces, we find between three and four hundred thousand people penned up in starvation stations and a prey to all kinds of epidemic diseases. They are without means and without food, and with only the shelter that the dried palm-leaves of their hastily erected bohios afford, and in the rainy season that is now upon them, there is no shelter at all. They have less clothing than the Patagonian savages, and, half naked, they sleep upon the ground, exposed to the noxious vapors which these low-lying swamp-lands emit. They have no prospect before them but to die, or, what is more cruel, to see those of their own flesh and blood dying about them, and to be powerless to succor and to save. About these starvation stations the savage sentries pace up and down with ready rifle and bared machete, to shoot down and to cut up any one who dares to cross the line. And yet, who are these men who are shot down in the night like midnight marauders? And why is it they seek, with all the desperate courage of despair, to cross that line where death is always awaiting their coming, and almost invariably overtakes them? They are attempting nothing that history will preserve upon its imperishable tablets, or even this passing generation remember. No, they are simply attempting to get beyond the starvation lines, to dig their potatoes and yams, to bring home again to the hovel in which their families are housed with death and hunger all about them. And they do their simple duty, not blinded as to the danger, or without warning as to their probable fate, for hardly an hour of their interminable day passes without their hearing the sharp click of the trigger and the hoarse cry of the sentry which precede the murderous volley; and every morning, through the narrow, filthy lanes upon which the huts have been erected the guerillas, drive along the pack-mules bearing the mutilated bodies of those who have been punished cruelly for the crime of seeking food to keep their children from starvation. This colossal crime, with all the refinement of slow torture, is so barbarous, so bloodthirsty and yet so exquisite, that the human mind refuses to believe it, and revolts at the suggestion that it was conceived, planned and plotted by a man. And yet this crime, this murder of thousands of innocent men, women and children, is now being daily committed in Cuba, at our very doors and well-nigh in sight of our shores, and we are paying very little heed to the spectacle.''

These words were written before the United States came to the rescue, and the criticism in the last sentence is, thank Heaven, no longer applicable. We are slow to act perhaps, but when we do act, our work is effective, and we never rest until our aim is accomplished.

CHAPTER X.

THE CRIME OF THE CENTURY.

To enlarge upon the sufferings of the Cubans is a painful task, but it is a task that must be accomplished, in the interests of justice and humanity, and also that the reader may clearly understand why it was the bounden duty of the United States to interfere.

Let us therefore proceed with the evidence.

Julian Hawthorne gives his testimony as follows:

"These people have starved in a land capable of supplying tens of millions of people with abundant food. The very ground on which they lie down to breathe their last might be planted with produce that would feed them to repletion. But so far from any effort to save them having been made by Spain, she has wilfully and designedly compassed their destruction. She has driven them in from their fields and plantations and forbidden them to help themselves; the plantations themselves have been laid waste, and should the miserable reconcentrados attempt under the pretended kindly dispensation of Blanco to return to their properties they would find the Spanish guerillas lying in wait to massacre them. No agony of either mind or body has been wanting. The wife has lost her husband, the mother, her children; the child its parents, the husband, his family. They have seen them die. Often they have seen them slaughtered wantonly as they lay helpless, waiting a slower end. The active as well as the passive cruelties of the Spaniards toward these people have been well nigh unimaginable."

Call Richard Harding Davis to the stand!

"In other wars men have fought with men, and women have suffered indirectly because the men were killed, but in this war it is the women herded together in the towns like cattle who are going to die, while the men camped in the fields and mountains will live."

General Fitz Hugh Lee says:

"General Weyler believes that everything is fair in war and every means justifiable that will ultimately write success on his standards. He did not purpose to make war with velvet paws, but to achieve his purpose of putting down the insurrection, if he had to wade through, up to the visor of his helmet, the blood of every Cuban, man, women and child, on the island."

Now hear General Lee relate the following incident, an incident which created much discussion and feeling in the United States:

"Dr. Ruiz, an American dentist, who was practicing his profession in a town called Guanabacoa, some four miles from Havana, was arrested. A railroad train between Havana and this town had been captured by the insurgents, and the next day the Spanish authorities arrested a large number of persons in Guanabacoa, charging them with giving information which enabled the troops, under their enterprising young leader, Aranguren, to make the capture; and among these persons arrested was this American. He was a strongly built, athletic man, who confined himself strictly to the practice of his profession and let politics alone. He had nothing to do with the train being captured, but that night was visiting a neighbor opposite, until nine or ten o'clock, when he returned to his house and went to bed. He was arrested by the police the next morning; thrown into an incommunicado cell; kept there some fifty or sixty hours, and was finally (when half crazed by his horrible imprisonment and calling for his wife and children) struck over the head with a 'billy' in the hands of a brutal jailer and died from the effects. Ruiz went into the cell an unusually healthy and vigorous man, and came out a corpse."

James Creelman, a brilliant newspaper correspondent, gives his testimony:

"Everywhere the breadwinners of Cuba are fleeing in terror before the Spanish columns, and the ranks of life are being turned into the ranks of death, for the Cuban who has seen his honest and harmless neighbors tied up and shot before his eyes, in order that some officer may get credit for a battle, takes his family to the nearest town or city for safety, and then goes out to strike a manly blow for his country."

Senator Thurston, who was sent to Cuba to investigate and report the condition of affairs, in a passionate address to the United States Senate testifies:

"For myself I went to Cuba firmly believing the condition of affairs there had been greatly exaggerated by the press, and my own efforts were directed in the first instance to the attempted exposure of these supposed exaggerations. Mr. President, there has undoubtedly been much sensationalism in the journalism of the time, but as to the condition of affairs in Cuba, there has been no exaggeration, because exaggeration has been impossible. The pictures in the American newspapers of the starving reconcentrados are true. They can all be duplicated by the thousands. I never saw, and please God I may never see again, so deplorable a sight as the reconcentrados in the suburbs of Mantanzas. I can never forget to my dying day the hopeless anguish in their despairing eyes. Huddled about their little bark huts, they raised no voice of appeal to us for alms as we went among them. The government of Spain has not and will not appropriate one dollar to save these people. They are now being attended and nursed and administered to by the charity of the United States. Think of the spectacle! We are feeding these citizens of Spain; we are nursing their sick; we are saving such as can be saved, and yet there are those who still say: 'It is right for us to send food, but we must keep our hands off.' I say that the time has come when muskets ought to go with the food."

Finally, Senor Enrique Jose Verona, who was at one time a deputy to the Spanish Cortes, sums up the situation as follows:

"Spain denies to the Cubans all effective powers in their own country. Spain condemns the Cubans to a political inferiority in the land where they were born. Spain confiscates the product of the Cubans' labor without giving them in return either safety, prosperity or education. Spain has shown itself utterly incapable of governing Cuba. Spain exploits, impoverishes and demoralizes Cuba.''

This is only a very small portion of the testimony which might be offered, but can the opinions of men of undoubted honor and veracity be impeached?

Not a tithe of the horrors which has existed in the island of Cuba has been told, and probably never will be told. Because a large proportion of the sufferers did not, like Du Barri shriek upon the scaffold, but, like De Rohan, died mute.

But still something further can be said as to ''The Butcher's,'' methods, and, worse still, as to the putting into practice of those methods. The insurgents have invariably been treated as if they were pirates. The tigerish nature of Weyler spared no one. Refugees, that is those who did not obey his barbarous proclamation, were shot down in cold blood. Starvation was his policy, and starvation too of those, whatever their sympathies might have been, had never raised a finger against the existing government. The reconcentrados, harassed beyond all measure, saw nothing before them but death, and the happiest among them were those who died first.

How would you, reader, like to be shut off, with no means of subsistence, for yourself, your wife and your children, within military lines, to cross which meant instant death?

The Butcher could not conquer this valiant people in honorable warfare, and therefore, worthy scion of his blood, he, without one qualm of conscience, determined to exterminate them. Young boys, not more than fifteen or sixteen years of age, were charged with the crime of "rebellion and incendiarism" (that was the favorite charge of Weyler), and sometimes with the pretence of a trial, sometimes with no trial at all, were shot down in cold blood by the score. Poor little starving babies clung to their mothers' breasts from which no substance was to be obtained. Weyler knew all this, and in his palace in Havana simply laughed, content so long as each day the death rate of the Cubans increased, and he himself was gaining favor with his government, and meanwhile had all that he wanted to eat and drink.

The merciless wretch, by the way, was ever careful not to expose his own precious person to bullet or machete.

But what could be expected of him? He was a Spaniard, a man after Spain's own heart, and one whom it was her delight to honor.

This picture is not over-painted. The colors if anything are laid on too thin.

Although the so-called rebels were not conquered and never could be conquered, Weyler was constantly sending reports home of the "pacification" of first this and then that portion of the island. This he probably supposed was necessary to placate the Spaniards, who are divided amongst themselves and ever ready to rise against the existing government whatever it may be

In spite of all this, brute Weyler has been and still is the idol of a certain class of Spaniards. In spite of all? No, we should have said, because of all.

One of his adherents, among other things, said to Stephen Bonsal, and this is the sort of utterance that the majority of Spain applauds:

"The only way to end this Cuban question is the way General Weyler is going about it. The only way for Spain to retain her sovereignty over these islands is to exterminate—butcher if you like—every man, woman and child upon it who is infected with the contagion and dreams of Cuba Libre. These people must be exterminated and we consider no measure too ruthless to be adopted to secure this end.

"I read in an American paper the other day that General Weyler was poisoning the streams from which the insurgents drink in Matanzas province. It was not true, but I only wish it had been.

"General Weyler is our man. We feel sure of him. He will not be satisfied until every insurgent lies in the ditch with his throat cut, and that is all we want."

Stop a moment and think! These words were spoken at the end of the nineteenth century by the representative of a professed Christian country. How have the teachings of Christ, who always and primarily advocated charity, been forgotten or perverted!

The whole matter of Cuba under Spanish rule is a disgrace to the age we live in.

But (call it spread-eagleism if you like) the United States now has the affair in hand. It can and will right this wrong, and so effectively that there will be no possibility of its recurrence.

CHAPTER XI.

TWO METHODS OF WARFARE: THE SPANISH AND THE CUBAN.

Now let us turn to the one crime, so-called, that has been alleged against the Cubans.

We refer to the burning of the sugar crops.

That this has been done on each and every occasion, no one will deny. At first glance, it seems an act of vandalism. But is it so? Let us examine carefully into the causes and reasons for it.

The Spaniards claim that it is a notable example of the reckless and uncivilized methods of the insurgents. On the contrary, it is a policy which was carefully planned and systematically carried out by Gomez and the other Cuban leaders.

In a proclamation by Gomez, he ordered his lieutenants to burn the sugar plantations, but he did not tell them to destroy the mills, because he did not wish, in case of his succeeding in his purpose of liberating Cuba, to lay the producers flat upon their backs, from which position they could never, or, only with the utmost difficulty, arise.

The destruction of the sugar cane was a necessity of war. It must be remembered that from the sugar crop Spain has received her largest revenue from Cuba, and to cut off this source of revenue is to cripple Spain and take away from her a large sum of money with which she might otherwise wage warfare.

To show that the damage wrought is by no means irreparable, we cannot do better than quote Baron Antomarchi, a Frenchman who lived for a long time in Cuba, was there during the early part of the present insurrection, and knows of what he is speaking:

"Since the suppression of slavery, and as a result of the high price of labor the work of sugar making had been modified. In former times a sugar planter considered his plantation his most necessary possession. After the process of manufacture was modified, it was his sugar mill upon which he depended; his plantation was less important. So in burning the sugar crop, Gomez did not strike a death-blow at the producer. It is a well known fact that when the cane growth is cut by fire and the fields are burntclose to the ground, the yield of the following season is increased and improved; so we see that Gomez did not ruin the country when he burned the plantations. True, the fields have been burned, but they will spring up with a more vigorous luxuriance after the rest which was one of the conditions imposed upon the first agricultural community of which we have any reliable record, and if the mills which Gomez has left intact are not destroyed by some authority equally potent, when the country is reorganized, the sugar industry may flourish to a degree undreamed of before the Cuban war for liberty."

Besides depriving Spain of her revenue, Gomez had another though a lesser reason, for burning the sugar cane.   He knew that those who were thrown out of employment would flock to his standard, and his forces thereby be greatly augmented.

On the whole, we do not see that the criticism and blame which have been given to the insurgents for destroying the crops and for the time being laying waste the land, are deserved.   It was a measure of war, and one, which it seems to us, under the circumstances, was thoroughly justified.

Now let us contrast, for a moment, the different methods of the Spaniards and the Cubans in waging warfare.

In the first place, we do not mean to affirm that the insurgents have not committed actions, which, in the light of civilization, are indefensible, but they are few and far between, and they were forced upon them. After all the horrors to which they were subjected, they would have been less than human if they had not retaliated.

The Cubans, both in the Ten Years' War and in the present one, have been merciful to those of the enemy who fell into their hands.   The latter have been almost invariably treated with kindness and allowed to go free and unmolested.

But the Spaniards never reciprocated.   It has been their invariable policy not to exchange prisoners, a notable instance of this being their recent refusal to exchange the gallant Hobson and his comrades.   To be sure, according to international law they are not compelled to do this, but it is doubtful if there is another civilized nation (by the way, it is an undeserved compliment to intimate that Spain is civilized), which would have acted as the country which boasts of its chivalry has done.

Just here, let us say that those acts of cruelty which have been committed by the Cuban army have been very far from receiving the sanction of their leaders. On the contrary, they have been done in violation of the explicit orders of those leaders; and whenever the offenders have been discovered, they have been hanged as bandits to the limb of the nearest tree.

The hatred and barbarity which the Spaniards have without exception, evinced toward the Cubans have done much to alienate the latter, have been the chief causes why peace could not be maintained, and have made only one outcome possible—the freedom and independence of the island.

We have already seen the humanity with which Gomez, Maceo and the other Cuban chiefs treated the wounded of the enemy who chanced to fall into their hands.

But how was it on the other side? How did the Spaniards behave toward the insurgent wounded? When not killed at once and their sufferings ended immediately, they were cast into loathsome dungeons, with insufficient food and with no medical attendance whatever.

Now to a charge which has more than once been brought against Spain, which has been brought against her recently, which her government has indignantly denied, but which both in the past and the present has been proved beyond any question of a doubt.

The charge refers to an action which, with the exception of Spain, has never been committed but by the most savage tribes, the Indians of North America and the inhabitants of darkest Africa. We do not think that even the Turks were ever accused of such an atrocious, unspeakable act.

We mean the mutilation of the dead bodies (often in a horrible, obscene way) left upon the battlefield.

It is with regret and loathing that we approach the subject. But facts must be spoken.

There has been scarcely a combat between the Spaniards and the Cubans, in all the revolutions which have occurred, where the former have not been guilty of the revolting practice of the mutilation of dead bodies.

Indeed the most savage of tribes have never gone further in the demoniac wreaking of vengeance upon the fallen bodies of the enemy than the Spaniards have.

It has been a common custom with them to disfigure, mangle and commit nameless indignities upon the dead.

When Nestor Aranguren, who you will remember was one of the bravest of the Cuban leaders, the ''Marion,'' the ''Swamp Fox'' of the insurrection, was killed, his body, covered with honorable wounds was taken to Havana, and paraded before the citizens, subject to their jeers and curses.

When another insurgent leader, Castillo, was killed, the same frightful spectacle was witnessed.

Indeed, it has been the rule among the Spaniards

whenever the body of a so-called rebel leader fell into their hands, to drag his nude and mutilated body, tied at the end of a horse's tail, throughout the nearest town, and the excuse for this was—what? That the body might be fully identified.

Among the Cubans, there is only one instance related where they retaliated in kind. And this was when it is said that they sent a Spanish soldier back to Havana with his tongue cut out. But even this story, the only act of brutality alleged against them is not well authenticated, resting as it does entirely upon Spanish evidence. And we know well how much credence can be given to that evidence.

To come down to more recent occurrences.

When it was first reported that the bodies of our marines killed at Guantanamo were subjected to unmentionable mutilations by the Spaniards, we could not believe it. It was said that the condition of the bodies was caused by shots fired from the Mauser rifle. But the Mauser rifle inflicts a clean cut hole. It could not possibly have been responsible for the horrible condition of the bodies. It is impossible for us to explain further in print. Remember or look up what was done by the Apaches in some of our Indian wars, and then from your knowledge, or the knowledge gained by research, fill up the hiatus.

And the Spaniards cannot claim in this latter instance, if indeed they can in any other, that these barbarities were committed by irregular and irresponsible troops. It is beyond question that by far the greater portion of the troops employed against Colonel Huntington (we are referring now to the affair at Guantanamo) belonged to the regular army, under the command of General Linares.

The New York Herald, in an editorial on the subject, remarks most justly and forcibly: ''What sort of a degraded spectacle, then, does Spain present, going whining through Europe in search of intercession or intervention, with such a damnable record against her, made in the very first engagement of troops?

''We can hear good old John Bull sputter out his righteous indignation, but will his Holiness the Pope recognize such degenerate child? Can the punctilious Francis Joseph of Austria afford to condone crimes like these? Will the Emperor William or the Czar of Russia lift his voice in behalf of such fiends? Can our sister republic, France, sympathize with the monsters who disgrace the very name of soldier?

''Not so! All Europe will join with our own government, now thoroughly aroused to the indignities put upon it, and voice the stern edict of humanity and civilization:

''Spain has now placed herself without the pale of the nations. Let her meet the retribution she so justly deserves.''

Senor Estrado Palma, the representative of Cuba in the United States, has declared in a manifesto that the Cubans threw themselves into the struggle advisedly and deliberately, that they knew what they had to face and decided unflinchingly to persevere until they should ree themselves from the Spanish government. Experience has taught them that they have nothing to envy in the Spaniards; that in fact, they feel themselves superior to them, and can expect from Spain no improvement, no better education.

Slavery is ended in Cuba, and the white and the colored live together in perfect harmony, fighting side by side, to obtain political liberty.

Senor Palma, by the way, asserts, with how much authority we are unable to state, that the colored population in Cuba is superior to that of the United States. He says that they are industrious, intelligent and lovers of learning; also, that, during the last fifteen years, they have attained remarkable intellectual development.

There are certain utterances of Senor Palma in this manifesto which deserve to be quoted in full, so pregnant are they with truth, and so full of food for thought to the average American citizen, whether he agrees with them or not. Senor Palma says:

"We Cubans have a thousandfold more reason in our endeavor to free ourselves from the Spanish yoke than had the people of the thirteen colonies, when, in 1775, they rose in arms against the British government. The people of these colonies were in full enjoyment of all the rights of man; they had liberty of conscience, freedom of speech, liberty of the press, the right of public meeting and the right of free locomotion. They elected those who governed them, they made their own laws, and, in fact, enjoyed the blessings of self-government. They were not under the sway of a captain-general with arbitrary powers, who, at his will could imprison them, deport them to penal colonies, or order their execution even without the semblance of a court-martial. They did not have to pay a permanent army and navy in order that they might be kept in subjection, nor to feed a swarm of hungry employees yearly sent over from the metropolis to prey upon the country. They were never subjected to a stupid and crushing customs tariff which compelled them to go to home markets for millions of merchandise annually which they could buy much cheaper elsewhere; they were never compelled to cover a budget of twenty-six or thirty millions a year without the consent of the taxpayers and for the purpose of defraying the expenses of the army and navy of the oppressor, to pay the salaries of thousands of worthless European employees, the whole interest on a debt not incurred by the colony, and other expenditures from which the island received no benefit whatever; for, out of all those millions, only the paltry sum of seven hundred thousand dollars was apparently applied for works of internal improvement, and one-half of which invariably went into the pockets of Spanish employees.

"If the right of the thirteen British colonies to rise in arms in order to acquire their independence has never been questioned because of the attempt of the mother country to tax them by a duty upon tea, or by the Stamp Act, will there be a single citizen in this great republic of the United States, whether he be a public or private man, who will doubt the justice, the necessity in which the Cuban people find themselves of fighting to-day and to-morrow and always, until they shall have overthrown Spanish oppression and tyranny in their country, and formed themselves into a free and independent republic?"

Now, honestly, all prejudice aside, this is not a bad brief for the plaintiff, is it?

There is one more document to which we desire to call your attention. And that is, a letter written to Professor Starr Jordan, of the Leland Stanford, Jr., University of San Francisco, by a Havanese gentleman of undoubted integrity and of Spanish origin.

Professor Jordan declares that this letter seems to show that "the rebellion is not a mere bandit outbreak of negroes and jailbirds, but the effort of the whole people to throw off the yoke of a government they find intolerable."

The letter states, among other things, that the insurrection was begun and is kept up by Cuban people; that the Spanish government has made colossal and unheard-of efforts to put it down, but has not succeeded in diminishing it; on the contrary, the insurrection has spread from one extreme of the island to the other; that the flower of the Cuban youth is in the army of the insurrection, in whose ranks are many physicians, lawyers, druggists, professors, artists, business men, engineers and men of that ilk.

Professor Jordan's correspondent declares that this fact can be proved by the excellent consular service of the United States.

He admits that destruction has been carried on by

both sides, but affirms that the insurgents began by destroying their own property, in order to deprive the troops of the government of shelter and sustenance.

He further declares that the insurgents will continue in their course until they fulfill their purpose, carrying all before them by fire and blood.

He concludes as follows:

"All eyes are directed toward the north, to the republic which is the mother of all Americans. The people of the United States must bear strongly in mind now, as never before, that profession is null and void, if action does not affirm it."

But action has come at last, as the fiendish Spaniards have already found out to their cost.

What is Cuba, the "Pearl of the Antilles," at the present time of writing? The answer to that question is as follows:

A land devastated and temporarily ruined; a gem besmirched almost beyond recognition; a heap of smoking ashes; a population of starving men, women and children, with an iron hand clutching remorselessly at their hearts; a horrible, ghastly picture of what savage men are capable of in the way of destruction.

Now, Americans, people of the free and independent United States; you who enjoy all the blessings of liberty; you who can pursue your avocations without let or hindrance; you who are the jury in this case—the evidence is before you.

You have undoubtedly heard it said that the interference of the United States was unwarrantable; that there was no real reason for the present Spanish-American war; that a stronger country took advantage of a weaker; and other arguments add nauseam.

But is there one of our readers who would see a woman, or a weak though honorable man, attacked by a savage foe, without interfering, and doing the best he could to give life and freedom to the oppressed?

Think it all over, Americans, and think it over carefully and judiciously.

At your own doors, is a poor, miserable, starving wretch, starving from no fault of his, and with a bulldog, not your own, but belonging to a neighbor (a neighbor, grant you with whom you have always hitherto been at peace) about to fasten its fangs in the throat of this unhappy man.

Would you hold your hands, saying that it was no affair of yours, or, with your superior strength, would you fly to the rescue?

Once more, Americans, you have heard the whole evidence. The case is in your hands.

What is your verdict?

CHAPTER XII.

THE BUTCHER'S CAMPAIGN.

Now let us go back to the making of history, to the time when the butcher Weyler came to Cuba to assume the governor-generalship.

By this time the Cuban question had been brought authoritatively before the United States Senate, the people were beginning to be strongly roused with indignation at the state of affairs in Cuba, and there was considerable excitement when the news of Weyler's appointment became known.

Strange to say, the insurgents rejoiced rather than grieved at this appointment, the cause of which is not far to seek. They knew thoroughly well Weyler's character, and what his policy was more than likely to be. They thought that it would drive all the Cubans, who were wavering, into their ranks and would at last force the United States, whose people, when all is said and done, were their natural allies and defenders, to intervene.

After the battle of Coliseo, Gomez and Maceo made their way through Madruga, Nueva-Paz and Guines. Then they destroyed, at a large number of points, the very important railway which connected Havana with Batabano, and also cut the telegraph wires. When they had accomplished this, the two leaders separated,

Gomez to advance in the direction of Havana, and Maceo to invade Pinar del Rio, which is in the extreme west of the island.

Gomez succeeded in burning several more or less important suburbs of Havana.

Almost the first military movement that Weyler made was an attempt to cut off Maceo and prevent his communication with the other detachments of the Cuban army. It seemed to be his chief purpose to compass the death of the mulatto leader, a purpose which at last was most unfortunately accomplished, but then only through treachery.

In emulation of his predecessor, Weyler also tried his hand at trocha building. He constructed a fence of this description across Cuba between the port of Artemisa and the bay of Majana, about twenty-five miles from Havana.

It may be of interest to describe this particular trocha, as it was one of, if not the most important, and a good example of the others.

As its name, trocha, signifies, it was a ditch, or rather two ditches, some three yards wide and the same in depth, with a road between them broad enough to allow cavalry to pass. On each bank was a barbed wire fence, to stop the assailants' progress. Beyond the two ditches, were trous-de-loup, or wolf-traps, from twenty to seventy feet apart. At every hundred yards or so there were fortifications. After night fell, this fortified line was lighted by electricity. Twelve thousand men comprised the garrison, besides outposts of half as many more.

Weyler prided himself greatly upon this trocha, which was intended to keep the rebels at a distance.

But, in spite of all the precautions taken, the wily Maceo and his men more than once crossed the trocha, and the Spanish were not the wiser until it was too late to prevent them.

Once, when they had passed the obstruction without a shot being fired, the insurgents tore up some distance of a railway line on the further side of the trocha, the Cuban leader remarking:

"We did this just to show the enemy that we noticed their plaything."

The headquarters of the insurgents was and is up to the present writing, a place called Cubitas, the top of a mountain, something over a score of miles from Puerto Principe. It is practically impregnable, only a very narrow spiral path leading up to it. A handful of men could defend it against a large army. The little plain on top of the mountain has an area of more than a square mile. It is arable land, and many food products are raised there. The insurgents have constructed here quite a number of wooden buildings, and they have also a dynamite factory. It would take a long time to capture the place by storm or to starve the defenders out.

The Cubans have had one great advantage, that is, they are acclimated. Quite the contrary is true of the Spanish army of invasion, and their ranks have suffered far more from the climate than they have from the bullets of the foe. Added to this, their wages are greatly in

arrears and the rations provided for them are unwhole-
some and insufficient. The surgeons have a very small
supply of quinine and antiseptics, both of which are absolutely essential.

The strength of the two armies, at the time of Weyler's arrival in Cuba was about as follows: The government has 200,000 men, including the 60,000 volunteers,
while the insurgents numbered not much more than a
fourth of this, some fifty or sixty thousand men, which
were scattered among the various provinces, the largest
proportion being massed in Santiago de Cuba.

There were twenty-four generals in the Cuban army,
nineteen being white, three black, one a mulatto, and
one an Indian; of the thirty-four colonels, twenty-seven
were white, five were black, and two were mulattoes.

The record of the mortality among the Spanish soldiers is an appalling one, something simply ghastly to
contemplate.

Harper's Weekly has published statistics concerning
Spanish losses in Cuba, which were obtained from a
source that it was forbidden to disclose. In two years
from March, 1895 to March, 1897, 1,375 were killed in
battle, 765 died of wounds, and 8,627 were wounded,
but recovered. Ten per cent. of the killed and fatally
wounded were officers, and 5 per cent. of the wounded
died of yellow fever, while 127 officers and about 40,-
000 men succumbed to other maladies.

Another authority gives the following rates of losses:
Out of every thousand, ten were killed, sixty-six died
of yellow fever, two hundred and one died of other dis-

eases, while one hundred and forty-three were sent home, either sick or wounded.

Out of two hundred thousand men sent to Cuba in two years, only in the neighborhood of ninety-six thousand, capable of bearing arms, were left the first of March, 1897.

During our own civil war one and sixty-five one-hundredths per cent. of all those mustered into the United States service were killed in action or died of their wounds; ten per cent. were wounded, and a little less than two per cent. died of wounds and from unknown causes.

That we lost during the civil war, 186,216 men from disease is terrible enough, but to equal the percentage of the Spanish losses from the same cause, during twice the time that our war lasted, would bring the total up to a million and a half of men.

From the very beginning, the insurgents held possession of the two eastern provinces, Santiago and Puerto Principe. It was only by unremitting efforts and the loss of many lives that the Spaniards retained their hold on the district about Bayamo.

Late in 1890 General Calixto Garcia, now second in rank to Gomez, and playing an important part in the aiding of the American troops, landed on the island with strong reinforcements. Garcia, who was also a veteran of the Ten Years' War had several more or less important engagements with the Spanish, in almost all of which he was victorious.

Antonio Maceo, in order to consult with Gomez,

crossed the trocha on the night of December 4, 1896. The next day, at the head of five hundred men and within an hour's ride of Havana, he was killed in a skirmish, just as he had made the declaration that all was going well. A young son of Gomez, who was suffering from an old wound, and who refused to leave the ground until his chief was carried away, was also killed.

There is not the shadow of a doubt but that this double catastrophe was due to the treachery of one of Maceo's companions, a certain Dr. Zertucha.

One of Maceo's aides tells the story as follows: "Firing was heard near Punta Brava, and Zertucha, who had ridden off to one side of the road, came galloping back, crying: "Come with me! Come with me! Quick! Quick!" Maceo at once put spurs to his horse, and, followed by his five aids, rode swiftly after the physician, who plunged into the thick growth on the side of the road.

The party had only ridden a few yards, when Zertucha, bent low in his saddle, and swerved sharply to one side, galloping away like mad.

Almost at the same moment, a volley was fired by a party of Spanish soldiers hidden in the dense underbrush, and Maceo and four of his men dropped out of their saddles, mortally wounded."

The single survivor, the man whose words are quoted above, contrived to get back to his own party and brought them to the scene of the tragedy. The Spaniards were driven away, Maceo's body was found stripped, and young Gomez had been stabbed, and his skull was broken.

The traitor Zertucha surrendered to the Spanish by whom naturally he was treated with the utmost kindness and consideration.

Afterwards Zertucha attempted to blacken Maceo's memory by declaring that he was disheartened and desperate, and that his death was the result of his own folly.

Senor Palma says of this:

"General Maceo was loved and supported by all men struggling for Cuban independence, whether in a military or civil capacity. If a man was ever idolized by his people, that man was General Maceo. Dr. Zertucha knows that, but perhaps he has an object in making his false assertions."

An object? Of course he had an object—the currying of favor with the Spaniards, the saving of his own wretched carcass sand the obtaining of the blood-money due him.

So perished the last of the Maceos, eight brothers, all having died before him in the cause of Cuban liberty.

The following poem on Maceo's death appeared in the New York Sun:

Antonio Maceo.

"Stern and unyielding, though others might bow to the
    tempest;
Slain by the serpent who cowered in hiding behind
    thee;
Slumber secure where the hands of thy comrades have
    laid thee;

Dim to thine ear be the roar of the battle above thee.
Set now is thy sun, going down in darkness and men-
    ace,
While through the thick-gathering clouds one red ray
    of vengeance
Streams up to heaven, blood red, from the place where
    thou liest.
Through the sword of Death's angel lies cold on thy
    forehead,
Still to the hearts of mankind speaks the voice of thy
    spirit:
Still does thine angry shade arrest the step of the
    tyrant.   "V. B."

Maceo's death was a terrible blow to the insurgents, but, with indomitable spirit they rallied and plunged with renewed energy into the fray.

Maceo was succeeded by General Rius Rivera, who does not seem to have been in any way the equal of his predecessor.

Having accomplished by low treachery what he had not succeeded in doing by open, honorable warfare, Weyler increased his efforts to put down the rebellion in Pinar del Rio, where Maceo had been in command.

The trochas now became of advantage, and Weyler succeeded in confining Rivera's scattered bands to the province. Early in 1897, Rivera was made a prisoner, and since then nothing of importance, from a military standpoint, has occurred in Pinar del Rio.

In 1897 there were but few incidents of interest in the war. The Cubans were holding back, evading conflicts wherever they could, and waiting for the long-delayed interposition of the United States.

Guines, however, was taken by them, and General

Garcia captured the fortified post of Tunas after a fight of three days. The Spanish commander and about forty per cent. of his force were killed. Finally the remainder of the garrison surrendered. The spoils which fell into the hands of the Cubans comprised a large amount of rifles and ammunition, besides two Krupp guns.

The victory was a notable one, especially as Weyler had cabled his government that Tunas was impregnable. Its fall gave rise to much harsh criticism and bitter feeling in Spain.

Weyler was constantly proclaiming the "pacification" of certain provinces, statements that were most transparently absurd and false. He even immediately followed up his proclamations by the most severe and brutal measures in those very provinces.

Finally even Madrid, to whom it would have mattered little if the policy had proved a success, became convinced that Weyler's savage procedure was a failure.

The butcher had gained absolutely no advantage, but had simply been the cause of untold and undeserved suffering.

The insurrection, taking it all for all, was just as strong, if not stronger, than it was the day Weyler arrived in Cuba.

So, in October, 1897, he was withdrawn from his post, and summoned back to Spain.

It is to be hoped that the world will never again witness such a shameful and shameless exhibition as was his administration.

Before dismissing him from these pages, let us quote

from Stephen Bonsal, with whose words no unprejudiced person can quarrel.

Mr. Bonsal says:

"Should they be wise, and they will have a moment of clairvoyance soon, or they will disappear as a nation, the Spaniards should seek to cast a mantle of oblivion and forgetfulness about the wretched name of Weyler and all the ignoble deeds that have characterized his rule. While it cannot be expected that the bishop will be displaced by the butcher, there is one whom Weyler will displace upon his unenviable pinnacle of prominence in the temple of infamy, and that is Alva. His name is destined to become in every tongue that is spoken by civilized people a synonym of bloody, relentless and pitiless war waged upon American soil, upon the long-disused methods of the Vandals and the Visigoths; and Alva, who had the cruel spirit of his age and a sincere fanaticism as his excuse, will step down and out into an oblivion which will doubtless be grateful to his shade, and most certainly so to those who bear his execrated name.

"I could ask no more terrible punishment for him (Weyler) than many years of life to listen to the voices of despair he has heard ring out upon his path through Cuba; to hear again and ever the accusing voices which no human power can hush, and to review the scenes of suffering which he has occasioned which no human power can obliterate from his memory.''

CHAPTER XIII.

AMERICA S CHARITY AND SPAIN'S DIPLOMACY.

The new governor-general of Cuba was Don Ramon Blanco, as to whose character accounts differ. It is probable that while he is not the high-minded, honorable gentleman that Campos was, he is far, very far from being such an unmitigated beast as his predecessor.

Before he reached Cuba, which was the last of October, 1897, he stated in an interview:

"My policy will never include concentration. I fight the enemy, not women and children. One of the first things I shall do will be to allow the reconcentrados to go out of the town and till the soil."

This sounds very just and right, but, as a matter of fact, the policy enounced was never carried out, not even in minor particulars. The persecution of the pacificos remained as bitter and relentless as ever.

Perhaps General Blanco is not entirely to blame for this, as the pressure brought to bear against his expressed ideas both by the home government and by the "peninsulars" in Havana, who had been in full accord with the methods of the "Butcher," was so strong as scarcely to be resisted.

Blanco issued an amnesty proclamation soon after his arrival in Havana, but the insurgents paid little or no attention. Their experience in such matters in the past had been too stern to be forgotten.

In the field, Blanco was also most unsuccessful, gaining nothing but petty victories of no value whatever. The pay of the Spanish soldiers was terribly in arrears, and their rations were of the most meagre description. No wonder that they were disheartened, and in no condition to fight.

In a word, Blanco absolutely failed, as completely as had his predecessors, in quelling the rebellion.

The people of the United States were becoming more and more enraged at the atrocities committed at their very door, and more and more anxious that the Cubans should have the independence which they themselves had achieved.

Moreover, there was a large number of Americans in the island who were made to suffer from the policy of reconcentration. Citizens of the United States, a large number of them being naturalized Americans, were constantly being seized and imprisoned, on suspicion alone, no proof whatever being advanced, of their furnishing aid and comfort to the insurgents. They were placed in filthy cells, no communication with the outside world being allowed them. This is what the Spaniards term ''incomunicado.''

No writing materials were allowed them and nothing whatever to read. The windows were so high up that no view was to be obtained. The cells were damp with the moisture of years and had rotten, disease-breeding floors, covered with filth of every description. Moreover, they were overrun with cockroaches, rats and other vermin.

The sustenance furnished the prisoners was wretched, and even such as it was, it was not given to them regularly. More often than not, they were left for long hours to suffer the pangs of hunger and thirst.

A notable instance of Americans being seized and imprisoned in these loathsome dungeons is the following:

A little schooner called the ''Competitor'' attempted to land a filibustering expedition. She was captured, after most of her passengers had been landed, and her crew, numbering five, were tried by a court which had been instructed to convict them, and sentenced to death. They would undoubtedly have been executed, as some years before had been the prisoners of the ill-fated Virginius, had it not been for the prompt intervention of the United States, spurred thereto by General Fitz Hugh Lee.

The conviction was growing stronger and stronger in the United States that something should be done to mitigate the terrible suffering in Cuba.

The Red Cross Association, a splendid charitable organization, at the head of which was Miss Clara Barton, undertook this noble work of relief. The government of the United States lent its assistance and support. Large sums of money and tons of supplies of food were contributed throughout the Union, both by public and private donations. The newspapers everywhere, North, East, South and West, did magnificent service in furthering the good work.

Spain, instead of showing gratitude, rather resented this, and there was considerable difficulty to prosecute the labor of charity. Still, the efforts, in the interests of suffering humanity were by no means unavailing.

President McKinley speaks of the movement as follows:

"The success which had attended the limited measure of relief extended to the suffering American citizens of Cuba, by the judicious expenditure through consular agencies, of money appropriated expressly for their succor by the joint resolution approved May 24, 1897, prompted the humane extension of a similar scheme of aid to the great body of sufferers. A suggestion to this end was aquiesced in by the Spanish authorities. On the twenty-fourth of December last, I caused to be issued an appeal to the American people, inviting contributions, in money or in kind, for the starving sufferers in Cuba, following this on the eighth of January by a similar public announcement of the formation of a Central Cuban Relief Committee, with headquarters in New York city, composed of three members representing the American National Red Cross Society, and the religious and business elements of the community. The efforts of that committee have been untiring and have accomplished much. Arrangements for free transportation to Cuba have greatly aided the charitable work. The president of the American Red Cross and representatives of other contributory organizations have generously visited Cuba and co-operated with the consul-general and the local authorities to make effective disposition of the re-

lief collected through the efforts of the Central Committee. Nearly $200,000 in money and supplies has al-
ready reached the sufferers and more is forthcoming.
The supplies are admitted duty free, and transportation
to the interior has been arranged, so that the relief, at
first necessarily confined to Havana and the larger
cities, is now extended through most if not all of the
towns through which suffering exists. Thousands of
lives have already been saved. The necessity for a
change in the condition of the reconcentrados is recognized in the Spanish government.''

And yet Spain resented these charitable efforts, as being opposed to her policy. The people of the United
States, in sending this money and these supplies, had
nothing else in view but charity, a longing to do all
that they could to relieve the anguish of an oppressed
and tortured people. There was no ulterior motive
whatever.

A large amount of the sums contributed was diverted
to a purpose very different from that for which it had
been intended.

The Spanish government, more through fear of the
condemnation of the other European nations than anything else, voted about six hundred thousand dollars for
the relief of the starving reconcentradoes.

But this was a ruse, a sum chiefly on paper. General
Lee, and his testimony is incontrovertible, says:

''I do not believe six hundred thousand dollars, in
supplies, will be given to those people, and the soldiers
left to starve. They will divide it up here and there; a

piece taken off here and a piece taken off there. I do not believe they have appropriated anything of the kind. The condition of the reconcentrados out in the country is just as bad as in General Weyler's day. It has been relieved a good deal by supplies from the United States, but that has ceased now.

"General Blanco published a proclamation, rescinding General Weyler's bando, as they call it there, but it has had no practical effect. In the first place, these people have no place to go; the houses have been burned down; there is nothing but the bare land there, and it would take them two months before they could raise the first crop. In the next place, they are afraid to go out from the lines of the towns, because the roving bands of the Spanish guerillas, as they are called, would kill them. So they stick right in the edges of the town, just like they did, with nothing to eat except what they can get from charity. The Spanish have nothing to give."

The government and people of Spain now became very much afraid of the attitude of the United States. They knew that something had to be done, so to speak, to throw a sop to Cerberus. Therefore Sagasta, the premier of Spain, conceived the idea of granting to Cuba a species of autonomy. But, with the usual Spanish diplomacy, it was not autonomy at all. It purposed to be home rule, but every article gave a loop-hole for Spain not to fulfill her obligations.

It was a false and absurd proposition, intended to deceive, but too flimsy in its fabric to deceive any one. It was rotten clean through, and was opposed by everyone except the framers of the autonomistic papers, General Blanco, his staff and a few others, who hoped, but hoped in vain, great things from the proclamation.

The Cuban leaders, who at one time would have hailed with joy such a concession, if they had been assured that the provisions would have been followed out loyally and without fraud, now rejected the autonomistic proposition with scorn and loathing.

Their battle cry was now, and they were determined it ever should be: "Independence or death!"

It was too late. There was no possibility now of home rule under Spanish domination.

Gomez even went so far as to declare that any one who should attempt to bring to his camp any offer of autonomy would be seized as a spy and shot.

General Lee, speaking of the proposed autonomy, says:

"Blanco's autonomistic government was doomed to failure from its inception. The Spanish soldiers and officers scorned it because they did not desire Cuban rule, which such autonomy, if genuine, would insure. The Spanish merchants and citizens were opposed to it because they too were hostile to the Cubans having control of the island, and, if the question could be narrowed down to Cuban control or annexation to the United States, they were all annexationists, believing that they could get a better government, and one that would protect in a greater measure life and property under the United States flag than under the Cuban banner. On the other hand, the Cubans in arms would not touch it, because they were fighting for free Cuba. And the Cuban citizens and sympathizers were opposed to it also.''

Senor Palma sums up the question of autonomy as follows:

''Autonomy would mean that the Cuban people will make their own laws, appoint all their public officers, except the governor-general, and attend to the local affairs with entire independence, without, of course, interference by the metropolis. What then would be left to Spain, since between her and Cuba there is no commercial intercourse of any kind? Spain is not and cannot be, a market for Cuban products, and is moreover unable to provide Cuba with the articles in need by the latter. The natural market for the Cuban products is the United States, from which in exchange Cuba buys with great advantage flour, provisions, machinery, etc. What then, I repeat, is left to Spain but the big debt incurred by her, without the consent and against the will of the people of Cuba? We perfectly understand the autonomy of Canada as a colony of Great Britain. The two countries are closely connected with each other by the most powerful ties—the mutual interest of a reciprocal commerce.''

Murat Halstead, who is invariably logical and correct, puts the whole matter in a few trenchant words:

''There is nothing to regard as possible in any of the reforms the Spaniards are promising with much animation and to which they ascribe the greatest excellence, to take place after the insurgents have surrenderd their arms. Spain is, as always, incapable of changing her fatal colonial policy, that never has been or can be reformed.''

Spain's fatal colonial policy. Could there be truer words?

Let us pause for a moment to contemplate what this fatal colonial policy has cost her.

At one time she swayed the destinies of Europe and had possessions in every continent. Samuel Johnson, in writing of her, said:

> "Are there no regions yet unclaimed by Spain?
> Quick, let us rise, those unhappy lands explore,
> And bear oppression's insolence no more.''

The whole reason of Spain's downfall is the ruthless and savage character of the Spanish people.

Due to her oppression, note the following list of colonies which she has lost:

1609. The Netherlands.

1628. Malacca, Ceylon, Java and other islands.

1640. Portugal.

1648. Spain renounced all claim to Holland.

1648. Brabant and other parts of Flanders.

1649. Maestricht, Hetogenbosch, Breda, Bergen-of-Zoom, and many other fortresses in the Low Countries. In this year also she practically surrendered supremacy on the seas to Northern Europe.

1659. Rousillon and Cardague. By the cession of these places to France, the boundary line between France and Spain became the Pyrenees.

1668. Other portions of Flanders.

1672. Still more cities and towns in Flanders

1704. Gibraltar.

1704. Majorca, Minorca and Ivizza.

1791. The Nootka Sound settlements.

1794. St. Domingo.

1800. Louisiana.

1802. Trinidad.

1819. Florida.

1810-21. Mexico, Venezuela, Colombia, Ecuador, Peru, Bolivia, Chili, Argentina, Uruguay, Paraguay, Patagonia, Guatemala, Honduras, Nicaragua, San Salvador, Hayti and numerous other islands.

Spain has now not a foot of territory on the American continent, and very shortly she will not have a foot anywhere except within the confines of her own home.

To return again to the proposed autonomy of Cuba.

At the time it was offered Gomez, that grand old man of Cuba said:

"This is a war to the death for independence, and nothing but independence will we accept. To talk of home rule is to idle away time. But I have hopes that the United States, sooner or later, will recognize our belligerency. It is a question of mere justice, and, in spite of all arts of diplomacy, justice wins in the long run. The day we are recognized as belligerents, I can name a fixed term for the end of the war.

"With regard to paying an indemnity to Spain, that is a question of amount. A year ago we could pay $100,-000,000, and I was ready to agree to that. Now that Spain owes more than $400,000,000, we will not pay so much."

It was too late now to speak of reforms or of home rule in any shape. The Cubans were not willing to nurse illusions. They were resolved on absolute freedom or nothing.

Any form of Spanish rule would mean the entire subjection of the Cubans, and, had they accepted the proposed autonomy, there is no doubt but that the future would have been as bad, if not worse, than the past.

Public opinion in the United States was never so deeply aroused as it was now. Citizens in all ranks of life were calling loudly for interference, which, in the name of civilization and humanity, should end the horrible state of affairs in Cuba.

The United States was Cuba's natural defender and protector, and now, both press and public declared, was the time to act.

The president was fully aware of the gravity of the situation, but with rare discretion, for which future historians will give him due credit, he bided his time, preferring, if possible, peace with honor.

In his first message relating to the Cuban situation, President McKinley said:

"If it shall hereafter appear to be a duty imposed by our obligations to ourselves, to civilization and humanity, to intervene with force, it shall be without fault on our part, and only because the necessity of such action will be so clear as to command the support and approval of the civilized world."

General Stewart L. Woodford, our minister to Spain,

behaved with the utmost courtesy and did everything in the power of mortal man to avoid hostilities.

One cause of the American people's irritability, and in all justice there was much reason for it, was Spain's pretence that the Cuban war had been prolonged because of America's inability or non desire to maintain neutrality. Nothing could be falser or more absurd, for the United States had invariably, whenever possible, stopped all filibustering expeditions to Cuba. The records will bear out this statement, without any possibility of refutation. More than two millions of dollars had been expended by the United States in Spain's interest. Certainly, gratitude or its equivalent is a word that does not appear in the Spanish lexicon.

CHAPTER XIV.

THE LAST DAYS OF PEACE.

Then came the De Lome incident which served to inflame further passions already aroused.

Senor Enrique Depuy De Lome was the Spanish minister to this country.

He wrote a letter, strongly denunciatory of the president's message, and of the president himself; with the worst taste possible, he alluded to Mr. McKinley as a low politician, one who catered, for political purposes, to the rabble.

This letter was intercepted and a copy given to the press. The original was sent to the State Department. Of course De Lome at once became persona non grata, which the Spanish government recognized, and even before Minister Woodford could make a ''representation,'' De Lome was recalled from his position and Senor Polo appointed in his place.

President McKinley showed the most admirable self-poise through all this affair, evincing outwardly no resentment for what was a personal insult to himself.

It was declared that we ought to have a ship of war in Havana harbor to protect American citizens, and for that purpose, the Maine was sent there.

It was the visit of a friendly ship to, at that time, a friendly country.

The Maine was received by the Spanish officials with every outward show of respect, the firing of salutes and the raising of the American and Spanish flags on the vessels of different nationalities.

And yet what was the result? Once more came an exhibition of Spain's perfidy. We know it is very much like the Scotch verdict of "non proven," but still there is no doubt among fair-minded men.

A tragedy ensued, a tragedy in which Spain played the part of the villain, and such an unconscionable villain as has never been seen upon the boards of any stage.

On the night of Tuesday, February 19, 1898, the United States battleship Maine, presumably in friendly waters, was lying calmly anchored in the harbor of Havana. Suddenly, with no warning whatever, for there was no suspicion on the part of either officers or men, the magnificent battleship was blown up. Two officers and two hundred and sixty of the crew perished, but their names and memories will ever be cherished affectionately and gratefully by the American people.

All on board behaved in the most heroic manner, Captain Charles D. Sigsbee, the commander being the last to leave the fated ship. The famous naval historian, Captain Mahan, says:

"The self-control shown in the midst of a sudden and terrible danger, of which not one of the men on board knew, showed that in battle with known dangers about them, and expecting every minute the fate that might overtake them, the fellow sailors of the men of the Maine would stand to their guns and their ship to the last. It was evident that the old naval spirit existed, and that the sailors of the new navy were as good as those who manned the old-time ships."

The Maine was one of the very best vessels in the American navy; with her stores and ammunition, she represented an expenditure of close upon five millions of dollars.

The blowing up of the Maine and the loss of our brave men aroused the most intense excitement throughout the United States, but the request of Captain Sigsbee that public opinion should be suspended until thorough investigation had been made, was followed, and the people behaved with admirable and remarkable control.

A naval board of inquiry was at once organized by the United States government. This board consisted of experienced officers, who were greatly assisted in their labors by a strong force of experts, wreckers and divers.

The investigation was most searching. The 21st of March, 1898, the board presented a unanimous verdict. The report was most voluminous, embracing some twelve thousand pages.

The verdict was practically that "the loss of the Maine was not in any respect due to fault or negligence on the part of any of the officers or members of her crew; that the ship was destroyed by the explosion of a submarine mine, which caused the partial explosion of two or more of her forward magazines; and that no evidence has been obtainable fixing the responsibility of the destruction of the Maine upon any person or persons."

Although it was not possible to obtain evidence which should convict the guilty parties, there was not and never has been the faintest doubt in the mind of any fair-minded person as to who was responsible for the tragedy. When Congress afterward spoke of the crime or the criminal negligence of the Spanish officials, the words found an ardent response in the heart of every true American.

There is no doubt but that the destruction of the Maine was the lever that started the machinery of war.

Like "Remember the Alamo!" "Remember the Maine!" is a clarion cry of battle that will go echoing down the centuries.

In Cuba we were most fortunate in having a superb representative in the person of General Fitz Hugh Lee, a man of rare intellectual ability, ever courteous but ever firm, a fine specimen of Southern chivalry.

The Spaniards, as was but natural, hated him, but when his withdrawal was suggested by the Spanish government President McKinley cabled to Minister Woodford at Madrid that the services of General Lee at Havana were indispensable and his removal could not be considered.

The relations between Spain and the United States became every day more and more strained. Every effort was made by the President to bring about a peaceable solution of the Cuban question, but Spain, stiff necked and suicidal, refused to cooperate with him.

On April 11, the president sent his famous message to Congress.

In it, he alluded to the way in which we had been forced to police our own waters and watch our own seaports in prevention of any unlawful act in aid of Cuba.

He spoke of how our trade had suffered, how the capital invested by our citizens in Cuba had been largely lost, and how the temperance and forbearance of our own people had been so sorely tried as to beget a perilous unrest among our own citizens.

The President, also, made some strong arguments against both belligerency and recognition, especially against the latter.

He quoted Jackson's argument, on the subject of the recognition of Texas, concluding as follows:

"Prudence, therefore, seems to dictate that we should stand aloof, and maintain our present attitude, if not until Mexico itself or one of the great foreign powers shall recognize the independence of the new government; at least until the lapse of time or the course of events should have proved beyond cavil or dispute the ability of the people of that country to maintain their separate sovereignty and to uphold the government constituted by them. Neither of the contending parties can justly complain of this course. By pursuing it we are but carrying out the long established policy of our government, a policy which has secured us respect and influence abroad and inspired confidence at home."

It is necessary to quote still further from President McKinley's message, a message so fine, so just and so true, that we are sure it will go down into history praised by all future historians, as it well deserves to be.

He says:

"The spirit of all our acts hitherto has been an earnest, unselfish desire for peace and prosperity in Cuba, untarnished by differences between us and Spain, and unstained by the blood of American citizens.

"The forcible intervention of the United States as a neutral to stop the war, according to the large dictates of humanity and following many historical precedents where neighboring states have interfered to check the hopeless sacrifice of life by internecine conflicts beyond their borders, is justifiable on rational grounds. It involves, however, hostile constraint upon both parties to the contest, as well as to enforce a truce as to guide the eventual settlement. The grounds for such intervention may be briefly summarized as follows:

"1. In the cause of humanity and to put an end to the barbarities, bloodshed, starvation and horrible miseries now existing there, and which the parties to the conflict are either unable or unwilling to stop or mitigate. It is no answer to say that this is all in another country, belonging to another nation, and is, therefore, none of our business. It is specially our duty, for it is right at our doors.

"2. We owe to our citizens in Cuba to afford them that protection and indemnity for life and property which no government there can or will afford, and to that end to terminate the conditions that deprive them of local protection.

"3. The right to intervene may be justified by the

very serious injury to the commerce, trade and business interest of our people, and by the wanton destruction of property and devastation of the island.

"4. And, what is of the utmost importance, the present condition of affairs in Cuba is a constant menace to our peace and entails upon this government an enormous expense. With such a conflict waged for years in an island so near us, and with which our people have such trade and business relations—when the lives and liberty of our citizens are in constant dread, and their property destroyed and themselves ruined—where our trading-vessels are liable to seizure and are seized at our very door, by warships of a foreign nation, the expeditions of filibustering that we are powerless to prevent altogether, and the irritating questions and entanglements thus arising—all these and others that I need not mention, with the resulting strained relations, are a constant menace to our peace, and compel us to keep on a semi-war footing with a nation with which we are at peace."

In his message, the President also gives utterance to these notable and memorable words:

"The long trial has proved that the object for which Spain wages war cannot be attained.

"The fire of insurrection may flame or may smoulder with varying seasons, but it has not been, and it is plain that it cannot be, extinguished by present methods. The only hope of relief and repose from a condition which cannot longer be endured is the enforced pacification of Cuba.

"In the name of humanity, in the name of civilization, in behalf of endangered American interests, which give us the right and the duty to speak and to act, the war in Cuba must stop."

The President then refers the whole matter to Congress to decide as that body may think best.

A somewhat acrimonious debate, of several days duration followed, chiefly over the side issue of the recognition of the Republic of Cuba.

On April 19, 1898, by the way, the date of the first battle of the Revolution at Concord, Massachusetts, the following joint resolution was agreed upon.

"Joint resolution for the recognition of the independence of the people of Cuba, demanding that the government of Spain relinquish its authority and government in the Island of Cuba, and withdraw its land and naval forces from Cuba and Cuban waters, and directing the President of the United States to use the land and naval forces of the United States to carry these resolutions into effect.

"Whereas, the abhorrent conditions which have existed for more than three years in the Island of Cuba, so near our own borders, have shocked the moral sense of the people of the United States, have been a disgrace to Christian civilization, culminating, as they have, in the destruction of a United States battleship, with two hundred and sixty-six of its officers and crew, while on a friendly visit in the harbor of Havana, and cannot longer be endured, as has been set forth by the President of the United States in his message to Congress of

April 11, 1898, upon which the action of Congress was invited; therefore,

"Resolved, By the Senate and House of Representatives of the United States of America in Congress assembled,

"1. That the people of the Island of Cuba are, and of right ought to be, free and independent.

"2. That it is the duty of the United States to demand, and the Government of the United States does hereby demand, that the Government of Spain at once relinquish its authority and government in the Island of Cuba and withdraw its land and naval forces from Cuba and Cuban waters.

"3. That the President of the United States be, and he hereby is, directed and empowered to use the entire land and naval forces of the United States, and to call into the actual service of the United States the militia of the several States to such extent as may be necessary to carry these resolutions into effect.

"4. That the United States hereby disclaims any disposition or intention to exercise sovereignty, jurisdiction or control over said island except for the pacification thereof, and asserts its determination, when that is accomplished, to leave the government and control of the island to its people."

The President set his seal of approval upon these resolutions the following day, and the same day an ultimatum was sent to Spain, practically the same as what has been quoted above.

It was also stated that it was the President's duty to request an answer within forty-eight hours.

Within forty-eight hours the ultimatum was rejected by the Spanish Cortes.

The ministers and representatives of the two countries were immediately recalled from their various posts, and a state of warfare proclaimed.

The United States now stood pledged to aid and succor agonized Cuba, to strike the shackles from off her bruised and bleeding limbs, and raise her to a position which her valor had long deserved, amongst the free and independent nations of the world.

CHAPTER XV.

THE TOPOGRAPHY AND RESOURCES OF CUBA.

Cuba lies in the northern portion of the torrid zone, and immediately south of Florida. From Key West to the nearest point on the Cuban coast, the distance in 86 miles.

The form of Cuba is an irregular crescent, with a large number of bays or indentations. The coast line is about 2,200 miles, exclusive of the indentations; or, if we include the latter, nearly 7,000 miles.

The island is about 760 miles long. Its breadth varies from 127 miles at a point some fifty miles west of Santiago to 28 miles from Havana to the south.

Its area is 43,314 square miles, which includes the Isle of Pines and several smaller islands.

Cuba is intersected by a range of mountains, more or less broken, which extends across the entire island, from east to west, and from which the rivers flow to the sea. This range is called the Sierra del Cobra, and it includes the Pico de Turgino, with an altitude of 7,670 feet, the highest point on the whole island. There are other ranges, and the eastern portion of the island is particularly hilly. We must not forget the famous Pan of Matanzas which received its name from its resemblance to a loaf of sugar. It is 1,300 feet high, and has been of great service to mariners in enabling them to get their bearings.

Naturally the rivers are small, but they are numerous. The principal one, and the only one that can properly be called navigable, is the Canto. Schooners ascend this for about sixty miles. It rises in the Sierra del Cobre, and empties upon the south coast, a few miles from Manzanillo. Mineral springs abound, and their medicinal qualities are in high repute.

Of lakes there are only a few, and most of these lie in the marsh lands.

The Scientific American says:

"The country may be broadly divided into the region of the plains the rolling uplands and the forest lands. The lowlands form a practically continuous belt around the island, and in them are to be found the great sugar plantations. Above these and on the lower slopes are found the grazing and farm lands, upon, which, among other things, is raised the famous Havana tobacco. The remainder of the island, especially the eastern portion is covered with a dense forest growth."

The vegetation of Cuba is of the most luxuriant and beautiful description. The forests are full of a large variety of trees, almost all of them most valuable for mechanical purposes. Some of them are almost as hard as iron. One of these is called the quiebra hacha (the axe breaker). There are other woods such as the jucaro, which are indestructible, even under water. Still others are lignum vitae, ebony, rosewood, mahogany, cedar, lancewood and many other species. There are over fifty varieties of palm, and the orange and lemon trees are indigenous. Although the forests are so dense so to be almost impenetrable, there are no wild animals in them larger than the wild dogs, which closely resemble wolves both in appearance and habits.

The fruits are those natural to the tropics, but only oranges, pineapples and bananas are raised for exportation.

The land is not suited to the cultivation of cereals, and there is no flour mill on the island. At one time, the coffee plantations were in a flourishing condition, but the recent outbreak has largely interfered with this industry.

By far the chief industries in the island are the cultivation of sugar and tobacco, both of which are famous the world over.

The soil of Cuba is simply a marvel of richness, practically unrivalled in any other part of the world. Except occasionally in the case of tobacco, fertilizers are not used. Crops have been grown on the same ground without an atom of fertilization for over a hundred years. This superb soil gives the Cuban sugar planter an enormous advantage over his competitors in other countries. For instance, in Jamaica, one to two hogsheads of sugar is considered a good yield, but in Cuba, three hogsheads are the average.

The introduction of modern machinery, which is very expensive, has done much to drive out the small planters, and the tax imposed by the Spanish government almost trebled the cost to the planter.

In times of peace, the sugar production of Cuba averaged a million of tons a year, but this is nothing like what the island might be made to yield under a decent government and proper enterprise. It has been estimated that if all the land suitable to the growth of sugar cane were devoted to that industry, Cuba might supply the entire western hemisphere with sugar.

Mr. Gollan, the British consul general, says:

"Until a very recent date the manufacture of sugar and the growing of the cane in Cuba were extremely profitable undertakings, and the reasons for their prosperity may be stated as:

"1. The excellence of the climate and the fertility of the soil, which allow of large crops of good cane. The rainfall, about 50 inches, is so distributed that irrigation is not a necessity, though it would in many cases be advisable.

"2. The great movement toward the centralization of the estates which took place in the early eighties, planters having understood the value of large sugar houses and overcome their difficulty in this way.

"3. The proximity of the United States, affording, as it does, a cash market for the sugar."

To show how the sugar trade has been injured by the Cuban uprising, the following figures are of interest:

Description.	Tons in 1895.	Tons in 1896.
Exports . . .	832,431	235,628
Stocks	135,181	36,260
	967,612	271,888
Local consumption	50,000	40,000
	1,017,612	311,888

Stock on January 1

    (previous crop)   .   13,348   86,667
                         ———————   ———————

    Total production   .   1,004,264   225,221

The decrease in 1895-96 was 779,043 tons, equivalent to 77.574 per cent.

While the tobacco crop of some portions of Cuba is unsurpassed, notably that of Vuelta Alajo and of Mayari, it is of excellent quality all over the island, the poorest of it being quite as good as that of Hayti. The entire crop is estimated at $10,000,000 annually. Yet, owing to the extortions of the government, which loaded it with restrictions and exactions of every description, the tobacco industry has always been an uncertain one. It is said that the tobacco growers, disgusted with their treatment, have always been in favor of the revolutionists.

The mineral riches of the island have never been exploited to any considerable extent and yet it is known that they are by no means unimportant. Gold and silver exist. Some specimens of the finest gold have been obtained, but at an expense of time and labor that could not remunerate the parties engaged in the enterprise. There are copper mines near Santiago of large extent and very rich in ore. There are also several iron mines. Numerous deposits of manganese have been found in the Sierra Maestra range. As nearly all the manganese used in the United States comes from the Black Sea, it is thought that these mines will prove very valuable, when the conditions for operating them are more favorable. Bituminous coal is very abundant. Marble, jasper and slate are also to be found in many parts of the island.

The trade of the United States with Cuba since 1891 is given as follows by the bureau of statistics, Treasury Department:

	Imports.	Exports.
1891	$61,714,395	$12,224,888
1892	77,931,671	17,953,570
1893	78,706,506	24,157,698
1894	75,678,261	20,125,321
1895	52,871,259	12,807,661
1896	40,017,730	7,530,880
1897	18,406,815	8,259,776

The commerce of Spain with Cuba since 1891, the figures up to 1895 being taken from a compilation by the department of agriculture, and those for 1896 from a British foreign office report was:

	Imports from Cuba.	Exports to Cuba.
1891	$7,193,173	$22,168,050
1892	9,570,399	28,046,636
1893	5,697,291	24,689,373
1894	7,265,120	22,592,943
1895	7,176,105	26,298,497
1896	4,257,360	26,145,800

The railways are insufficient and wretchedly managed, while the roads are in a deplorable condition, sometimes, in wet weather, being almost impassible.

In regard to the future commercial prosperity of

Cuba, Mr. Hyatt, who until recently was our consul at Santiago, gives the following opinion:

"Railroads and other highways, improved machinery and more modern methods of doing business are among the wants of Cuba; and with the onward march of civilization these will doubtless be hers in the near future. Cuba, like other tropical and semi-tropical countries, is not given to manufacturing; her people would rather sell the products of the soil and mines and buy manufactured goods. The possibilities of the island are great, while the probabilities remain an unsolved problem."

When the tropical position of Cuba is taken into consideration, it may be stated that its climate is generally mild. In fact, we can say that it is one of the best, if not the very best, of the countries lying within the tropics; and, during the dry season, it is unsurpassable anywhere. In this season, the days are delightful, and the nights, with the clear, transparent air, and the sky spangled with myriads of stars (many of which, notably the constellation known as "The Southern Cross," are not visible in more northern countries), are veritable dreams of beauty.

The heat and cold are never extreme, and there is only a slight difference in the temperature all the year round. The warmest month at Havana is July, with an average temperature of 82 degrees Fahrenheit, and the coldest is January, with an average temperature of 70 degrees.

The rainy season lasts from the first of May till the

first of October. The popular impression is that it rains pretty nearly all the time during this season, but this is a mistake. On an average there are not more than ten rainy days a month, and the rain generally comes in the afternoon. The temperature of Havana in the summer is but little higher than that of New Orleans, while its rainfall is infinitely less. Yellow fever exists in the coast cities all the year round, but it rarely makes its appearance in the interior. The western part of the island is as habitable as is Ohio.

It is certain that the effects of the climate upon the Spanish soldiers has been disastrous, but much of the mortality among them have been due not to the climate alone, but to a bad system of hygiene, wretched diet, unsuitable clothing and a criminal disregard on the part of the military authorities of the health of the men under their control.

The Medical Record, in an article on the subject, says:

"There is no evading the fact, however, that the landing of a large body of more or less raw, unacclimatized men in the lowlands of a reputed unhealthy coast at the beginning of the rainy season is an experiment that must from the very nature of things be attended with much risk."

But the danger to our own soldiers must also from the very nature of things, be much less than it has proved to the Spaniards. Our army is composed of a much higher class of men intellectually, and besides that, they will be infinitely better taken care of.

The next point to be considered is the population of Cuba. There has been no official census taken since 1887. Then the entire population was estimated at 1,631,687. Of these about one-fifth were natives of Spain, 10,500 were whites of foreign blood, 485,187 were free negroes, about 50,000 were Chinese and the rest native Cubans.

It may be interesting to note the percentage of whites and blacks, and to see how the negro element has been decreasing both relatively and absolutely during late years. At the present time the negroes are in all probability not more than one-fourth of the entire population.

Year.	White.	Negro.	Per Cent.
1804	234,000	198,000	45.8
1819	239,830	213,203	47.
1830	332,352	423,343	56.
1841	418,291	589,333	58.4
1850	479,490	494,252	50.75
1860	632,797	566,632	47.
1869	797,596	602,215	43.
1877	985,325	492,249	33.
1887	1,102,689	485,188	30.55

The island is divided into six political divisions, each province taking the name of its capital city: Havana, Matanzas, Santa Clara, Puerto Principe, Santiago de Cuba and Pinar del Rio.

The figures in the following table give the population by provinces, as well as the density of population (number of inhabitants per square kilometer.)

Provinces.	Inhabitants.	Square Kilometers.	Density.
Pinar del Rio .	225,891	14,967	15.09
Habana . . .	451,928	8,610	52.49
Matanzas . .	259,578	8,486	30.59
Santa Clara .	354,122	23,083	15.34
Puerto Principe .	67,789	32,341	2.10
Santiago de Cuba	272,379	35,119	7.76
Totals . .	1,631,687	122,606	13.31

In Cuba, under Spanish rule, the Roman Catholic is the only religion tolerated by the government. There are no Protestant or Jewish places of worship. A decree promulgated in Madrid in 1892 declares that, while a person who should comply with all other requirements might be permitted to remain on the island, he would not be allowed to advance doctrines at variance with those of the established church. As Catholicism is a state religion, its maintenance is charged to the revenues of the island, and amounts to something like $400,000 a year.

Education in Cuba is, or has been, at a very low ebb. That is due, as many other things are, to the wretched, short-sighted policy of Spain, the country which has never completely emerged from the darkness of barbarism. She was afraid to give education to the Cubans, thinking that she could better dominate them in their ignorance. There is a royal university in Havana, and a collegiate institute in each of the six provinces, the number of students in all amounting to nearly three thousand, but these come almost without exception from the ranks of the well-to-do.

Less than one out of every forty-five of the children in Cuba attend the public schools. There was a farcical law passed in 1880, making education compulsory. How could such a law be of any effect when there was neither the ability nor the desire to provide school-houses and instructors? Now let us take a brief glance at some of the chief cities of Cuba.

Havana, the principal and capital city of the island, is situated on the west side of the bay of Havana, on a peninsula of level land of limestone formation.

It is the seat of the general government and captain-generalcy, superior court of Havana (audencia,) general direction of finance, naval station, arsenal, observatory, diocese of the bishopric and the residence of all the administrative officers of the island (civil, military, maritime, judicial and economic).

Its strategic position at the mouth of the Gulf of Mexico has aptly given to the city the name of the Key of the Gulf; and a symbolic key is emblazoned in its coat-of-arms. The harbor, the entrance to which is narrow, is wide and deep, and a thousand ships could easily ride there at anchor.

It has always been supposed to be strongly fortified, its chief defences being Morro Castle, the Cabana, the Castillo del Principe, Fort Atares, the Punta and the Reina Battery.

The population of Havana, from the last official estimate, is about 220,000.

Before the present war, Havana was one of the most charming places in the world for the tourist to visit, more especially during the winter months.

There is scarcely a city in Europe which, to the American seemed so foreign as Havana. The whole appearance of the place, its manners and customs, were all totally different to what the American had been accustomed.

The streets are so narrow that vehicles by law are obliged to pass down one street and up another, while the sidewalks are not more than two feet wide and hollowed down in the centre by the constant trampling of feet. This applies to the city proper, for, outside the walls, there are many broad and beautiful avenues. The streets are very noisy and, as a rule, excessively unclean.

The houses, many of them palaces, wonderfully beautiful within, but situated on dark and dirty alleys, are all built about a central courtway. There are no fireplaces anywhere, nor a window shielded with glass in the whole city. The windows have iron bars, and within those of the first story is the inevitable row of American rocking chairs. Through these bars the Cuban lover interviews hisn iamorata. It would be the height of indecorum for him to approach nearer, to seek to speak with her within the walls of her own home, even in the presence of her father and mother.

Cows are driven about the streets and milked in front of your own door, when you desire the lacteal fluid. This custom is, at all events, a safeguard against adulteration.

Ladies do not go into the shops to make purchases, but all goods are brought out to them as they sit in their volantes.

By the way, the volante (flyer) is the national carriage and no other, practically, is used in the country. It consists of a two seated vehicle, slung low down by leather straps from the axle of two large wheels, and it has shafts fifteen feet long. The horse in the shafts is led by a postillion, whose horse is harnessed on the other side of the shafts in the same manner. The carriage is extremely comfortable to travel in, and the height of the wheels and their distance apart prevent all danger of turning over, although the roads in the country are for the most part, mere tracks through fields and open land. Ox carts and pack mules are used for conveying goods in the interior of the island outside of the meagre railway lines.

Havana has some beautiful public parks and some really fine statues, chiefly those of Spain's former rulers.

Its principal theatre, the Tacon, is celebrated throughout the world for its size and beauty. In regard to theatres, there is one peculiar custom in Havana: By the payment of a certain sum, beyond the price of admission, one is allowed to go behind the scenes between the acts. This privilege has caused great annoyance to many eminent artists.

The cathedral of Havana is rather imposing in architecture, although it is badly situated, but it is very interesting because there is an urn within its walls which is said, and with a large semblance of truth, to contain the bones of Columbus.

Space does not permit us to tell of all the charms of Havana, but, suffice it to say, that it was and will be again, under far happier conditions too, one of the most delightful cities in the world.

The city of Cuba, next in commercial importance to Havana, is Matanzas. It is beautifully situated on the north coast, about seventy miles from Havana, and has a population of about fifty thousand. The climate is fine, and Matanzas is considered the healthiest city on the island. With proper drainage (something that has hitherto been almost unknown in Cuba as are all other sanitary arrangements) yellow fever and malaria would be almost unknown. If it should ever come under American enterprise, the city would develop into a superb pleasure resort and be a fatal rival to the Florida towns. We cannot forbear to mention the Caves of Bellamar. These are not far from Matanzas and are subterranean caverns, of which there are a number in Cuba. The walls and roofs are covered with stalactites of every conceivable hue and shape, and forming pictures of beauty far beyond anything conceived of, even in the Arabian Nights.

The most modern city of importance is Cienfuegos (as its name signifies, the City of a Hundred Fires). It has a population of about twenty-six thousand and its harbor is one of the best on the southern coast, with a depth of 27 feet at the anchorage, and from 14 to 16 feet at the wharves.

Cardenas is a seaport on the north coast about 135 miles east of Havana. Its population is about the same as Cienfuegos. In the rainy season, its climate is distinctly bad and its sanitary conditions worse. It has some large manufactories, and carries on a flourishing trade.

Santiago de Cuba, on the southeastern coast, is the second city of size in Cuba (60,000 inhabitants), and the one on which all American eyes have been fixed, for it is there that our brave Sampson bottled up Cervera's illusive fleet, and on its suburbs a fierce battle was fought, July 1, 2 and 3, between the American troops under General Shafter and the Spanish army under General Linares, resulting in the defeat of the latter and the subsequent surrender of the city to the United States' forces on Sunday, July 17. ·

It is very difficult, by the way, to find the entrance to the harbor of Santiago. Approaching it from the sea, nothing is seen but lofty mountains. When quite near, two mountains seem to suddenly part, and a channel only 180 yards wide, but of good depth, is revealed.

It is the oldest city in America, many years older than St. Augustine, having been founded by Velasquez in 1514, and is exceedingly quaint and mediaeval.

Its chief fortifications are the Castillo of La Socapa and the Morro Castle, the largest and most picturesque of the three of that name. The latter was built about 1640, and is a fine specimen of the feudal "donjon keep" with battlemented walls, moats, drawbridge, portcullis and all the other paraphernalia of the days of romance.   The harbor itself, around which so much interest has clustered, is naturally one of the finest in the world, but no pains has been taken to improve it, the funds appropriated for that purpose having been stolen by the Spanish engineers and officials.

Santiago is Spanish for St. James, who is the special patron saint of Spain, on account of a myth that he once made a journey to that country.

Cuba, in short, is one of the most beautiful and fertile countries on the face of the globe, but man, in the shape of brutal Spain, has done everything he could, to ruin the gifts Nature so lavishly bestowed.

Let us hope and believe, as surely we have every reason to do, that upon the ''Pearl of the Antilles,'' the sun of prosperity will rise, driving away the gloomy shadows of oppression, and that the dawn will be not long postponed.

CHAPTER XVI.

WHAT WILL THE FUTURE BE?

It is unnecessary to refer except in a brief manner to the Spanish-American war, as the struggle is at the present time of writing only in its inception, and no one can tell how long it will last or what reverses each side may experience before peace is declared.

One thing is certain, however. The result is not problematical. It is assured. The United States will be victorious in the end, be that end near or distant, and Cuba must and shall be free.

If ever there was a war that was entered into purely from motives cf humanity and with no thought what-ever of conquest, it is this one. The entire people of the United States were agreed that their purpose was a holy one, and instantly the call of the President was re-sponded to from all parts of the country. Sectional differences, such as they were, vanished like mist be-fore the sun. There was no Easterner, no Westerner, no Northerner, no Southerner, but "Americans all."

We are proud of our army and navy, and justly so. Dewey destroyed a large fleet, without the loss of a man, a feat unprecedented in the annals of warfare, ancient or modern. Sampson bottled up Cervera's fleet in the harbor of Santiago, after the wily admiral had at-tempted a diplomacy which was nothing more nor less than absurd, and when Cervera, on the eve of the surrender of the city, attempted to escape from his self-constituted trap, his four armored cruisers and two torpedo boat destroyers were literally riddled and sunk outside the harbor by the skilful gunners of the American fleet. Hobson, in sinking the Merrimac, displayed a heroism that has never been surpassed. And on land, General Shafter's achievements have been brilliant in the extreme.

It is interesting here to examine for a moment the attitude of other countries toward us since the declaration of war with Spain.

Of course they all declared neutrality.

At first France apparently was very bitter against us, declaring that it was a war of aggression and one that was unjustified. We think we have already shown in these pages how unwarrantable such an accusation was. There was a reason for France's feeling, outside of the fact that her people, like Spain's, belong to the Latin race, and that reason was that a large proportion of Spanish bonds was held in France. Even the best of us do not bear with equanimity anything which depletes our pockets. But it was not long before a great change took place both in press and public and a wave of French sympathy turned toward us. This is as it should be and was inevitable. There could be no lasting rancor between us and our sister republic, the country who gave us Lafayette and presented us with the Statue of Liberty.

The press of Germany has unquestionably said some

very harsh things. But we are confident that the feeling is confined to the press and does not represent the mass of the people. We do know that it is in no way representative of the German government, which from the very beginning has showed itself most friendly to us. The ties between Germany and the United States are too strong ever to be severed, with the thousands and thousands of Germans in this country who rank among our very best citizens.

Russia, who from time immemorial has been our friend and given us her moral support in all our troubles, has treated us with the utmost cordiality.

But the pleasantest thing of all has been the attitude of Great Britain, our once mother country. She has stood by us through thick and thin, hurling defiance in the face of the world in her championship of us, and rejoicing in our victories almost as if they were her own. This has done more to bring the two great English-speaking nations together than anything else could possibly have done, and will probably have far reaching consequences in the future.

The Marquis of Lansdowne, the British Secretary of State of War, in a recent speech, thus expressed himself:

''There could be no more inspiring ideal than an understanding between two nations sprung from the same race and having so many common interests, nations which, together, are predominant in the world's commerce and industry.

''Is there anything preposterous in the hope that

these two nations should be found—I will not say in a hard and fast alliance of offense and defense, but closely connected in their diplomacy, absolutely frank and unreserved in their international councils, and ready wherever the affairs of the world are threatened with disturbance to throw their influence into the same scale?

''Depend upon it, these are no mere idle dreams or hazy aspirations.　The change which has come over the sentiment of each country toward the other during the last year or two is almost immeasurable.　One can scarcely believe they are the same United States with whom, only two years ago, we were on the verge of a serious quarrel.

''The change is not an ephemeral understanding between diplomatists, but a genuine desire of the two peoples to be friends, and therefore it cannot be laughed out of existence by the sort of comments we have lately heard.''

There is a poem which we cannot forbear to quote here, it is so fine in itself and so expressive of the existing situation.　The author is Richard Mansfield, the eminent actor:

THE EAGLE'S SONG.

BY RICHARD MANSFIELD.

The Lioness whelped, and the sturdy cub
Was seized by an eagle and carried up
And homed for a while in an eagle's nest,
And slept for a while on an eagle's breast,
And the eagle taught it the eagle's song:
''To be staunch and valiant and free and strong!''

The Lion whelp sprang from the eerie nest,
From the lofty crag where the queen birds rest;
He fought the King on the spreading plain,
And drove him back o'er the foaming main.

He held the land as a thrifty chief,
And reared his cattle and reaped his sheaf,
Nor sought the help of a foreign hand,
Yet welcomed all to his own free land!

Two were the sons that the country bore
To the Northern lakes and the Southern shore,
And Chivalry dwelt with the Southern son,
And Industry lived with the Northern one.

Tears for the time when they broke and fought!
Tears was the price of the union wrought!
And the land was red in a sea of blood,
Where brother for brother had swelled the flood!

And now that the two are one again,
Behold on their shield the word "Refrain!"
And the lion cubs twain sing the eagle's song,
"To be staunch and valiant and free and strong!"
For the eagle's beak and the lion's paw,
And the lion's fangs and the eagle's claw,
And the eagle's swoop and the lion's might,
And the lion's leap and the eagle's sight,
Shall guard the flag with the word "Refrain!"
Now that the two are one again!
Here's to a cheer for the Yankee ships!
And "Well done, Sam," from the mother's lips!

War is unquestionably a terrible thing. As General
Sherman put it, "war is hell." But there are other terrible and yet necessary things, also, such as the operations of surgery and the infliction of the death penalty.

War is justifiable, when waged, as the present one unquestionably is, from purely unselfish motives, simply
from a determination to rescue a people whose suffer-

ings had become unbearable to them and to the lookers-on. The United States, by its action, has set a lesson for the rest of the world, which the latter will not be slow to learn and for which future generations will bless the name of America.

Nobly are we following out the precepts of our forefathers, who declared in one of the most magnificent documents ever framed:

"We hold these truths to be self-evident: That all men are created equal; that they are endowed by their Creator with certain inalienable rights; that among these are life, liberty, and the pursuit of happiness; that, to secure these rights, governments are instituted among men, deriving their just powers from the consent of the governed; that, whenever any form of government becomes destructive of these ends, it is the right of the people to alter or abolish it, and to institute new government, laying its foundation on such principles, and organizing its powers in such form, as to them shall seem most likely to effect their safety and happiness."

We fought for these principles, in our own interests, a century and a quarter ago; in the interests of others, we are fighting for them to-day.

A question which has been universally asked is this: Can the Cubans, if they obtain freedom, govern themselves, or will not a free Cuba become a second Hayti with all the horrors of that island?

To this our reply is: Most emphatically Cuba will be able to govern herself; not in the beginning, perhaps, where mistakes must of necessity be made, but most certainly in the end.

The Cuban leaders are men of high intelligence and lofty purposes, and they know what reforms must be instituted. Some one has said that "love of liberty is the surest guarantee of representative government."

Surely these men have shown their love of liberty in the fullest degree and have proved themselves in every way fitted for self-government.

The Cubans, strange as the statement may seem to those who have studied the matter only in a cursory way, are not a people who love trouble. Though revolution after revolution has occurred in the island, the Cubans have never taken up arms until every peaceful means of redress had been resorted to.

It has been feared that the negro element would be a disturbing influence, but we can see little or no reason for this dread. The same thing was said of the emancipation of the slaves in our own South, but certainly, taken altogether, the behavior of the colored race in the United States, since the Civil War, has been most praiseworthy.

A Frenchman, Baron Antomarchi, who is naturally unprejudiced, says:

"When the time for the settlement of the Cuban question shall have come it will be an affair of give and take between the whites and the negroes, and if the negro does not succeed in convincing the white man that he is entitled to a full measure of civil authority, a measure which by reason of his numerical strength he will have a right, under a republican government, to exact, then we may have to stand by while Cuba engages in an internal struggle important enough to cripple or, to say the least, seriously hinder, her development. Should the war come to an end and should Cuba be free to develop the riches of the land for which she is now battling, an American protectorate would prevent all dangers of race conflict. The United States would be under a moral obligation to avert disorder. Aside from all considerations of a commercial character there would be the obligation resulting from an adherence to consistency of conduct. The stand taken by the American legislators, or some of them, to say nothing of the stand taken by the American people, would make this latter obligation even still more binding.

Not until her machetes shall have been returned to their original use can Cuba develop the riches bestowed upon her by Nature. After the dawn of peace, when her sons are free to settle down to the tranquil life of the untrammeled husbandman, there will be no hunted exiles in the long grass of her savannas. When Cuba has attained the quiet calm that her younger generation has never known, she will show the world that it was not for idle brigands that Maceo died. In the shadow of the feathered cocoa palms in the deep shade of the drooping heavy leaves where Gilard dreamed of liberty, great cities shall one day loom in the misty, tropic twilight, and peace shall brood over the land that now, seamed with the graves of Cuba's heroes, awaits the murdered bodies of Cuban victims. Not until that day has come will it be known how strong to endure torment and sorrow, how brave in time of danger, were the men who won the day for Cuban independence.''

It is absolutely certain that all the natural and political ties that have bound ''the Ever Faithful Isle'' to the mother country have been so completely severed that it is utterly impossible they should ever be united again.

The unique banner of Cuba, with its blue and white stripes and a single star upon a red triangle, has cost more blood and treasure than any revolutionary flag known to history.

When this war is over, and Spain has learned her lesson, severe but well-deserved, and we hope salutary, then shall that flag take its place among the honored ones of other nations; then will the Cubans show their ability to prize and cherish the liberty for which the blood of their heroes has been spilled; then, under the protectorate of the United States, but as an independent republic, will Cuba, in the words of our own General Lee, emerge from the dark shadows of the past, and stand side by side with those countries who have their place in the sunlight of peace, progress and prosperity.

Oh! Cuba Libre! as Longfellow said of our own Union, so do all Americans, who are now fighting with you shoulder to shoulder, say to you:

> ''Our hearts, our hopes, are all with thee;
> Our hearts, our hopes, our prayers, our tears,
> Our faith triumphant o'er our fears,
> Are all with thee—are all with thee!''

(THE END.)

PORTO RICO

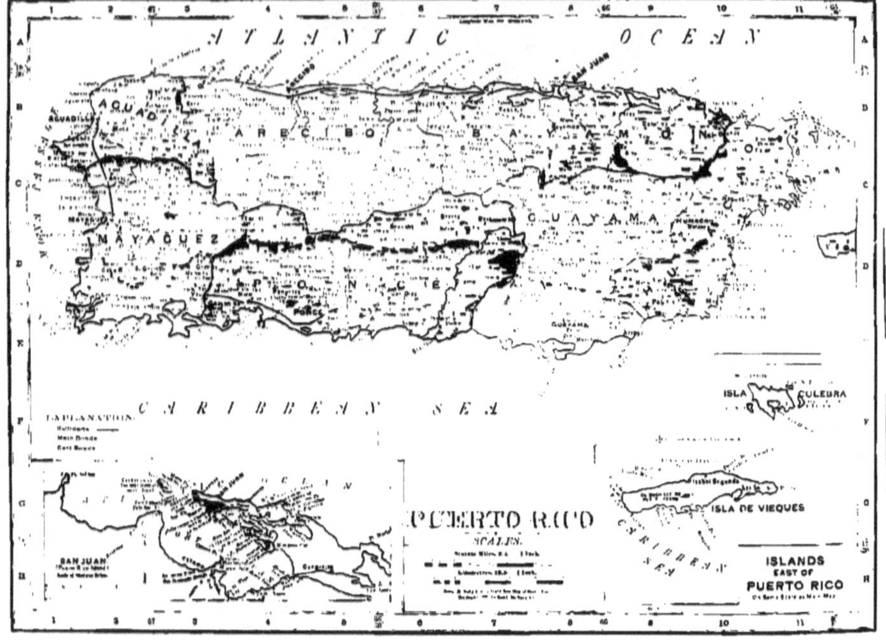

ATLANTIC OCEAN
AGUADILLA
AGUAD
ARECIBO
BAYAMO
San Juan
MAYAGUEZ
GUAYAMA
HUMACAO
PONCE
PONCE
Guayama
CARIBBEAN SEA
ISLA CULEBRA
EXPLANATION
SAN JUAN
ISLA DE VIEQUES
Isabel Segunda
PUERTO RICO
SCALES.
CARIBBEAN SEA
ISLANDS
EAST OF
PUERTO RICO

PORTO RICO.

Its History, Products And Possibilities . .

BY

A. D. HALL,

Author of "Cuba" and "The Philippines."

NEW YORK
STREET & SMITH, Publishers
81 Fulton Street

CONTENTS.

PORTO RICO.

CHAPTER I.

THE ABORIGINES OF PORTO RICO.

Porto Rico, or Puerto Rico, as it is sometimes called, has lately become of the first importance in the eyes of the world. To Americans it has assumed special interest, as it is now practically in the possession of the United States, and sooner or later will be represented by a new star in our beautiful flag, that flag which recently, by the magnificent exploits of our navy and army, has assumed a greater importance than ever among the standards of the universe.

Uncle Sam will certainly find this beautiful and fertile island a most valuable possession, every foot of which he could sell at a large substantial price, if he chose to do so.

Until recently there has been an impression in the United States that Porto Rico did not amount to much, that Cuba was the only island in the West Indies which was of any especial value. But this is the most grievous error, as we shall endeavor to show in the course of this little book.

The island, without much exaggeration, can really be called the garden spot of the world, and there is no doubt but that when the Stars and Stripes wave permanently over it, and there is an influx of American enterprise and wealth, there will be a marvelous increase in values of all kinds.

Like all Spanish colonies, Porto Rico has been wofully mismanaged. The Spaniards have looked upon it in the light of a more or less valuable cow from which every drop of milk must be squeezed. But now, under more fortuitous circumstances, under a more beneficent rule, the charming little island will undoubtedly ''blossom as a rose''; for those who have looked into the subject have declared that more can be raised on an acre of land in Porto Rico than in any other portion of the globe. Later on we shall examine in detail the truth or falsehood of this statement.

Porto Rico is older than the United States, for it was discovered by Columbus on November 16, 1493, during his second voyage to America. The great discoverer remained there only two days in the port of Aquadilla, but he did not come in contact with any of the ingenuous natives, for they fled in terror when they saw his ship.

During their subsequent conquests in the West Indies, the Spaniards paid no attention to Porto Rico until 1509. At this time Ponce de Leon, then governor of Hispaniola, afterward known as Hayti, determined to extend his dominion. With the idea of obtaining fresh supplies of gold, he went to Porto Rico and made a long visit to the chief of the natives, by whom he was received and entertained with the greatest kindness and hospitality. The chief willingly pointed out to his

Spanish guests all the great resources of the island, and when, with the greed which has ever distinguished the men of their country, they asked for gold, he took them to streams where the sands were loaded with the precious metal.

Ponce de Leon was so delighted with the beauty and fertility of the island that he imagined he could find there the fountain of perpetual youth for which he so long sought in vain. In this chimerical idea, however, as in Florida, he was doomed to disappointment.

The original name of the island is said to have been Borinquen, and the population of the natives, who were of the same race as the inhabitants of the other islands of the Greater Antilles, has been estimated at six hundred thousand.

Dr. C. T. Bedwell, recently British consul at Porto Rico, has published a most interesting report in regard to the aborigines, and from this report we have obtained considerable of the information which follows.

Among the Sibaros, or sallow people of to-day, one rarely sees a physical trace of Indian descent, although in their mode of living much of Indian character exists. Fray Inigo Abbad, who wrote a work on Porto Rico, published in Madrid in 1878, says that when the Spaniards first came to Porto Rico "it was as thickly populated as a beehive, and so beautiful that it resembled a garden." Fray Inigo says that the color of the Indians of Porto Rico was the copper color known to the aborigines of America, though they were of a sallow and somewhat darker complexion. They were shorter in stature than the Spaniards, stout and well-proportioned. They had flat noses with wide nostrils, bad teeth and narrow foreheads. Their heads were flat, both in front and at the back, "because," says the author, "they were pressed into this shape at the time of their birth." They had long, thin, coarse hair, and, according to Fray Inigo, they were without hair on their face or on other parts of their body. This, however, is disputed by some writers.

The small quantity and little substance of the food they used, the facility with which they supplied material wants without labor, the excessive heat of the climate, and the absence of quadrupeds for the exercise of hunting, caused them, he says, to be weak and indolent, and averse to labor of all kinds. Anything that was not necessary to satisfy the pangs of hunger, or that did not afford amusement, such as hunting or fishing, was regarded with indifference. Neither the hope of reward nor the fear of punishment would tempt them to, seek the one or to avoid the other.

Fray Inigo admits, however, that there were some exceptions among them, and says that some of the Indians displayed much bravery and strength in the contests with the Spanish soldiers.

Their forms were light and free, and there were no cripples among them.

They were governed by Caciques, whose eldest sons inherited the succession. In the absence of a son the chief was succeeded by the eldest son of his sister, that there might be no doubt as to true descent.

The tutelary deity was Cerni, who was made to speak by the Buhitis or medicine men, who were at the same time the priests. The Buhites hid themselves behind the statue of Cerni and declared war or peace, arranged the seasons, granted sunshine or rain, or whatever was required, according to the will of the Cacique. When announcements were not fulfilled the Buhites declared that the Cerni had changed his mind for wise reasons of his own, ''without on this account,'' says Fray Inigo, ''the power or credit of the pretended deity, or his mendacious ministers being doubted, such being the simplicity and ignorance of the Indians.''

The chiefdoms were divided into small provinces, which for the most part only comprised the inhabitants of a valley; but all were subject to the head Cacique, who at the time of the conquest was Aqueynoba. He was actually governor-in-chief, the others being his lieutenants, who carried out his orders in their respective districts.

Men and unmarried women wore no clothing, but painted their bodies abundantly, and with much skill, drawing upon them many varieties of figures with the ores, gums and resins which they extracted from trees and plants. In this uniform they presented themselves in their military expeditions, public balls, and other assemblies. To be well painted was to be well dressed, and they learned from experience besides that the resinous matter and vegetable oils with which they painted their bodies served to preserve them from excessive heat and superabundant perspiration. The paint also served to protect them from the changes of atmosphere, the dampness of climate, and the plague of the numerous varieties of mosquitoes and other insects, which, without this precaution, constantly annoyed them. They wore headdresses made of feathers with exquisite colors. They put small plates of gold on their cheeks, and hung shells, precious stones and relics from their ears and noses, and the image of their god Cerni was never forgotten. The chiefs used as a distinctive emblem a large golden plate worn on their breasts. Married women wore an apron which descended to about half their leg; but no clothing was worn on the rest of the body. The wives of the Caciques wore their aprons to their ankles; except at the national game of ball, when they also wore short ones.

The men took two, three or more wives, according to their ability to support them. The chiefs possessed a larger number of wives than their subjects, but one of them was generally preferred over all others. The women, besides their domestic duties, had charge of the agricultural pursuits and worked in the fields. Those best loved were buried alive with their husband on his demise. The men did not intermarry with relatives of the first degree, from a belief that such marriages resulted in a bad death.

Their huts were similar in structure and in character to those of the North American Indians.

The hammock was the chief article of furniture of the aborigines, and the calabash shell their only cooking utensil.

Their arms were a bow and arrow, in the use of which they were very skilful. They had canoes both for fishing and sea voyages. These were hewn out of the timber of enormous trees, the like of which, owing to fires and seasons of drouth, no longer exist upon the island. Some of the canoes were large enough to hold forty or fifty men.

When the Indians saw that the sick were near to death they suffocated them. Even the chiefs did not escape.

After death they opened and dried the body by fire, and buried it in a large cave, in which were interred also some live women, the arms of the deceased and provisions for the journey to the other world. Sticks and branches of trees were then placed on the top, and the whole was covered with earth, which was thus kept from the bodies of those interred.

They were accustomed to perform a national dance which was called the areito. At the conclusion of this dance, all became intoxicated with drinks made by the women of fruit, maize and other ingredients, and with the smoke of tobacco which they inhaled in their nostrils.

As has been said, at the time of the conquest the name of the native chief was Aqueynoba. He was friendly to the Spaniards at first and lived peaceably with them for some time.

There is no doubt but that the aborigines were confiding, generous and peaceful. But, like all savages, they were very superstitious. They worshipped a vast quantity of idols, but believed in one superior deity. With the exception of the Caribs, who occupied the eastern part of the island, they were not cannibals. They were in the habit of practicing quite a large number of domestic arts, such as the cultivation of the soil, the carving in wood and stone, and the manufacture of pottery and furniture.

The Spaniards have ever been treacherous, selfish and a nation of money-grubbers.

Now followed an instance which is only one of many to prove the truth of this statement.

After Ponce de Leon had won the confidence and had been the recipient of boundless hospitality from the islanders, he returned to Hayti and at once commenced to fit out an expedition for the invasion and subjugation of Porto Rico. From a purely selfish point of view, this was a most senseless proceeding on his part. He could have done much better without having any recourse to force, for at first the natives regarded the Spaniards as immortal visitors from Heaven, as superior beings whom they could not kill.

But they speedily recognized their mistake and discovered the abominable character of the invaders.

De Leon killed off all the natives that he could and made the rest slaves to work in the gold mines of Hayti.

When any one resisted he was killed, and if he attempted to escape he was hunted down by bloodhounds.

It is related that Ponce de Leon had a dog which became noted as a slave catcher. So valuable was he in this respect that his name was actually carried on the army payroll for the benefit of his master.

When the natives found that they were being slain or deprived of their liberty they naturally became exasperated and turned against their dastardly oppressors. But from their point of view it was absolutely necessary to find out if the Spaniards were mortal. If they were not, it would be an act of impiety to resist them.

This vital question must be settled, and therefore one of the native chiefs was detailed to try if he could kill a Spaniard. The trial was eminently successful. A young man named Salzedo was found alone and was drowned by the natives.

The action is thus related in the words of a competent authority:

"The guides conducted Salzedo to the bank of a small river through which they must pass, and to prevent his being exposed to the water one of the Indians kindly offered to take him on his shoulders and carry him over. Salzedo mounted to his high seat and was borne into the middle of the stream, when the Indian and his burden fell into the water. The other Indians immediately rushed into the river with the apparent purpose of rescuing their guest, but contrived, while professing to offer him assistance, to keep his head continually under water. The result of this practical biological experiment, so adroitly conducted, brought hope and joy to the despairing natives. The body was kept immersed until long after every sign of life had gone, but they still feared animation might return. Carrying the body to the bank, a new farce was acted; they lamented over him, they begged his pardon for the accident, and they protested their innocence of any design. In every way they provided themselves with a plausible defense in case he should recover or they should be suspected. After several days, putrefaction happily settled all their doubts about the mortality of their conquerors, and the glad news was communicated to their people.''

The natives then at once commenced to massacre the Spaniards. But this did not last long. Ponce de Leon immediately sent for reinforcements, and the Indians believed that these newcomers were the resurrected bodies of those they had killed. This idea caused them to lose all hope and courage, and they fell an easy prey to their enemies. It was not many years before the aboriginal population, large as it was originally, was completely exterminated.

The Spaniards now began to colonize the island and the town of Capana was the first one settled by them. Its site was found, however, to be too high and inaccessible. It was therefore abandoned and in 1511 the present city of San Juan was founded.

In this city Ponce de Leon built the governor's palace called Casa Blanca, a structure which is still in use.

After de Leon's unsuccessful expedition to Florida, where he received a mortal wound at the hands of the Indians, his remains were brought to Porto Rico and interred in the Dominican church.

The inscription upon his monument reads as follows:

*Mole sub hac fortis requiescunt ossa Leonis
Qui vicit factis nomina magna suis.*

These words may be translated into English as follows:

"This narrow grave contains the remains of a man who was a Lion by name, and much more so by his deeds."

His cruel treatment of the gentle natives, inspired though it may have been and probably was by the home government, by no means causes him to deserve so flattering an epitaph.

CHAPTER II.

STRUGGLES OF THE PAST.

Ever since the days of Ponce de Leon, Porto Rico has been a Spanish possession. It has never been captured, although many attempts have been made to take it both by external and internal forces.

None of these attacks seriously affected Spanish authority on the island.

But although the island has never been taken, it has been sacked. It may be said that it was pirates who did this, for while the commanders of several of the expeditions against the island bore great names, they were really little more or less than pirates.

The first to attack was no less than the famous English commander, Sir Francis Drake, who had Elizabeth behind him. This was in 1595, and Drake then scored his first failure, in spite of the fact that when he left his ballast consisted of ducatoons, and the shops of San Juan were in ruins.

It is rather a strange coincidence that Drake's failure was due to the fact that the Spaniards had recourse to the same scheme that was so daringly and successfully carried out by Lieutenant Hobson in the harbor of Santiago.

They sunk a ship in the neck of San Juan harbor, thereby preventing Drake's fleet from obtaining an entrance.

Dr. Griffin, the accomplished assistant librarian of the Congressional Library in Washington, has recently been making a study of Porto Rican literature which has been pregnant with interesting results.

Dr. Griffin discovered the following in an old English chronicle:

"Confession of John Austin, mariner of London, of the late company of Sir Francis Drake and Sir John Hawkins.

"Directions were given that if any of the fleet lost company they should make for Guadaloupe in the Indies; his ship did so, but having lost her rudder failed, and was taken by five Spanish frigates and the crew imprisoned in the Isle of St. John de Porto Rico. Sir Francis, who lost company of Sir John Hawkins, was told of this by a bark which saw the fight. The prisoners were examined and threatened with torture to tell what the English forces were. The Spaniards sunk ships in the harbor to hinder their entrance. Sir Francis summoned the town, and on their refusing to yield sent fifteen vessels to burn the frigates in the harbor. Two were fired, but the light thus made enabled the Spaniards to fire on the English ships and drive them away. The English attacked the fort, but Sir John Hawkins was killed. Sir Francis sent back to the governor five prisoners whom he had taken, and begged that the English might be well treated and sent home, in which there was an improvement in their diet, etc. Sir Francis then went to the south of the island, got provisions and water and went to Carthagena. This was reported by two frigates that watched him, and then the treasure ships in Porto Rico with $4,000,000 on board sailed for Spain, and reached St. Lucas, bringing the English prisoners, who still remain in prison, but the examinante escaped. Two fleets, each of twenty-five ships, and 5,000 men, are said to be sent out to follow Sir Francis Drake, March 25, 1599."

In Barrow's "Life of Drake," there are further particulars given of this unsuccessful attack on San Juan, which was under the command of Sir Francis Drake and Sir John Hawkins, the two greatest British naval commanders then living. Barrow says:

"The fitting out and equipment of this grand expedition were not surpassed by that of 1585 to the West Indies under Sir Francis Drake, Vice Admiral Forbesher and Rear Admiral Knolles. Its destination, in the first place, was intended for Porto Rico, where the queen had received information that a vast treasure had been brought, and intended to be sent home from thence for the use of the King of Spain in completing the third grand armament (the second having been destroyed by Drake) which he had in contemplation for the invasion of England. The object of the present fleet was to intercept the treasure and thereby cut off the main supply of his navy and army destined for that purpose.

"Their first intention, however, had been to land at Nombre de Dios and proceed direct from thence over the Isthmus of Panama in order to seize the treasure generally brought thither from the mines of Mexico and Peru; but in a few days before their departure from

Plymouth they received letters sent by order of the queen informing them that advices had been received from Spain announcing the arrival of the West Indian or Plata fleet, but that one of them, a very valuable ship, had lost her mast and put into the Island of Puerto Rico, and it was therefore her majesty's recommendation that they should proceed direct to that island to secure the ship and treasure which was on her."

The expedition left Plymouth, August 28, 1595. Before going to Porto Rico, Drake, against the protest of Hawkins, tried to take the Canaries and failed. The voyage was then continued.

"On the 30th of September," the historian continues, "Captain Wegnot, on the Francis, a bark of thirty-five tons, being the sternmost of Sir John Hawkins' division, was chased by five of the king's frigates, or zobras, being ships of two hundred tons, which came with three other zobras for the treasure at San Juan de Puerto Rico. The Francis, mistaking them for companions, was taken in sight of our caraval. The Spaniards, indifferent to human suffering, left the Francis driving in the sea with three or four hurt and sick men, and took the rest of her people into their ships and returned to Porto Rico.

"The squadron now intended to pass through the Virgin Islands, but 'here,' says Hakluyt, 'Sir John Hawkins was extreme sick, which his sickness began upon neues of the taking of the Francis.' Remaining here two days, they tarried two days more in a sound, which Drake, in his barge had discovered. They then stood for the eastern end of Porto Rico, where Sir John Hawkins breathed his last.

"Sir Thomas Baskerville now took possession of the Garland as second in command. The fleet came to anchor at a distance of two miles, or less, at the eastern side of the town of San Juan de Porto Rico, where, says Hakluyt, 'we received from their forts and places, where they planted ordnance, some twenty-eight great shot, the last of which stroke the admiral's ship through the misen, and the last but one stroke through her quarter into the steerage, the general being there at supper, and stroke the stool from under him, but hurt him not, but hurt at the same table Sir Nicholas Clifford, Mr. Browne, Captain Stratford, with one or two more. Sir Nicholas Clifford, and Master Browne died of their hurts.'

"Drake," continues Barrow, "was certainly imprudent in suffering the squadron to take up anchorage so near to the means of annoyance; but his former visit had no doubt taught the enemy the prudence of being better prepared for any future occasion, and it is somewhat remarkable that Drake should not have observed his usual caution. Browne was an old and particular favorite of Drake.

"The following morning the whole fleet came to anchor before the point of the harbor without the town, a little to the westward, where they remained till night-fall, and then twenty-five pinnaces, boats and shallops, well manned, and furnished with fireworks and small shot, entered the road. The great castle, or galleon the object of the present enterprise, had been completely repaired, and was on the point of sailing, when certain intelligence of the intended attack by Drake reached the island. Every preparation had been made for the defense of the harbor and the town; the whole of the treasure had been landed; the galleon was sunk in the mouth of the harbor; a floating barrier of masts and spars was laid on each side of her, near to the forts and castles, so as to render the entrance impassable; within this breakwater were the five zabras, moored, their treasure also taken out; all the women and children and infirm people were moved to the interior, and those only left in the town who were able to aid in its defense. A heavy fire was opened on the English ships, but the adventurers persisted in their desperate attempt, until they had lost, by their own account, some forty or fifty men killed, and as many wounded; but there was consolation in thinking that by burning, drowning and killing, the loss of the Spaniards could not be less; in fact, a great deal more; for the five zabras and a large ship of 400 tons were burned, and their several cargoes of silk, oil and wine destroyed.''

After thus being defeated in his main object, Drake did not return to San Juan. He contented himself with laying tribute upon Porto Rico, and burning the towns on the Caribbean side of the island.

He then sailed for Wombee de Dios, and, when the fleet was off the South American coast, he died on the 28th of January and was buried at sea. Drake was succeeded in command by Sir Thomas Baskerville.

When the latter was on his way back to England he encountered a Spanish fleet and engaged in battle off the Isle of Pines. The victory was decidedly with the English, but the Spaniards were apparently the same then as they are to-day. Everybody remembers Blanco's famous dispatches, famous for their absurd falseness. So then the Spanish admiral issued a bulletin in which he claimed a magnificent triumph. Baskerville was so angry that he publicly declared the admiral to be a liar and challenged him to a duel. Nothing, however, ever resulted from this challenge.

Three years later the Duke of Cumberland, who might also be called a corsair, but a private one, as he acted on his own hook, attacked San Juan, and after three days' fighting, laid the city in ruins. He was unable to follow up his victory, however, as the fever killed his men by the hundreds.

The English tried to take it in 1615, and again in 1678.

Once more in 1795, seeing the great advantage of owning the harbor of San Juan, the English attempted to capture it, but they were repulsed with great slaughter.

Spain has never given as much attention to Porto Rico as she has to her other colonies, and therefore the government, while practically of the same character, has not been so intolerable as in Cuba and the Philippines.

For nearly three hundred years the island was neglected. During all that time it was used chiefly as a watering station for ships and as a penal colony. In 1815 it was thrown open to colonization, and land was given free to all Spaniards who went there to settle. As a consequence a host of adventurers hastened to Porto Rico, as well as a number of Spanish loyalists, belonging to the better classes, who had been expelled by the decrees of other and rebellious colonies.

About this time there was a large importation of negro slaves to work on the sugar plantations. For these reasons the wealth and population rapidly increased.

Nevertheless there has been a large number of revolutions against the home government.

As early as 1820, long before Cuba had made any attempt to throw off the Spanish yoke, the Porto Ricans made an effort to obtain their independence. After a short guerilla war, this first rebellion was suppressed, as were also several other abortive attempts.

In 1868, the year of the great uprising in Cuba, the most formidable outbreak occurred in Porto Rico.

After two months of severe fighting the Spanish regulars were victorious, and the leader of the rebels, Dr. Ramon E. Bentances, who has since resided most of the time in Paris, was captured, as was also J. J. Henna, afterward a New York physician. All the prisoners were sentenced to be shot, November 4, 1868.

On the very day preceding that date news came to the island that Queen Isabella had been deposed, and in consequence the political prisoners were released.

But they were afterward banished, and in their exile

they have ever since been active in devising measures for the freedom of the island.

There is no reason whatever to think that there will be any discontent in the future under the liberal and beneficent government of the United States.

CHAPTER III.

TOPOGRAPHY AND CLIMATE.

Now that there is no doubt of the acquisition of Porto Rico by the United States, many of our people will be going there, and it is therefore of great interest to note how its general features will please and its climate be adapted to Americans.

The island is most eastern of the Greater Antilles, and it is the fourth in size and importance of all the islands of the West Indies. In fact, in point of density of population and general prosperity, it takes the first place. On the east, the Lesser Antilles extend in a curve toward Trinidad, on the South American coast, inclosing on the westward the Caribbean sea. A strait of seventy miles separates Porto Rico from Hayti on the west, and the distances from San Juan, the capital, to other points are 2,100 miles to the Cape Verde Islands, 1,050 miles to Key West and 1,420 miles to Hampton Roads.

Porto Rico lies near enough to the Gulf of Mexico to receive the benefit of the soft Gulf breezes and the very best and most desirable of the trade winds.

The island is almost a rectangle in shape. Its length from east to west is 108 miles and its breadth from north to south about 37 miles. Its area, including its dependencies, the isles of Vieques, Culebra and Mona is 3,530 square miles.

The coasts are generally regular, but there are a large number of bays and inlets, and the north coast is full of navigable lagoons.

The principal capes are San Juan, Mala Pascua, Rojo and Bruquen.

Generally speaking, the conformation of the island is slightly undulating, with the exception of a mountain range which traverses it from east to west, running through nearly its whole length in a zig-zag course, and on the average about twenty-five miles distant from the north coast.

This range divides the island into two unequal portions. The largest is on the north, and the rivers flowing through that section are much the longer. A part of the main range is called Sierra Grande or Barros. The northeast spur is known as the Sierra de Luquillo and the northwest as the Sierra Larea. The general height of these mountains is about 1,500 feet above the sea, but there is one peak, Yunque, which reaches a height of 3,678 feet. This can be seen seventy miles at sea, and would be a magnificent place for a shore signal for the benefit of the ships that sail the South Atlantic seas.

It is noticeable that there are no extensive lakes in the highlands of the interior, but there are many interesting caves in the mountains, the principal ones being those of Aguas Buenos and Ciales.

The elevated ridge which crosses the island intercepts the northeast trade winds which blow from the Atlantic and deprives them of their moisture. The consequence of this is that the rainfall in the northern portion of the island is very copious. It also has the effect of reducing the rain south of the mountains, so that there is a prevalence of droughts in that section and agriculture can be advantageously carried on by irrigation. Up to the present, however, this work of irrigation has been very imperfect and unsystematic, and the results on the whole have not been satisfactory.

The Luquillo range ends ten miles from San Juan. The capital is, therefore, to a certain degree sheltered by a mountain wall from the rain-bearing winds, which, in the warmest months blow mainly from easterly points. Still all the northern adjacent shores and lowlands are subject to flooding by torrents of rain.

Taking it as a whole, the island is approximately roof-shaped, so that the rainfall is rapidly drained off.

In the interior are extensive plains and there are level tracts from five to ten miles wide on the coast.

The soil of Porto Rico is exceedingly fertile. In the mountains it is a red clay, colored with peroxide of iron, in the valleys it is black and less compact, and on the coasts it is sandy, but capable of some culture.

The pasture lands in the northern and eastern parts of the island are superior to any others in the West Indies.

Porto Rico is essentially a land of rivers and streams. Of course none of them are of any great length, but of the entire number, some thirteen hundred, forty are navigable for more or less distances for commercial purposes.

Mr. John Beggs, a former planter of Porto Rico, says that the island is perfectly adapted for commerce. Sugar, coffee, cotton, corn and potatoes are constantly shipped down the navigable rivers, and were Porto Rico to be fully cultivated, many more streams could be opened and communication made between others by means of canals, so that the entire island would present a system of water ways which would make it an ideal place for the shipping of useful articles to the United States.

The water of the rivers and brooks and lakes is remarkably pure, and there is quite an industry in its shipment for sale to other West India islands. It is stated that more than twenty of these islands send to Porto Rico for water. Little boats sail up the harbor of San Juan, fill their tanks with water and sail away again. Havana's chief scourge is the lack of fresh water, but Porto Rico has all the water it can use and enough to supply islands hundreds of miles away.

The anchorages can not be said to be the best in the world, although a few of them are excellent, and most of them sufficiently deep for ordinary craft.

Mayaguez Bay on the west coast admits vessels of any size and is the best anchorage on the island. Guanica is the best on the south coast, of which it is the most western port. It was here that the American troops first landed. Still Guanica is not visited by much shipping. The district immediately surrounding it is low and swampy, and the roads leading from it are not good. Guanica has been the outlet for the produce of San German Sabana Grande and, to some extent, of Yanco, which is on the railroad. The western and southwestern parts of the island have been particularly over-run by the Porto Rican rebels, and this has undoubtedly done much to injure its commerce. But with the advent of the Americans all this will be changed.

The eastern coast is fairly indented and washed by a sea which is usually smooth.

On the rugged north side, where the ocean currents set to southward, there are no good anchorages between Arecibo and San Juan. The port of San Juan, however, affords good shelter and will be an important centre for merchant shipping as well as an attractive rendezvous for yachts on a pleasure cruise. The harbor is deep enough to admit large vessels, but its channel communicating with the sea is winding and difficult, and can be navigated safely only with the aid of a pilot.

One of the leading seaports of the island is Aquadilla on the west coast. This has the advantage of a spacious bay, which is sheltered from the trade winds. From this place are shipped the sugar and coffee produced in the northwest part of the island.

There are seven or eight other ports of minor importance.

The main highway of central Porto Rico runs from Ponce to San Juan, in a northeasterly direction, through Juana Diaz, Coamo and Abonito. From the latter place it proceeds almost eastward to Cayey, and there it takes a winding course to the north as far as Caquas. Thence it turns west o Aquas Buenos, and then goes straight north through Guaynola and Rio Piedras to San Juan. The entire length of this highway is about eighty-five miles.

The distance from Ponce to San Juan, as the bird flies, is only forty-five miles.

And now to take up a most important point—the climate. Of this much can be said in favor.

On the whole, it may be stated that Porto Rico, for a tropical region, is very healthful; in fact, by far the most so of any of the West India islands.

There have been no climatic observations which cover the whole of the Porto Rican territory, but the Spanish Weather Bureau has published certain observations which show the general conditions prevailing in San Juan and the vicinity.

The climate, though hot, is agreeably tempered by the prevailing northeast winds. At night there is always a pleasant breeze which carries sweet fragrance along the northern coast. A temperature as high as 117 degrees has been recorded, but this is most unusual. At San Juan, the average temperature in August is about 81 degrees Fahrenheit; in September, 80.5 degrees, and in October, 79.3 degrees. At night it sinks to 68 or 69 degrees, which is more than it frequently does in New York or Chicago during heated spells. The most marked feature of the climate is that the summer's heat and rainfall keep up until late autumn. In the hottest months the calm days average not far from ten a month, and these have a very relaxing effect. For this reason it is advisable for residents of temperate climes not to visit Porto Rico until November, when the weather becomes beautifully fine and settled, and almost always continues good during the winter and early spring.

The rainfall in San Juan, which can be taken as a fair index of that along the northeastern coast, averages about 6.65 inches during August, 5.30 during September and 7.10 during October. But in some years the heaviest fall was in September. Not infrequently the cultivated fields and plantations are inundated, and swamps are formed. As has been intimated, the southern part of the island is relatively much drier than the northern, though the former is apt to experience excessive rains during the passage of a hurricane.

It is fortunate for Porto Rico that it does not lie directly in the track of West Indian cyclones. It has been visited, however, at long intervals by devastating hurricanes, notably those of 1742 and 1825, which destroyed a vast deal of property, and during the passage of which many lives were lost. The terrible tornadoes of the tropics are very erratic in their course, and are so apt to be deviated from their accustomed paths that it is unsafe to assume that danger has passed for Porto Rico until late in the autumn. Captains of all vessels during the summer months should therefore exercise extraordinary vigilance to avoid being caught in a hurricane.

The prevailing diseases of the island are yellow fever, elephantiasis, tetanus, March fever and dysentery. There is no question but that a lack of proper sanitary measures is responsible for much of the illness. Even the most to be dreaded of these diseases, yellow fever, could in all probability be rooted out if proper precautions were taken and every available means employed to prevent its recurrence. As it is, yellow fever never scourges Porto Rico as it does parts of Cuba.

In the winter and early spring Porto Rico is less subject than Cuba to those chilling winds that blow from the freezing anticyclones moving east from the American coast toward Bermuda. Under American auspices and enlightened systems of sanitation, there will doubtless spring up a number of attractive winter resorts, which will prove formidable rivals to those of Florida, especially if, as is not unlikely, San Juan Bay becomes the headquarters of the North Atlantic naval station from November until April.

In this regard, the manager of a prominent life insurance company has spoken as follows:

"Let me raise my voice in prophecy and then wait and see if events do not bear me out. I want to prophesy right now that five years from date that island will be a great popular winter resort. No one can appreciate its natural attractions unless he has been there, and when to them have been added a few good American hotels it is bound to become a popular resort.

I was in Porto Rico several years ago, and I then expressed surprise that it was not boomed as a winter resort. The Porto Ricans to whom I spoke shrugged their shoulders and smiled. The ground is high, the climate is fine, and the place is healthful.

It has many attractions of its own that are lacking in the other West Indies.

Close on the heels of the army will march some enterprising American hotel man, and then look out for results.''

CHAPTER IV.

POPULATION AND TOWNS.

According to the latest statistics, the entire population of the island of Porto Rico is estimated at 900,000. Of these about 140,000 are *peninsulares*, as the natives of Spain have been termed throughout her former colonies. From 12,000 to 14,000 are foreigners, mostly Frenchmen, Germans, Italians, Englishmen and Americans. Other nationalities have little or no representation. The so-called native population is composed of two-thirds whites who are descendants of Spaniards and people of other European countries, and one-third negroes and mulattoes or those of mixed blood, half castes, as they are denominated.

It is valuable to note the large proportion of whites, which is very unusual for a tropical country.

The census, which was taken December 31, 1887, states that the women outnumbered the men by about one thousand. As the immigrants from Spain are mostly men, however, the actual ratio between the two sexes, as far as the native population is concerned, would be greatly in favor of the feminine.

The area of Cuba is thirteen times larger than that of Porto Rico, and yet even before the butcher Weyler exterminated a third of the native Cubans, it contained not quite double as many people as the smaller island.

This will give some idea of the density of the population of Porto Rico.

Thirty per cent. of the whites and seventy-five per cent. of the negroes were classed in the census of 1887 as laborers.

The western part of the island is far more densely populated than the eastern. The reason for this probably lies in the fact that the east coast is on the windward side, and offers less protection for shipping. Consequently it is not so conveniently situated for trade. All the larger towns of the east are situated inland, or, at least, some distance from the coast. They are in the hilly portion of the island and surrounded by rich coffee plantations and grazing lands of large extent.

The inhabitants of Porto Rico are scattered all over the country, and the land is greatly subdivided. The Spanish authorities have made many efforts to collect the people into villages, but the people themselves have frequently resisted a change which they considered would not suit the conditions of their lives or tend to improve their finances.

Still, in the last fifty years more than half of the population has gravitated to and around the towns, especially those which are situated on the seashore. Most of these people live in comfortable houses, and have the means to provide themselves with all the necessities and many of the luxuries of life.

The population, by the way, has been steadily increasing since the beginning of the present century.

Ponce, named after Ponce de Leon, is the largest city

and the one of the most commercial importance upon the island. It is beautifully situated about three miles north of the port of Ponce, in a fertile plain, and is surrounded by plantations and gardens. It is the terminus of one of the three short railroads which have been constructed, and along the beach in front of the port are large warehouses, where the produce, forwarded through Ponce, which is the trading centre, is stored for shipment. The population of Ponce has been estimated at 44,500 inhabitants, and this is probably not far from the actual truth.

Ponce has quite a number of fine buildings, including the town hall, the theatre, two churches, the charity and the woman's asylums, the barracks, the Cuban House and the market. Between the city and the seashore is an excellent road which forms a beautiful promenade.

Near Ponce are hot springs which are quite famous and held in high estimation by invalids.

The capital of Porto Rico is San Juan, which in many respects has always been the most important city. It is on the north coast, and as has already been stated, was founded by Ponce de Leon in 1510. It now has a population of 31,250 inhabitants, which includes the town and its suburbs.

The situation of San Juan is somewhat peculiar, as it is built on a high and narrow peninsula, which is separated from the mainland by shallow water spanned by a bridge known as the San Antonio.

The town is about half a mile wide, inclosed by high walls of masonry, which are very picturesque, and with their portcullis gates and battlements recall vividly to one's mind the description of mediæval times.

The bluff is crowned by Morro Castle, rendered familiar to Americans in the recent war.

San Juan is really quite a beautiful place with straight and narrow streets and many imposing buildings. It has a number of public institutions and colleges, several churches, and seven small parks. Among the latter may be mentioned the Plazuela de Santiago, in which is an excellent statue of Columbus.

It was on the western end of the island that Ponce de Leon built the governor's palace, which is enclosed within the Santa Catalina fortifications, where are also the cathedral, town house and theatre. This portion of the city is now known as Pueblo Viego, and is the seat of an Episcopal see, which is subordinate to the bishop of Santiago de Cuba.

The city is lighted by gas, which is controlled by an English company, and it also has an electric plant under local management.

There is a local telephone company.

There are eleven newspapers of various descriptions, the chief one being La Correspondencia, a local political paper, which has a circulation of seven thousand copies, more than that of all the other papers put together.

The water is obtained entirely from cisterns. About fifty years ago a project was formed to build a reservoir, and the plans were approved by the government. But, with that spirit of procrastination so characteristic of the Spanish, in all public and private walks of life, and which is known as manana, the reservoir has never been completed.

The harbor of San Juan is in almost all respects a very fine one. On the east and south it is surrounded by swamps, and on the west it is protected by the islands of Cabra and Cabrita, which are practically connected to the mainland by sandbars. There are strong fortifications which guard the entrance to the outer harbor.

The inner harbor is spacious and landlocked. It has been dredged to a uniform depth of twenty-nine feet from the docks to the anchorage.

The old city is divided into four wards, three of which are outside of the fortifications. The houses are of stone, or brick, and from the roofs beautiful sea views may be obtained. In the patio or court of almost every house there is a garden.

Besides Ponce and San Juan, the largest towns on the island are Arecibo (30,000 inhabitants), Utuado (31,000), Mauaguez (28,000), San German (20,000) Yanco (25,000), and Juana Diaz (21,000). There are also about a dozen other towns with a population of 15,-000 or over.

These figures are only approximate, as no regular census has been taken in ten years, and even then the Spanish officials were none too correct.

Railways on the island can as yet be said to be only in their infancy. There is only about 150 miles of railroad, with about as much more in construction. It is intended to have stretches of railroad parallel with the coast, which shall make the entire circuit of the island. From these there will be short branches to all the seaports and inland markets.

The cart roads are very primitive, some of them being little better than cattle tracks. There is, however, be it remembered, one fine road, which extends across the island from San Juan to Ponce.

The telegraph system is also in a very incomplete state and is poorly managed.

There is one line of cable which runs to Cuba, Mexico, Panama and the coasts of the South American continent, and another which connects the island with St. Thomas, Jamaica, and thus the rest of the world.

CHAPTER V.

RESOURCES.

It is somewhat difficult to tell exactly what is the commercial value of the new colonial possessions which the Spanish-American war has placed at the disposal of the United States. The figures are naturally based upon the conditions which prevailed under Spanish rule.

But, all for all, it may be said that Porto Rico, taking into consideration its area, has been the most valuable of all Spain's colonial possessions.

For some reason, which seems to be inscrutable, Spain has given the inhabitants of Porto Rico far better treatment than she accorded to the natives of Cuba. She dealt with the island more as if it were a Spanish province than a colony to be bled to the fullest extent possible for the financial benefit of Spanish officials and the mother country. Quite the contrary has been the case in Cuba and the Philippines.

It may be stated that, as a matter of fact, Porto Rico has been, in a political sense, a province of Spain for the past twenty years.

Spain has paid but little attention to internal improvements, but this has been an advantage. For with her heavy hand relaxed, the people have had a certain opportunity to develop such spirit of enterprise as they possessed.

Porto Rico, in proportion to its size, is immensely

wealthy. It is very doubtful if the Philippines can equal it in richness, square foot for square foot.

With the island in the possession of the United States and with the abolishment of the differential duties in favor of the Spanish government, its geographical position will undoubtedly cause most of its commerce to flow to and from the ports of the United States.

There will be a market furnished for great quantities of food products, textile fabrics, iron, steel and coal. From the island the United States will chiefly receive coffee, tobacco and sugar. Indeed it may be said that in the line of coffee cultivation, the greatest development of Porto Rico may be expected in the near future.

Mr. John Beggs, whom we have quoted before, says that Porto Rico is one of the finest pieces of property on the earth's surface. May it prove so in the hands of the United States!

The soil of Porto Rico is of remarkable fertility. Its dominant industries may be said to be agriculture and lumbering.

In the elevated regions, most of the vegetable productions of the temperate zone can be grown.

More than five hundred varieties of trees can be found in the forests of the island, many of which are very valuable, and the plains are full of palms, oranges and other fruit-bearing trees. There are several very interesting trees, especially a beautiful *Talauma*, with immense white odorous flowers and silvery leaves. This tree is exceedingly ornamental. It is used for lumber and called Sabino. A *Kirtella* with crimson flowers is also rather common.   A tree which is called Ortegon by the natives is found at high altitudes, but chiefly near the coast.   It has immense purple spikes, more than a yard long, and is very striking.   It seems to be confined to Porto Rico and Hayti.   There are many varieties of cabinet and dye woods, including mahogany, ebony, lignum vitæ, cedar and logwood.   Plants valuable in the arts and pharmacy abound.   Tropical fruits grow everywhere to perfection.

The chief products of Porto Rico, outside of lumber, may be said to be sugar, coffee, tobacco, rice, honey and wax, and these have greatly enriched the island, making many of the people well-to-do.

Sugarcane is cultivated on the fertile plains, yielding three hogsheads on an average per acre without any manure.

An excellent grade of coffee is produced, and it does not appear that as yet any blight has perceptibly affected the shrubs.

Rice is very commonly cultivated on the hills in the Sierra.   It must be a kind of mountain variety, as no inundation or other kind of watering is used.

Rice and plaintain are in fact the staple food of the natives.

Cotton and maize are also raised to a certain extent.

There should in the future be an industry from the manufacture of tannin extracts from the bark of Cocco-lala, Rhizophora and the pods of various acacias, the latter of which are a great nuisance on account of their rapid growth.

There are a long number of fruits on the island, such as cherries, guava plums, juicy mangoes and bell apples.

Edwin Emerson, Jr., a war correspondent, speaks of some of the fruits as follows:

"The most astonishing and the best of all was a fruit called pulmo—in our language, sour-sap. It is about as large as a quart bowl, and so nourishing and full that a single fruit was enough for a good meal, although that did not deter my horse from eating four. Later I found that they are also relished by dogs. Of springs and streams there were so many that I had no fear of dying of thirst. If water was not handy, I could always climb a cocoanut tree and throw down the green nuts, which were filled with an abundance of watery milk, more than I could drink at one time. Other nuts there were in plenty; but many were more curious than edible, even to my willing appetite. One had a delicious odor. I tasted a little, and thought it ideal for flavoring candy. But it soon dissolved in my mouth in a fine dust, absorbing all the moisture, so that I had to blow it out like flour. Nothing ever made me so thirsty in my life, and even after rinsing out my mouth I felt for a long time as if I were chewing punk or cotton. The fruit of the tamarind only added to my torments by setting all my teeth on edge. When we reached the next spring I fell off my horse for fear he would get all the water. Only after I had satisfied my thirst would I let him drink."

The poverty of the fauna and flora is remarkable, there being scarcely any wild animals, birds or flowers.

There is a great deficiency of what may be called *native* animals of any sort.

The most troublesome quadruped is the wild dog, which chiefly attack pigs and other small domestic animals. Mice are probably the greatest pest of the island, but they are considerably kept down by their natural enemies, the snakes. The latter not infrequently reach a length of from six to nine feet. There are a good many mosquitoes, but they are no worse than they are in New Jersey. Numerous species of ants and bees exist as well as fireflies. The latter occasionally fly in great masses, producing beautiful effects in the tropical nights.

It may be stated that, on the whole, Porto Rico is singularly free from those noxious reptiles and insects which seem to inherit the rest of the West Indies as their peculiar possession.

Immense pastures occupy a part of the lowland, and feed large herds of cattle of an excellent quality. St. Thomas and the French islands all obtain their butcher's meat from Porto Rico. Even Barbadoes comes there for cattle. Sheep always thrive in a hot country, and they grow big and fat in Porto Rico. Fresh lamb and mutton are constantly shipped from there. A very numerous class of the people are shepherds, and these live upon mutton and the kind of highland rice, already alluded to, which is very easily prepared for food.

Poultry is most abundant, and the seas and rivers are full of the finest fish.

Agriculture has hitherto been almost exclusively in the hands of the natives, but most of the business and commerce have been controlled by foreigners and Spaniards from the Peninsula.

Although the island is certainly well developed agriculturally, it certainly admits of considerable expansion in this direction. Under a different political system, and when it is freed from the oppressive and vexatious taxation, Porto Rico will certainly become far more productive and prosperous even than it is now.

There is no question but that the island, richly endowed as it is by Nature, has been miserably governed.

But agriculture in the near future will certainly not be the main industry of the island. For there are known to be gold, copper, iron, zinc and coal mines, which have never been developed. In fact, strange as it may appear, none of these valuable mines is worked at all. The vegetable productions have been considered so valuable that in order to cultivate them the minerals have been neglected. There are also extensive sponge fields, which are very valuable, but which have not been touched, owing to several causes, chiefly the lack of capital. The same can also be said of the quarries of white stone, granite and marble.

Then there is the question of salt, which is sure to be of importance. There are large quantities of salt obtained from the lakes. Salt works have been established at Guanica and Salinas, on the south coast, and at Cape Rojo, on the west. This constitutes the principal mineral industry of Porto Rico.

Hot springs and mineral waters are found at Juan Diaz, San Sebastian, San Lorenzo and Ponce, but the most famous are at Coamo, near the town of Santa Isabella.

It is now interesting to see what the trade of Porto Rico has been with other countries, and especially the United States during recent years.

A very large part of the island's trade has been carried on with the United States, where corn, flour, salt-meat, fish and lumber have been imported in return for sugar, molasses and coffee.

The natives are not a sea faring people, and care little or nothing for ships of their own. Therefore, by far the larger part of their trade with other countries has been carried on by the means of foreign ships.

Porto Rico has paid into the Spanish treasury about 4,000,000 pesos annually, which is equivalent to about $800,000.

In normal years, that is, when no war was going on, the total value of imports into the island amounted to about $8,000,000, and the exports to about $16,000,000.

The latest Spanish statistics, that is, during 1896, give the importations into Porto Rico as amounting to $18,945,793, and the exports to $17,295,535.

The average entrances of ships into the ports have been 1919 vessels of an aggregate of 327,941 tons, of which 544 of 81,966 tons were British. Articles of import have been distributed by countries as follows:

From Spain come wines, rice, oils, flour and textiles; from England, machinery, textiles, salted provisions, rice and coal; from France, a small amount of textiles, some jewelry and perfumery, and some fine wines and liquors; from Italy, wines, vermicelli and rice; from Germany, glass and porcelain wares, textiles, paper, cheese, candied fruits, beer and liquors; from Holland, cheese; from Cuba, rum, sugar and tobacco; from the United States, petroleum, ironware, glassware, chemicals, textiles, paper, lumber, barrels, machinery, carriages, dried and salted meats, butter, grease, codfish, flour, coal, fruits, vermicelli and cheese.

A commercial arrangement was entered into between the United States and Spain in 1895, in consequence of which the following proclamation was issued by the Spanish Government:

PROCLAMATION:

The executive is authorized to apply to the products and manufactures of the United States which coming from the ports of the United States be admitted into the ports of Cuba and Porto Rico, the benefits of the second column of the tariffs in said islands; provided that the United States, in their turn apply their lowest rates of duty to the products of the soil and of the industry of Cuba and Porto Rico.

This modus vivendi shall be in force until a permanent commercial treaty between the two parties concerned is concluded, or until one of them gives notice to the other, three months in advance of the day on which it wishes to put an end of it.

Therefore, I command all the courts, justices, chiefs, governors and other authorities, civil, military and ecclesiastical, of all classes and dignities, to observe

and cause to be observed, obeyed and executed this pres
ent law in all its parts. Given in the palace, February 4,
1895.   I, the Queen Regent.

Alejandro Groizard, Secretary of State.

The above is translated from the Gaceta de Madrid of
February 6, 1895.

This agreement, if so it can be called, is of course
now at an end. Hereafter Porto Rico will enjoy all the
privileges of a colony of the United States.

But still it is interesting to note the duty on the leading articles of export from the United States to Porto
Rico, as expressed in the second column of the Spanish
tariff.

This was as follows:

Wheat flour, rice flour, buckwheat flour, corn-
   meal, oatmeal, barleymeal, ryemeal, per 100
   kilograms, gross, ... $4 00
Pork, per 100 kilograms, net 9 90
Beef and all other meats, per 100 kilograms, net . 6 50
Sausage, per 100 kilograms, gross 20
Hay, per 100 kilograms, gross 80
Pig iron, per 100 kilograms, net 50
Bar iron, per 100 kilograms, net 2 15
Barb wire (for fencing), per 100 kilograms, net . 40
Coal, per 100 kilograms, net 60
Patent medicines, including weight of container
   and wrapper 35

One hundred kilograms amounts to something over
two hundred pounds.

The people on the island are rather luxurious, so much so that in one year five million dollars worth of goods were carried there. These goods consisted principally of manufactured products, such as clothing and household wares.

The principal exports from the United States have been flour, pork, lard, lumber and shooks.

But, of course, all this will be largely increased now that Porto Rico is practically a portion of the United States, and the increased commerce will be to the advantage of both.

During the five years from 1893 to 1897, the trade of Porto Rico with the United States has been as follows:

	Exports to United States:	Imports from United States:
1893	$4,008,623	$2,510,007
1894	3,135,634	2,720,508
1895	1,505,512	1,833,544
1896	2,296,653	2,102,094
1897	2,181,024	1,988,888

Whatever disadvantages Porto Rico may possess, and when all is said and done, they are beyond question few, it is certainly lovely enough and prolific enough to make one forget them all.

A writer in Ainslee's Magazine concludes his very clever article as follows, and undoubtedly every word he says is true:

"Unfortunately for the development of Spanish coun-

tries the mental activity of the people is principally
manifested in an exuberant imagination which finds expression in superlative and poetical language. If there
were any corresponding creative genius and executive
ability in material affairs such a fertile and well-watered
land as Puerto Rico would be the home of one of the
richest communities on the globe. By her situation she
is adapted to become the centre of a flourishing commerce whose goods might be carried down dozens of
navigable rivers from the interior of the island. Under
a good government, with enterprising colonists, the
natural resources of the island, some of which have been
scarcely touched, would bring comfort and wealth to a
large population.

CHAPTER VI.

MANNERS AND CUSTOMS.

Let us examine briefly in the first place what has been the management of Porto Rico under Spanish rule, or, rather, perhaps we should call it mismanagement, for no one of Spain's colonies has ever been properly directed.

Porto Rico has been governed under a constitution voted by the Spanish Cortes in 1869. The government has been administered by a captain-general, assisted by an administrative council appointed at Madrid.

The revenue has been about four millions of dollars a year, considerably more than half of which has been derived from customs, and the rest from taxation, direct and indirect.

The captain-general was president of the superior tribunals of justice and of the superior juntas of the capital; but the fiscal administration had a special chief called intendant. The supreme judicial power lay in a royal *audience*. Justice was administered in the cities and in the country by judges of the first instance and by alcaldes. There were nine special tribunals: civil, ecclesiastical, war, marine, artillery, engineers, administration, probate and commerce.

Ecclesiastical affairs were presided over by a bishop chosen by the crown and approved by the pope.

For administrative purposes the island and its dependencies were divided into nine districts: Porto Rico, Bayamon, Arecibo, Aquadilla, Mayaguez, Ponce, Humacoa, Guayama and Vieques.

The Spanish administration in Porto Rico, although not so bad as in other colonies, has, nevertheless, been one of cruelty and oppression. The Spaniards, as will be remembered, began by exterminating the native Indian population in less than a century.

There was not a branch of the administration which was not conducted under a system of corruption. The law was constantly violated by the Spaniards, and the natives deprived of their rights.

When elections took place the Spanish or Conservative party always won, and this in spite of the fact that this party was in a large minority. No more corrupt and farcical elections have even been known to take place.

Such a thing as liberty of the press was utterly unknown. Articles that had been printed in the Madrid or other Spanish papers attacking the government could not be reproduced in any Porto Rican papers, without the editors being arrested and punished. And this occurred even if the article in question had not been considered as offering ground for the prosecution by the authorities in Spain.

The papers, by the way, were ridiculously inadequate in every sense of the word. Only one attempt was ever made to establish a magazine. This was about eleven years ago. It was called the *Revista Puertorriquena* and was intended "to carry the highest expression of our intellectual culture to all the people of Europe and America where the magnificent Castilian language is spoken.''

The magazine was conducted by a committee composed of a director, two editors, ''and other illustrious persons'' elected by the subscribers. The founder of the magazine lamented that the ''race of artists'' who first settled in Puerto Rico ''were so overwhelmed by the exuberant and pompous beauty of the tropics that the natural means of artistic expression were exaggerated to the detriment of ideas,'' and that the crying evil of the periodical press of the island was ''the abundance of sonorous and high-sounding articles having nothing to say to the understanding.''

The founder of the magazine was Don Manuel Juncos, who is the author of several books of travel. He speaks of the Brooklyn bridge as ''a magic vision of the Thousand and One Nights,'' while the smoke that rose from myriads of New York chimneys ''formed the holy and blessed incense of a mighty and busy population, rising directly up to God from the fecund altar of labor.'' In the streets he was amazed at the ''incessant avalanche of men, all having the purpose of certain or probable utility.''

No more than nineteen persons, under the old regime, were allowed to meet in any place of the island, without special permission from the government, and the mayor of the town was obliged to attend the meetings to see that nothing was said or done against ''the integrity of the nation.''

Licenses were required for everything, even for an ordinary dancing party.

The manner of life in the large towns of Porto Rico is not dissimilar from that of European countries, with the exception of some slight differences due to the heat of the climate. The fashions for men and women alike are imported, especially from Paris and London. Those who are in comfortable circumstances dress just like people in European countries. The men wear woolen clothes all the year round. The young women dress very elaborately and all wear hats, the Spanish mantilla being adopted by elderly women only.

In the small towns, men dress after the fashion of the cities, except that their clothes are made of linen. Woolen fabrics are uncomfortable, and they are considered a luxury to be donned only on Sundays and holidays.

Laborers and farm hands wear neither coats nor shoes. They do not care to do so, in the first place, and, in the second, they could not afford to, as their earnings are very small.

In San Juan the streets are rectangular and are closely built with brick houses usually two or three stories, stuccoed on the outside, and painted in different colors. In one house live several families, and the degree of rent, as well as of social position, rises with the height of the floor above the ground.

The lower floors, as a rule, are very dirty, and are crowded in a most unhealthful way by negroes and the servants of those who live above.

Sanitary conditions, by the way, as in all Spanish possessions, are the very worst possible, and much will have to be done in this respect when the United States takes permanent possession.

There is one feature which strikes every foreigner, and that is the roof gardens. In many parts of the island, especially in the smaller towns, the whole population enjoys itself at night on the housetops. The houses are built a little off the ground, and they look not unlike castles in the air which have been built for pleasure rather than for living purposes.

In all tropical countries people have the habit of sleeping in the daytime, and do their shopping and attend to their social duties in the evening. In Porto Rico this custom is almost universal.

Every man of any means is the possessor of two houses, a town house and a country house. At carnival times, or when any special celebration is going on, he takes his family to town and brings them back again when the sport is over.

Poverty is almost unknown in Porto Rico, for almost every man owns his horse and every woman is the possessor of chickens. Horseback riding is an almost universal pastime. There are many fine horses on the island, and they are used daily by men and women.

The inhabitants have but few wants which are not satisfied by Nature without any effort on their part. They lead a *dolee far niente* existence, swinging to and fro in their hammocks all day long, smoking cigarettes and strumming guitars.

Life at San Juan and the other principal towns is more or less monotonous, amusements being few. There is a *retreta* or concert by the military bands twice a week and theatrical performances three or four evenings a week. Matinees are very seldom given. The theatres are owned by the cities and rented to European and American companies traveling through the island at so much an evening.

Unlike Cuba, there are no bull fights, but cock fighting may be called the national sport, and is universally indulged in. Game cocks are the greatest attraction of the markets. Every Sunday there are public fights in the cockpit, and these are invariably accompanied by betting, often very large amounts being involved.

Gambling, by the way, may be said to be universal. Every one, from the rich planter down to the lowest laborer and beggar, is given up to this vice, and will squander away every dollar if the mood takes him.

There is nothing but hospitality on the island. The people are exceedingly polite to strangers, and the traveler who offers money deeply offends his host.

A curious feature of the streets is the milk delivery, which is not unlike that prevailing in Cuba.

This takes place before and during the noon, or breakfast, hour, breakfast being taken here between 12 and 2 o'clock. Sometimes the milk is still being sold at 4 or 5 o'clock. The milkman drives from door to door from one to four or five cows, each branded with a number and usually one or more of them accompanied by a calf. The driver cries his approach, and the customer fetches er sends out a pan, pail, bottle, or cup, which he hands to the milkman. The milkman puts into the receptacle the quantity of milk paid for, which he induces the cow to yield after the usual manner.

Mr. W. G. Morrisey gives an interesting description of how funerals are conducted in Porto Rico. He says that when a native dies preparations are immediately made for the burial.

No women are allowed to attend the funeral and the casket is carried on the shoulders of four natives. The cemetery being reached, the remains are deposited in one of the many vaults in the place, provided the sum of four pesos per year is paid to the authorities. If this sum is not forthcoming the corpse is placed in a corner of the graveyard and left there to decay. Mr. Morrisey said it was a common occurrence to see seven or eight funerals pass by every day.

Another thing that struck Mr. Morrisey was the railroad that runs from Ponce to Playo. The train is made up of an old-fashioned engine and three cars. There are first, second and third class coaches, the only difference between the first and second class being the seats in the first class coach, which are cushioned. It is first class in name only, and very few of the visitors and the better class of natives use it, because of the fact that the cushions are full of vermin. Everything seems to be filthy, from the Hotel Ingleterra, which is considered the best house in Ponce, to the most miserable of huts on the outskirts of the city.

Mr. Morrisey said that it is not a question of one place

being cleaner than the other, but one place not being as filthy as another.

The facilities for lighting the city at night were investigated, and it was found that very little light is used. The stores are lighted with one or two incandescent lights, which are put in by the managers of a small electric light plant that has been in operation for some time. Kerosene oil cannot be bought for less than forty cents a pint, and consequently is not used to any great extent. An ice plant has also been established in Ponce, where they manufacture ice in small cakes about the size of a brick. This sells at $1.50 per hundred-weight.

There is no public school system, and a large number of even the white population can neither read nor write. The daughters of the well-to-do are sent to convents on the island, while the sons go abroad to be educated. Among this latter class there is considerable culture and refinement, and most of them speak English.

The women are of medium size, but exquisitely formed. They have all the coquetry which is typical of the women of the tropics, and no one who visits Porto Rico can fail to be impressed with their beauty, delicacy and grace.

It has been affirmed that Porto Rico has been in the past a perfect Mecca for fugitives from justice. At one time no less than one hundred of this description were traced there.

It is really possible to live on very little money there, and lives are prolonged to an incredible period. Fugitives therefore find it a haven in which to turn over a new leaf and begin a better life.

The Porto Ricans are naturally Roman Catholics and are very devout.

The manner of keeping Sunday would be apt to shock our New Englanders of Puritan descent.

A correspondent of the New York Sun, who was with the army in Porto Rico speaks of this as follows:

"Sunday at Ponce, if it continues as at present, will add still further variety to the somewhat different observances of the day which now characterize the territory of the United States.

" 'To-morrow,' said a native last Saturday, 'to-morrow I shall go to the theatre.'

" 'It's Sunday,' said his American soldier companion. 'You should be going to church.'

"An elevation of the shoulders.

" 'The same thing,' said the native.

"The show at the theatre that day, by the way, was given by an American troupe that has been touring the Indies.

"There is, of course, nothing new in the custom in Catholic countries of giving Sunday mornings to church and Sunday afternoons to pleasure. In Ponce the merchants are not willing to close their stores for the religious observances of the day, but hold that it would be wholly wrong to mar the hours of pleasure by business attentions. The stores are all open Sunday mornings as on other days, but shut tight Sunday afternoons. Vesper services are all but unknown. There may be a change regarding services presently. The priests have not been paid since the arrival of the American army. It was the Spanish custom to pay them from the customs receipts. Colonel Hill has refused to give them any money since he has been in charge of the custom-house, and has told them that hereafter their people will have to support them voluntarily. What the people will say to this at the start it is hard to guess. They may not wholly understand it. Under existing laws they are taxed for the support of the church. What their voluntary support of it will be remains to be seen. Protestants have almost a clear field for mission work here. The only Protestant church on the island is at Ponce, and that was opened on the Sunday after the Americans' arrival, for the first time, it is said, in ten years.

"The chief service at the cathedral is held at 9 o'clock Sunday mornings, mass being said hourly from 5 o'clock until then. At the 9 o'clock service many Americans drift in. Even the Catholics among the soldiers who have attended have appeared to drift in rather than go with the purpose of doing their devotions. It may be that there seemed something inconsistent in kneeling before the altar with a row of cartridges girded around the body. One man crept into the nave behind the seats, took off his cartridge belt and laid it beside him, and, kneeling, bowed his head very low, while he joined in the prayers. When the service was over he carried the war belt in his hand to the door and there stopped and buckled it on. Fifty yards from the door a company of the Nineteenth Infantry was encamped on guard duty in the principal public square, on one end of which the cathedral stands.

"While the services were going on late comers of the native congregation edged their way in at the rear doors, and, passing round the screen beneath the choir loft, dropped to their knees on the marble floor, there remaining until the close. Noticeable among these worshippers were the old and widowed and the very poor. The last recked little or not at all of the filthy floor, trailed with dirt and spotted with tobacco juice. Some of the others brought with them prayer rugs, even though they were but ragged strips of carpeting."

The same correspondent has also this to say about the shops, which is interesting:

"One of the things revealed by a shopping tour is the absence from the shops of anything distinctly characteristic of Porto Rico. The tourist has not made the island a favorite stopping place, and the people seem to prefer when buying anything not edible to buy foreign-made articles. The only things that even bore a stamp indicative of Porto Rico found by several hunters after curios were fit relics of a Spanish city—case knives inscribed "Viva Ponce." Fortunate seekers after mementoes secured a few of the peculiar native musical instruments called guiros. It is straining courtesy as well as language to call them musical instruments, but they are used by the natives to make what to the natives is music, and one of them is included in each group of street or cafe musicians. The instrument is a gourd shaped like some of our long-necked squashes, hollowed out through two vents cut in one side, and the surface over half the perimeter slashed or furrowed so as to offer a file-like resistance to a metal trident, which is scraped over it in time to the music made by the guitar, or whatever other instrument or instruments make up the orchestra. There are times when the result is suggestive of the couchee-couchee music and scratching."

For nearly three centuries slavery existed in Porto Rico, but it was finally abolished by the Spanish Cortes in March 1873.

The New York Herald in its special correspondence has much to say about the inhabitants that is of undoubted interest, and from this article we have culled considerable that follows. The article in question was written after the virtual surrender of Porto Rico.

These people have been accustomed to military rule all their lives, and to withdraw it in toto and tell them to go in and govern themselves is an experience which many regard as dangerous. Of a race excitable, with blood that courses quickly and with wrongs of many years' standing, the natives are intoxicated with their freedom. Their delirium has but one course—revenge— and when the entire population is fully awake to the opportunity offered there may come a break from all restraint, and then it may be shown that the depletion of our army was a blunder.

Without the menace of the Spanish soldiery, without the fear of the Church, and without the guiding hand of a good American officer and wisely-located American army of occupation, there may be trouble ahead.

With the going of the soldiers comes the influx of the mercantile classes. Salesmen are arriving in large numbers and promoters and speculators abound. Everything is being boosted from its former lethargic tropical calm. Prices of commodities are rising. Land has quadrupled in value in the owners' minds, and even the street gamins now demand twenty-five cents American money for a single button alleged to be cut from the coat of a Spanish soldier, which they formerly had trouble at disposing of at the rate of twelve and one-half cents per dozen.

These commercial avant couriers are bright, active 'hustlers,' who make the native nabobs gasp at their breezy ways, but, all the same, these nabobs are pretty shrewd persons and know how to buy closely.

There is one thing the native merchants have to learn, and that is to display their goods and wares. Not a single show window exists, and if some enterprising Yankee will just tear out the forbidding front of one of these business houses, replace it with one on the show-case style and set forth a dazzling array of merchandize, arranged by the deft hand of the artistic window decorator, there will be a revolution in trade in this place.

Another portion of the business life to be renovated is the sugar industry. The crudest system exists for the transformation of the juice of the cane into the saccharine crystals of commerce. Machinery so ponderous that it requires a volume of steam all out of proportion to the energy actually needed, and wasteful methods in the extraction of the syrup residue after crystallization, obtain. Yankee machinery, coupled with Yankee push, will cause a wonderful difference in the cost of the finished product.

"At the same time the manner of herding the hangs on these huge plantations must surely be changed. Such conditions exist in the quarters that a mere recital would be unprintable, and from an examination I made of the quarters of a very large estate I came away ill mentally and physically."

Members of the Society for the Prevention of Cruelty to Animals have a great field before them in this island. The inhabitants are the most cruel in their handling of beasts of burden and, in fact, of all living creatures below the grade of mankind that could be imagined.

Oxen and bulls furnish the principal means of merchandise transportation. They are yoked together with a huge horn rising upon the neck just back of the horns and held in place by bandages around the forehead. The driver carries a goad about five feet in length, in the end of which is inserted a sharp steel point about one inch long. This is used so freely that it is common to see streams of blood running down the sides of the poor maltreated beasts. Not satisfied with using the sharp end, the inhuman drivers frequently deliver terrific blows with the butt across the tender noses of their charges.

Many an American soldier has knocked down these cruel drivers for their abuse of the patient beasts, but the drivers do not improve with the thrashing. The American military authorities have imported several

American yokes and an effort is to be made to compel their use instead of the timber of torture which now obtains.

An author of the last century has this to say about the Porto Ricans:

"They are well proportioned and delicately organized; at the same time they lack vigor, are slow and indolent, possess vivid imaginations, are vain and inconstant, though hospitable to strangers, and ardent lovers of liberty."

Referring to the mixture of races, the same author continues:

"From this variety of mixture has resulted a character equivocal and ambiguous, but peculiarly Porto Rican. The heat of the climate has made them lazy, to which end also the fertility of the soil has conduced; the solitary life of the country residents has rendered them morose and disputatious."

A writer of more recent times declares that they are "affable, generous, hospitable to a fault, loyal to their sovereign, and will to the last gasp defend their island from invasion. The fair sex are sweet and amiable, faithful as wives, loving as sisters, sweethearts and daughters, ornaments to any society, tasteful in dress, graceful in deportment, and elegant in carriage. In fact, visitors from old Spain have frequently remarked their resemblance to the *doncellas* of Cadiz, who are world-renowned for their grace and loveliness."

"The truth is that they all have the Spanish *cortesia*," says Frederick A. Ober, in the Century Magazine, when commenting upon the above opinions, ''and are more like the polite Andalusians of the south of Spain than the boorish Catalans of the northeast. Even the lowliest laborer, unless he be one of the four hundred thousand illiterates, signs his name with a *rubrica*, or elaborate flourish and styles himself 'Don,' after the manner of the Spanish grandees, and the humblest innkeeper, when receipting a bill, will admit he 'avails himself with intense pleasure of this occasion for offering so such a distinguished gentleman the assurance of his most distinguished consideration!'

''This need not imply affectation, nor even insincerity, but merely a different conception of the social amenities from that of the all-conquering American, who, it is to be hoped, will not treat this foible with the contempt which, in his superior wisdom, he may think it merits.''

CHAPTER VII.

THE DAWN OF FREEDOM.

When the United States declared war against Spain for the purpose of freeing Cuba from Spanish misrule under which she had suffered for so long, and also with the desire to avenge the dastardly blowing up of the Maine, but little or no thought was given to Porto Rico. That island was an unknown quantity, but still one which was destined to play a considerable part in the near future.

This was in the natural sequence of events. After the terrible havoc wrought by our navy at Manila and at Santiago de Cuba, attention was turned toward Porto Rico.

The feeling became widespread throughout the United States that the war would fail in its object if Spain were not driven from the possession of all her colonies in the West Indies. Even those who in the beginning thought that the war was unnecessary, gradually came round to this point of view. It was quite sure that the expulsion of Spain from the western hemisphere would prevent the provoking of another war of the same character, and this desirable result could not be achieved so long as Spanish rule was maintained in any part of the West Indies.

The demand for the freeing of Cuba, the possession of

Porto Rico, as well as a protectorate over the Philippines, was just, and the nation demanded it.

The Boston Herald aptly remarked:

''This may well stand in the place of any exaction of money. The United States is much too rich to desire to compel money payment from an exhausted and practically beggared nationality. Such a course would be belittling the war in the eyes of the nations of the world, and it is not at all in accordance with ideas of our own national dignity. Here is the substantial concession of Spain, and it involves all and more than all for which the war was declared.''

The invasion of Porto Rico was not commenced until after the result of the war had been definitely decided.

But the Spaniards with that unfailing belief in ''manana'' (to-morrow) behaved like true Orientals, as they are in part, and acted as if time gained was halfway toward victory. With scarcely an exception, they are all indolent and fatalists.

The prime minister, Senor Sagasta, put off everything with that word which has proved so fatal to Spain, which undoubtedly precipitated the war, and which was at the bottom of all Senor Sagasta's policy—''manana.''

It is related that one day in the Cortes, a deputy criticized the idleness and indolence of Senor Sagasta, and the latter replied:

''*A nadie le ha sucedido nado por no hacer nada.*''

A free translation of this is: ''Nothing happens to him who does nothing.''

Both Sagasta and the Spaniards have doubtless found

out by this time the falsity of the saying. To show the feeling prevailing in Spain, it may be well to quote a Madrid correspondent of the London Times:

"Though peace is regarded as assured, it may not be attained so quickly as is generally expected. Senor Sagasta objects to be hustled, and insists upon everything being done in a quiet, orderly and dignified manner. He considers it necessary to have full and satisfactory explanations as to all doubtful points, in order to enable him best to protect the national interests against the aggressive tendencies of the Washington Cabinet.

"He has also to examine very minutely the exigencies of the internal situation and home politics, so as to avoid popular dissatisfaction and political unrest. The Spanish people, though sincerely desirous of peace, are disposed to admire this hesitancy and tenacious holding out till the last, although aware that it implies greater sacrifices.

"As an illustration of this feeling, while General Toral is blamed for capitulating at Santiago, Captain-General Augustin, in continuing a hopeless resistance at Manila, bids fair to be a popular hero."

About this time, before any attack by the Americans, Macias, captain-general of Porto Rico, discovered a conspiracy, which if it had not been quickly checked would have placed the island in a state of insurrection.

Eduardo Baselge and Danian Castillo, both prominent Porto Ricans, were active leaders in the incipient insurrection.

The Spanish postal authorities discovered the conspiracy through a letter written by Castillo to Baselga. General Macias was informed of this discovery, and a quiet investigation disclosed the fact that there were involved in it all of the most prominent residents of the city of San Juan, both native and foreign.

The headquarters of the conspirators were located and a quantity of dynamite, arms and provisions was found.

It was the intention of the leaders, after their plans had been perfected, to give wide publication to a proclamation calling upon all native and patriotic Porto Ricans who hold liberty dearer than life, to join them and accomplish the overthrow of the Spanish government and the death of the governor and his officials. The plans of the conspirators were so carefully laid that had it not been for the accidental discovery of Castillo's letter, they would unquestionably have been carried out.

The discovery of the conspiracy occurred about the time of the visit to Washington of Dr. J. J. Henna and Ramon Todd, both prominent Porto Ricans, of whom we have had occasion to speak before, and whose purpose in going there was to hold a conference with President McKinley relative to the establishment of a provisional United States government in the island after the Spaniards had been driven out.

Within twenty-four hours after the arrest the two leaders, Baselga and Castillo, were shot.

The residents became very much excited over the affair, and feeling against the Spanish officials ran high.

From the very beginning the real Porto Ricans, as we

shall see hereafter, were in favor of the Americans. The Spaniards, however, were most bitter, and as had been the case in Havana and Manila, kept up an absurd show of superior strength. This is well manifested by a proclamation which, signed by Jose Reyes, Celestins Dominguez and Genara Cautino, was issued to the people of Guayama on May 20, 1898. As one of the curiosities of the war, it can only be compared to the celebrated and laughable manifesto which Captain-General Augustin issued at Manila just before the appearance of Admiral Dewey's fleet.

The Porto Rican proclamation ran as follows:

"To the people of Guayama. Hurra for Spain!

"A nation that is our enemy, by its history, by its race, and because she is the principal cause of our misfortunes in Cuba, having fomented in this island that is our sister a war in which she supplied all kinds of resources, taking away at last the mask with which she concealed her fictitious friendship, has excited us to-day to vowed war.

"There is a deep abyss between the manner of being of that people and ours, which established antagonism that we should never be able to remove. Our sonorous language, our habits, the religion of our ancestors, and our necessities are conditions of our life so different from those of that race, so opposite to those of that people, that we are frightened in thinking that we should be constrained to accept a manner of being that is repugnant to our origin, our heart and our feelings. We are a people entirely Spanish, and we were born to a civilized life under a flag that was, and we hope ever will be, that of our wives and children. For four hundred years the warmth of the mother of our native country has given life to our organisms, ideas to our brains, majestic thoughts to our souls, and generous undertakings to our hearts, and in those four centuries the glories of the Spanish house have been our glories, her gayeties our gayeties, and her misfortunes our own misfortunes.

"We have been full of haughtiness when, being considered as the Conqueror's sons, we know that we had participation in the heroic actions of our brothers, and that the laurels with which they crowned their hero's front were also our laurels. When in tranquil hours we heard in our hearths our predecessors' epopee, describing as superfluously exact their achievements; giving them lively color that always inspires our tropical fancy, our nerves felt the thrill produced by enthusiasm; at those moments, our being all affected, our breast with its strong aspirations and our fiery tears rolling down the cheeks reminded us, obliging the cords of patriotism to vibrate, that we were Spaniards, and we neither could nor would like any other thing than to remain Spaniards.

"As if it could be that the country of Sergeant Diaz, of Andino, and Vascarrondo's, and all those conspicuous countrymen that irrigated with their blood Martin Pena and Rio Piedras camps could measure either the vigor or the haughtiness of an enemy who has not yet exhibited his face after so many ostentatious and angry vociferations. No! and thousand times no! The light fishermen of Porto Rico's shores, merchants, lawyers, musicians, mechanics, journeymen, all persons who may have strength to grasp a gun must ask for it. All united, with a solid front we shall go to intercept the invader. Behind us and as a reserve legion will come down from the highlands like a raging storm, if it is necessary, the *jibaros*, our fields' brothers, the most accomplished exemplar of abstinence, probity and bravery; the same that formed the urban militia; the same that were sent to Santo Domingo to defend gentile honor; they, who in number of more than 16,000, covered the plains of the north shore of the island, and compelled the Englishmen in 1797 to re-embark hastily, leaving their horses and artillery park.

"Porto Ricans! the moment is rising when not a single man of this country gives a step backwards, as it is said commonly; the hour of organizing ourselves for defense is sounded. The Spanish lion has shaken his dishevelled mane, and our duties calls us around him. Our temper is to fight, and we shall fight. Our fate is to overpower, and we shall overpower. Honor imposes upon us the obligation of saving home, and we shall save it in this land of our loves. Before North American people carry their boldness so far as to tread our sea-coasts it is necessary that we must be ready to receive them; that they may find in every Porto Rican an inexorable enemy, in every heart a rock, in each arm a weapon to drive them away; that that people feels that here it is detested intensely, and that Porto Rico's spirit is Spanish, and she will ever be so; therefore, inhabitants of Guayama, we invite you for a meeting at the Town House next Tuesday and offer our kind offices to the government, who will give us arms.

"It would be unworthy of our so gentle history, we should deny our blood, if in these moments of struggle we should endure indifferently. Let our enemies know that we are a brave people, and that if we are soft in peace days, we are also fit for war chances; that all his command, all his pride, and all his arrogance may fall out with a wall composed of all Porto Rican breasts."

In the light of ulterior and posterior events, this document is really as comical as anything in opera-bouffe.

"We have no means of knowing," says the New York Sun, in commenting upon this precious effusion, "whether Senor Jose Reyes, Senor Celestino Dominguez and Senor Genaro Cautino actually grasped their guns and immolated themselves upon the altar of four centuries and in the presence of the ostentatious and vociferous invader; or whether they prudently joined the light fishermen, merchants, lawyers, musicians and *jibaros* of Porto Rico, to whom they had vainly appealed in the name of Spain in yelling themselves hoarse as the Stars and Stripes went up in town after town. Perhaps they took the latter course. Perhaps they will turn out good Americans. In Porto Rico, as elsewhere, times change, and men's minds change with the changes of time and destiny."

CHAPTER VIII.

NAVAL LESSONS TAUGHT BY THE WAR.

After the remarkable victory at Santiago de Cuba, where Admiral Cervera's fleet, which attempted to steal out of the harbor, with the loss of but one man on the American side, Admiral Sampson, with a portion of his fleet, proceeded to San Juan in Porto Rico. This city he bombarded, directing his principal fire against Morro Castle.

What followed bears strong testimony to the remarkable gunnery of our ''jackies.''

Morro Castle and the buildings on the high ground in its rear were simply riddled. Great holes were in places blown out by our large shells and the walls were pitted by the hail of the smaller ones.

There was one entire building which was blown to pieces, and a whole section of the Cuartel was laid in ruins. To be sure, many of our shells were wasted in the sea wall, but this is not to be wondered at, as the parapet had embrasures for guns, and from where our ships were lying, these would naturally be mistaken for a sea battery.

Neither in Morro Castle nor in the more pretentious fortifications known as San Cristobal, were there any great number of modern guns. There were a few Krupp guns, but the remainder consisted of muzzleloaders of an ancient pattern; most of the latter were mounted upon parapets of masonry. It may be said that the defences of San Juan were opposed to every theory of modern military science. The defenses might have been considered impregnable some fifty years or so ago, but to-day they are by no means formidable.

Our marvelous naval victories have taught a lesson to the entire world, and America to-day stands stronger than she ever did before. In fact, there is not a nation that does not respect us and fear us, which possibly could not have been said before the American-Spanish war. Prior to that, it was rather the fashion to sneer at the Yankee army and navy, but that will never be done again.

Foreign nations know now what the United States really is.

"Dewey's and Sampson's victories must be very depressing to French, German and Russian naval aspirations," observes a gentleman of Washington, who is a most competent authority. "For years they have been measuring up against England, and quietly calculating what combinations they could make to overthrow British sea power. France, particularly, has been building a navy which she hoped, in spite of past experience, might cope with England's. She has spent immense sums upon it, and relative to the interests it has to guard, it is larger and stronger than England's. But Spain's experience reiterates the old story that it is not so much the ships as the men on them who win victories. Had the Americans been on Spanish ships and the Spanish on the American there would have been a very different story to tell. While the French are very superior to the Spanish, they are of the same Latin blood, and there is just enough similiarity between the two peoples to hint at the success French ships would have in encountering with Anglo-Saxons, either sailing under the Star Spangled Banner or the Cross of St. George. Germany is likely to have the same sort of a chill. The Germans have never been a maritime nation. A German war vessel has never fired a hostile shot, and Germans may well have solicitous thoughts as to the result of a struggle with men who have shown themselves past masters in the art of naval warfare. Russia is in the same situation. She has never actually fought anybody at sea but the Turks. The wiser among these peoples are very likely to begin thinking that their dreams of sea power are vain illusions, and that they had better save the money they have been spending on navies and resign the dominion of the sea to the English-speaking races.''

There is no doubt that our naval victories have taught many and valuable lessons, and it is perhaps proper to make a slight digression here and show what some of these lessons are.

Let us then consider the deliberations of a board of naval officers, some of the ablest experts in the service, appointed by Admiral Sampson, after the battle of Santiago de Cuba, to report upon the condition of Cervera's sunken fleet, the extent of damages done by American shells and the lessons to be learned therefrom to guide the United States in its future ship construction.

The conclusions reached by the board were as follows:

The use of wood in the construction and equipment of war ships should be reduced to the utmost minimum possible.

Loaded torpedoes above the water line are a serious menace to the vessels carrying them, and they should not be so carried by vessels other than torpedo boats.

The value of rapid-fire batteries cannot be too highly estimated.

All water and steam pipes should be laid beneath the protective deck and below the water line and fitted with risers at such points as may be considered necessary.

The board also found that the ships Infanta Maria Teresa, Almirante Oquendo and Viscaya were destroyed by conflagration, caused by the explosion of shells in the interior, which set fire to the woodwork. The upper deck and all other woodwork on their ships was entirely consumed except the extremities. This shows the importance of fireproofing all woodwork on board ships.

Many of the guns on board the burned ships were found loaded at the time of the board's visit, indicating the haste with which the crews were driven from the guns.

With talks with experts the following was developed as to what the war showed:

First—That the gun is still the dominating factor in war.

Second—That rapid-fire guns are especially valuable, but that it is advisable to retain guns of large calibres.

Third—That smokeless powder is absolutely essential for modern warfare.

Fourth—That there should be a great reduction in the amount of woodwork on board ship and that that left on board should be fireproof, some going so far as to say that woodwork should be eliminated entirely, its place to be taken by some other substance.

Fifth—That armor should be distributed over the entire ship rather than be limited to the section where its vitals are located.

Sixth—That monitors are useless for cruising purposes or for fighting in rough waters.

Seventh—That the United States should have a larger navy, with speedier battleships and fast armored cruisers, and with coaling stations in different sections of the globe, where men-of-war can procure supplies and make repairs if necessary.

Captain Charles O'Neil, chief of the bureau of ordnance, gave his opinion as follows:

"I do not think the battle off Santiago de Cuba demonstrated that we should abandon the heavy calibres of guns. Serious injury to an enemy's thickly-armored battleships can be inflicted only by large-calibre guns.

"It is possible that with rapid-fire guns you may shoot away the lightly armored superstructure, but as long as the vitals are protected and the turret armor is intact the guns in the turret will be able to do execution, and large-calibred guns will be necessary to perforate the armor and disable those weapons. Even with her 12-inch guns the Texas can fire at the rate of one round per minute, and this record is as good as that made by any foreign ships. Rapid fire consists in good facilities for handling ammunition and loading the gun with a quick-working breech mechanism.

"We are now building at the Washington gun factory an experimental 6-inch rapid-fire gun, different from the rapid-fire guns we have now in service, which are supplied with what is termed fixed ammunition. The powder and projectile to be used in the experimental gun will be separate, and two operations consequently will have to be employed in loading. This can be done so quickly that it is expected that a very rapid fire will be obtained.

"It is the policy of the Department to have our ships a little ahead of those of any other nation, to have them equipped with armor of greater resistive power, and guns capable of doing more execution. The 13-inch gun, as at present designed, is a more destructive gun than a 12-inch ordinarily, and its energy is very much greater, the result naturally being that it has superior armor-piercing powers.

"I think we should keep the 13-inch gun on board of our battleships. On account of the light armor which protected the Spanish men-of-war, it is difficult to compare the ships and the effect of their fire, or to draw conclusions. We would have learned more if the Spanish fleet had been made up of battleships, and the fire of their gunners had been more accurate. As it is, the value of the secondary battery was certainly demonstrated.

"The necessity of eliminating wood to the greatest extent possible and fireproofing what remains, was shown by the destruction of the Spanish men-of-war. Fire mains should be kept below the protective deck. The battle proved that ships moving rapidly can attack other vessels also under way and inflict serious injury.

"The excellent gunnery of the American sailors is entirely due to the practice which they had undergone, but the target fired at was stationary, while their ship was moving. The conditions were different in action. The Spanish were under way, yet the American gunners fired as well as if they were merely practising."

The New York Herald speaks as follows of our naval victories:

"Ramming, that expedient of despair, was not attempted. Torpedoing, despite the opportunities afforded, was estopped by the quick service of rapid-fire guns on board an inferior but superbly handled construction, and that final effort, a 'charge through,' was never allowed to challenge the combined energies of our fleet. If audacity could have merited success, these Spaniards deserved much, but here the marrow of the war proverb was not with them.

"Pitted against similar ships, even in superior numbers, some of the fleeing cruisers might have slipped seaward in hot haste for the breaking of the Havana blockade. Failing that, all might have concentrated an assault upon certain selected vessels and found consolation for final defeat in the foundering hulls of their enemy. But audacity did not count, individual bravery went for naught; because, while heavier constructions barred the way, and superior guns smashed the pathways of escape, energized skill overcame untrained courage and patient discipline crushed unorganized effort.

"The battleships not only fought the armored cruisers in a long, stern chase down the shore, but destroying as they ran, finally forced them blazing in their own wrecks upon a hostile coast. The torpedo boat destroyers engaged single handed by the Gloucester succumbed so quickly to inferior armament and speed that their value in a day attack, or, indeed, their value at any time save as weapons of surprise, need no longer be reckoned with. This will be a rude awakening to the zealots who had seen in this weapon the downfall of the ship of the fighting line, but it will be a heart-cheering confirmation to the loyal seamen who in season and out have never ceased to proclaim that the integrity of sea nations rests on battleships and the well-served guns of a fleet."

"I think sometimes if it had not been for the work of the Oregon the Colon might have got away," was the statement made by an admiral on the retired list. "I am not sure that the Brooklyn, with all her speed, could have stopped the Colon, but I think it quite likely that the New York would have finally overtaken the Colon and stopped her."

More emphasis was laid upon the speed of the Oregon and the closeness of her position than upon her 13-inch shells, one of which played such havoc. The admiral was not seemingly impressed with the difference in effectiveness between the guns of large and small calibre, but continued to lay stress on the admirable speed of the Oregon.

"But," he continued, "the war has proved nothing so far as the navy is concerned. The Spaniards showed no enterprise. If we had come up against the navy of England there would have been some basis for a conclusion, but shooting in the air, as the Spaniards did, proves nothing. They had a fine fleet, with most modern equipment, and yet they could kill only one man in the whole encounter."

Admiral Sir George Elliot, of the British Navy, considers that at least five important lessons have been taught by the war. His opinions are as follows:

"First, in state of peace be fully prepared for war in every respect; second, the value of adequately-protected coaling stations; third, the value of superior speed for the cruiser class, and especially for the more weakly-armored vessels; fourth, the naval defense of seaports by gunboats and the raising of the naval volunteer corps as an integral portion of the naval reserve forces; fifth, that great importance be attached to a steady gun platform for quick-firing guns, looking to the small number of hits compared with numerous shots fired.

"In this connection," said Sir George Elliot, "I am informed that the Americans are likely to adopt Captain Hodgett's form of bottom for their new ships, which must give greater steadiness than bilge keels."

Admiral Sir Henry Nicholson, who was captain of the Temeraire at the bombardment of Alexandria, and has since been commander in chief at the Cape of Good Hope and at the Nore, has spoken thus:

"This war has taught us nothing. The state of the Spanish navy has been for years so hopelessly rotten that when the moment for action arrived its military value was nil. The Spanish gunners hardly seem to have got a hit in on any American ship. Nothing is taught us as to the relative value of the belt or deck armor."

As regards ships versus forts, he said:

"The Spanish forts seem to have been, probably from various reasons, as inefficient as their ships. Both the Spaniards and the Americans in their use of torpedo craft have shown very remarkable absence of dash. Practically neither side has made any use of this dreaded arm."

Captain Montagu Burrow, who is professor of modern history at the University of Oxford, had this opinion to offer:

"There are no new lessons to be learned, but only confirmation of some that are very old. The state of unreadiness in Spain when the war suddenly. broke out might, from the unfortunate circumstances of that country, have been expected, but if the United States had had to deal with a Power anything like its own strength it would have found its own position intensely difficult. The war will probably have the effect of inducing their government to keep up a standing army and navy of a very superior kind to that of their present system. The recent warning of their admirable writer, Captain Mahan, will now have a chance of being listened to, but the Americans have only to expand what is already proved to be good. The training of their officers and men must have been of a superior kind to enable them to handle their ships and point their guns with such excellent effect. It was at one time considered doubtful whether modern guns could be as accurately fired at great distances as the old armament at shorter ranges, but they were laid quite as accurately, and were far more destructive.''

As the New York Herald declared at the time, the United States had now attained their majority. They were now of age, and their voice must be heard in the council of nations.

There were misgivings all over Europe, especially in Germany and France, old and bitter foes though they are.

A prominent Parisian thus summed up these misgivings:

''The young American giant,'' he said, ''is only trying his strength on Spain, but what if he should use it against us?''

CHAPTER IX.

WHAT OUR ARMY ACHIEVED.

Now to turn from the navy to the army, and see what the latter achieved in Porto Rico.

On July 21, 1898, General Miles sailed from Guantanamo Bay with a force of 3,415 men. General Wilson had sailed the day before from Charleston with 4,000 men, and General Schwan and his command sailed from Port Tampa two days later.

The entire army of invasion numbered about eleven thousand men.

The hardships on the transports were very great.

The Massachusetts carried three troops of cavalry from New York and Pennsylvania to Porto Rico and the events of the voyage have been thus narrated by an eye-witness:

"With the penetrating of the tropics come days of languor and nights of inactivity so delicious it seems profanation to move. More than one thousand men, who boarded the Massachusetts with the vigor of the North in their veins, have succumbed, one by one, to the lethargy of the soft breeze of the Bahamas.

But an awakening is at hand. Pumps that have been running steadily day and night slow down and stop. Troopers had become so accustomed to the quick beating of the smaller machines that the cessation of throbs between the slower pulsations of the heavier engines is noticed instantly. A quick inquiry as to the cause brings the answer from one less well-informed: "Only the water pumps broken down." That is all, only eleven hundred parched horses awaiting the answer to the bugle call they had learned so well—"Water horses!"—which sounded at the moment of the fatal break in the pumps. Only a transport carrying ten hundred and thirty men, and no means of extinguishing a fire!

Twenty minutes; one-half hour, and Captain Read, who has gone down into "the hole," asks for five Troop A men. "No hurry," so the order said. Somebody knew better, and the troopers go, hand over hand, down into the ship's hold. A few bales of hay come up and over the side of the ship, and sizzle as they strike the water. The troopers nurse a few burned fingers, and Captain Read reappears on deck, smoked, wet with perspiration, and makes his usual answer to a question, "What's the trouble?" with "Nothing at all." But five men of Troop A and Captain Read knows that a dangerous fire has been extinguished for the third time in one day with men's bare hands.

"Three-quarters of an hour, and no sound from the engine-room, except the steady throb of the propeller.

" 'Thirty men from Troop A, thirty men from City Troop, and thirty men from Troop C!' and ninety men in three squads silently are lined around that entrance to Hades—the hole. 'Another fire,' was the quick alarm, but it was worse than that. 'Water! water! water!' the cry comes from the sunken eyes that look pleadingly at men; from harsh breathing; from parched throats; from hanging heads of eleven hundred horses and mules that had not been watered since receiving a scant quart eighteen hours before. 'Let's see,' said the United States cavalrymen, quietly, 'the pumps are hopeless, but we can draw up one bucketful every minute from the hold aft, and one every minute from the forward hatch. We ought to water all in ten hours. Form lines and water solid. The horse you skip will be dead .in the morning.'

"The horses stand with swollen legs far apart, instinctively to prevent a fall. Once down, they know they never can get up. Their heads hang low and their breathing comes in a whistle from parched lungs through a long, dry throat and dusty mouth. There is an occasional form in the black galleys. It is some trooper, his big arms around the neck of his beloved dying mount, with tears in his eyes, but petting and talking to the animal as if it understood. Then ropes over blocks begin to draw buckets of water from sixty feet below. Immediately each horse or mule has its draught, it is bathed in perspiration, and skin dry and shriveled becomes soft and pliable. One can feel in the dark, whether a horse has been missed or not.

"There is a delay and an anxious inquiry from above: 'What's the matter?' 'Haul away,' is the response, and the bucket comes heavy this time. Oh, it's only a man, stark naked, fainting, with a rope beneath his arms, and head away to one side. 'Hospital case, overcome, haul away,' and another bucket swings upward."

Of course the objective point of the whole campaign

was the capital, San Juan, on the northeastern coast of the island. Nevertheless the troops were mostly landed on the southern coast not far from the southwestern corner. The plan was to drive all the Spanish troops upon the island into San Juan, where they could be captured upon the surrender of that city.

The Spaniards abandoned precipitately the whole southern coast line, and this seemed to promise an easy march for the Americans across Porto Rico.

But this was not exactly the case, as we shall proceed to demonstrate.

There were several causes why the Spaniards fled before the invading Americans.

One was that in the beginning the Spanish forces, from lack of knowledge as to where the Americans would land, were widely scattered. By retreating, the coast garrisons were brought together in bodies of more or less magnitude. More than this in the interior could be found stronger positions for defense, and there only land forces would have to be dealt with.

It is probable that the Spaniards in Porto Rico, knowing as they must have, that the war was virtually over, hoped by a show of resistance at the end to come out with a certain degree of credit, and had resolved to give up the fight only when they received an order to do so from Madrid.

At all events, the Spanish troops disputed the American advance at several points. At Fajardo the American forces raised the Stars and Stripes, but the Spaniards, several hundred in number, pulled it down and even sought to drive away the landing party that held the lighthouse on the shore. This attempt was most manifestly absurd, as in the harbor was a squadron, consisting of the monitor Amphitrite, the protected cruiser Cincinnati and the Leyden. No time was lost in landing men to support the lighthouse force, and to open fire from the ships. The Spaniards were driven back and suffered much from their foolish temerity.

In the beginning the plan of campaign included an advance along three lines.

The first division, under General Schwan, was to advance along the western coast to Aguadilla, in the northwestern corner of the island, and then to push to the east until Arecibo, on the northern coast and about halfway between Aguadilla and San Juan, was reached. The second division, under General Henry, was to push directly to the north from Ponce, forming a union with Schwan at Arecibo. The main advance was to be along the military road from Ponce to San Juan. As this road runs for some distance parallel to the southern coast, a division was dispatched under General Brooke to land at Arroyo and capture Guayama, an important city on the military road, about forty miles east of Ponce. By this means, whatever detachments of Spanish troops might be stationed on the road between these two points were exposed to attack from both front and rear.

Before any of these movements could be completed, however, came the armistice and the consequent cessation of hostilities.

Much, though, had been accomplished before this, enough to show what American arms were capable of.

In the east, General Brooke, after landing at Arroyo, had taken Guayama; in the centre, General Wilson had advanced on the military road, occupied Coamo, and had made a demonstration before Aibonito, where there was a large Spanish force; further to the west, General Henry had marched to within fifteen miles of Arecibo; in the extreme west, General Schwan had marched along the coast and taken Mayaguez, the principal port in that end of the island, after a sharp skirmish with a force that outnumbered his own. The slight opposition met by General Brooke at Guayama, General Wilson at Coamo, and General Schwan near Mayaguez, indicated that there would be little difficulty in reaching the capital, and officers and men alike felt that the capture of San Juan was a matter of but a few days.

The third landing of American troops in Porto Rico took place on August 2, at Arroyo, from the St. Louis and the St. Paul. The army then took the place of the navy and accepted the surrender of the town. There was no defense and no Spanish flag was flying. The surrender of Arroyo was important, as there were a large number of manufacturing enterprises there.

The attitude of the civil authorities and the ineffective character of the defense made by the Spanish troops, says the San Francisco Argonaut, was illustrated by the advance made by General Henry's division. General Roy Stone was sent in advance with a small body of about one hundred men to reconnoiter the road and determine its fitness for military operations. The character of the expedition may be gathered from the fact that General Stone and his officers rode in carriages. Yet town after town surrendered to these outposts until they were encamped before Arecibo, on the northern coast of the island. The main body had nothing to do but follow and furnish flags for the surrendered municipalities.

One of the most extraordinary things in the whole campaign was the surrender of the city of Ponce. This was done in response to a telephone communication from Ensign Curtin. Not a single shot was fired.

After the surrender of Ponce it was reported that a large Spanish force had gathered about ten miles in the interior. Two companies of soldiers were sent out by General Ernst to see what this meant. On the outskirts of the town a party of Spanish soldiers, loaded down with guns and swords, was met with. As soon as the Spaniards caught sight of the Americans they ran toward them crying, ''Don't shoot!''

They declared that they were coming in to surrender. Although the party was small, they had arms enough to stock a regiment. They were taken before General Wilson, gave up their arms and signed a parole.

There was quite a strong resistance made at Coamo, a town on the main military road between Juana Diaz and the Spanish mountain stronghold at Aibonito. General Wilson effected the capture of this place with the most consummate skill. His plan was simple enough. It was nothing more nor less than an ordinary flank movement, such as Grant and Sherman used so successfully during the Civil War.

General Wilson advanced against the town on the main road with sufficient infantry, cavalry and artillery to drive out the Spanish garrison. But when the latter attempted to retreat they found their way blocked by the Sixteenth Pennsylvania, under Colonel Hulings, which General Wilson had sent round to the rear of the town the night before.

The attack in front was timed so as to allow this force to get into position.

The Battle of Coamo, if indeed, it can be so called, for it was nothing more than a lively skirmish, has been thus described:

"Just as darkness fell, the regiment left the military road and struck at a right angle for the hills to the northward. Porto Rican guides led the way over paths so rough and narrow that the men could move only in single file. It was toilsome progress. Absolute silence was enjoined; no smoking was permitted lest the fitful flash of a match should betray the movement to the watchful Spaniards on the hills. For hours the men toiled on. The officers were compelled to walk and lead their horses. Creeks and rivulets were waded; lofty hills were climbed or skirted; yawning ravines were crossed. The men dripped with perspiration, although the night air was chilly.

"At dawn both General Wilson and General Ernest were in the saddle, and long before the shadows lifted from the valleys the main body of the army was in mo-

tion to drive the enemy out of the town and into Hul-
ing's net.   Nearer than the village and off to the right
was the blockhouse of Llamo de Coamo.   The blockhouse was the first place attacked.   There was a heavy,
jarring rumble over the macadam of the military road.
Anderson's battery came along at a sharp trot.   At a
turn in the road where the blockhouse came into view it
halted.   Two minutes later the fight opened.   For a few
minutes the Spanish returned the fire with Mausers, but
as shell after shell crashed through the blockhouse, they
abandoned it and fell back toward Coamo.   Soon flames
leaped upward from the roof, and an hour later the fort
was but a smoldering ruin.

"Meanwhile the infantry was pressing rapidly forward.
General Wilson was wondering what had become of
Hulings.   Not a warlike sound came from the village, a
mile and a half away. Had the garrison escaped?   Suddenly from beyond the town came the rattle of mus-
ketry. Soon the sound swelled into a steady roar, which
the mountains echoed again and again."

The same writer tells a story in regard to one whom
he terms a real hero of the war, and he calls attention to
the callous manner in which Spanish soldiers were sacrificed to protect political adventurers at home.   To
quote his own words:

"His name was Don Rafael Martinez.   There was no
military justification for attempting to hold Coamo
under the circumstances.   Yet Major Martinez stayed.
He was still in the prime of youth and in fine health.
In Spain his family is aristocratic and influential, and

could have protected him from the consequences of a quixotic court-martial. Martinez knew that resistance was utterly hopeless. But Colonel San Martian had been practically disgraced by Governor-General Macias for evacuating Ponce, and all commanders of garrisons in the path of the American army were ordered to fight. So Major Martinez kissed his young wife and children good-by one day last week and sent them into San Juan for safety. His scouts brought word that an American column of double the garrison's strength was slowly creeping around to his rear. Then Martinez knew that he was trapped, and decided to go out and meet the enemy. He rode in advance of his slender column until he sighted Hulings's men, who were immediately apprised of the enemy's presence by a volley. Soon bullets were flying like hail. Martinez, mounted upon a gray horse, rode up and down in front of his troops, uttering encouraging words. The soldier's death which Martinez sought was not long coming. For a while he reeled in his saddle, maintaining his seat with evident difficulty. Then his horse went to his knees, and Martinez slowly slid from the saddle, a lifeless form. When Major Martinez was found, five wounds, three of which were mortal, were discovered. His horse was shot in four places."

The result of the attack on Coamo was the capture of about one hundred and eighty men, or most of the garrison except the cavalry who took to the mountains by paths better known to them than to the Americans. Of General Wilson's force, none was killed and only a few were wounded.

The whole affair was splendidly managed. As has been said before, all General Miles's plans could be put into action, the war was practically ended.

On the afternoon of August 12, Secretary of State Day and M. Cambon, the French ambassador, who was representing Spain, affixed their signatures to duplicate copies of a protocol establishing a basis upon which the two countries, acting through their respective commissioners, could negotiate terms of peace.

The provisions of the protocol were practically as follows:

1. That Spain will relinquish all claim of sovereignty over and title to Cuba.

2. That Porto Rico and other Spanish islands in the West Indies, and an island in the Ladrones, to be selected by the United States, shall be ceded to the latter.

3. That the United States will occupy and hold the city, bay and harbor of Manila, pending the conclusion of a treaty of peace which shall determine the control, disposition and government of the Philippines.

4. That Cuba, Porto Rico and other Spanish islands in the West Indies shall be immediately evacuated, and that commissioners, to be appointed within ten days, shall, within thirty days from the signing of the protocol, meet at Havana and San Juan respectively, to arrange and execute the details of the evacuation.

5. That the United States and Spain will each appoint not more than five commissioners to negotiate and conclude a treaty of peace. The commissioners are to meet at Paris not later than October 1.

6. On the signing of the protocol, hostilities will be suspended and notice to that effect will be given as soon as possible by each Government to the commanders of its military and naval forces.

The President at once signed the following proclamation, declaring an armistice:

"By the President of the United States of America:

"A PROCLAMATION.

"Whereas, By a protocol concluded and signed August 12, 1898, by William R. Day, Secretary of State of the United States, and his Excellency Jules Cambon, Ambassador Extraordinary and Plenipotentiary of the republic of France at Washington, respectively representing for this purpose the Government of the United States and the Government of Spain, the United States and Spain have formally agreed upon the terms on which negotiations for the establishment of peace between the two countries shall be undertaken; and,

"Whereas, It is in said protocol agreed that upon its conclusion and signature hostilities between the two countries shall be supended, and that notice to that effect shall be given as soon as possible by each government to the commanders of its military and naval forces;

"Now, therefore, I, William McKinley, President of the United States, do, in accordance with the stipulations of the protocol, declare and proclaim on the part of the United States a suspension of hostilities, and do hereby command that orders be immediately given through the proper channels to the commanders of the military and naval forces of the United States to abstain from all acts inconsistent with this proclamation.

"In witness whereof, I have hereunto set my hand and caused the seal of the United States to be affixed.

"Done at the city of Washington, this 12th day of August, in the year of our Lord one thousand eight hundred and ninety-eight, and of the independence of the United States the one hundred and twenty-third.

"William McKinley.

"By the President. William R. Day, Secretary of State."

It may be interesting to pause here for a moment and note what the London press had to say as to this suspension of hostilities. It will be observed that the comments were extraordinarily favorable to the United States.

The Standard, commenting on the signing of the protocol by the representatives of Spain and the United States, said: "Thus ends one of the most swiftly decisive wars in history. Spanish rule disappears from the West. The conquerors have problems of great difficulty before them. Doubtless they will face them with patriotic resolution."

The Daily News said: "August 12, 1898, will be a memorable day in the history of the world. It is the day which witnessed the death of one famous empire and the birth of another, destined perhaps to more enduring fame. It must be admitted that the results achieved are a substantial record for four months of war."

The Morning Post said that the protocol leaves open the two questions regarding which future difficulties that may not concern the United States and Spain alone are likely to arise. It advises Spain, assuming that the United States only holds Manila, to sell the Philippines.

The Daily Telegraph was impressed by the indifference of the bulk of the Spanish nation to the sentiment of national pride, which seems to be extinct. For this reason national life, in the true sense of the word, must sooner or later cease to exist.

The paper discussed the decadence of Spain in connection with the contention that France and Italy have become stationary, and predicts the ultimate disappearance of the Latin race as a factor in the human drama.

The Chronicle said that the American people will never regret the sacrifices they have made to remove the Spanish colonies from the map.

It added that many more difficulties and sacrifices await them, but the result will be the growth of freedom and the extension of human happiness and prosperity.

The Times said it hoped it was not a violation of neutrality to express the satisfaction felt by a great majority of Englishmen at the success of the United States. It added:

"Historians will wrangle for a long time respecting the propriety of the methods by which the war was brought about, but once begun it was eminently desirable for the interests of the world, and even, perhaps, ultimately to the interests of Spain herself, that it should result in the success of the Americans.

The factor in the situation which is of the greatest immediate importance to ourselves is the fate of the Philippines."

The Times thought it very remarkable that the New York newspapers discovered on the same day that the United States were bound to put themselves in the best possible position for defending the common interests of themselves and Great Britain in China. It concluded:

"Providence in the nick of time has given them the Philippines."

The armistice proclamation was followed at once by orders from the War Department to the several commanding generals in the field directing that all military operations be suspended.

This was the text of the message to General Miles:

"Adjutant-General's Office,
Washington, Aug. 12, 1898.

"Major-General Miles, Ponce, Porto Rico:

"The President directs that all military operations against the enemy be suspended. Peace negotiations are nearing completion, a protocol having just been signed by representatives of the two countries. You will inform the commander of the Spanish forces in Porto Rico of these instructions. Further orders will follow. Acknowledge receipt.

"By order Secretary of War.

"H. C. Corbin, Adjutant-General."

These orders, coming as they did, undoubtedly prevented the sacrifice of many valuable lives before San

Juan. But they were anything but popular among the American troops, for they reached the various divisions just as each was about to strike a decisive blow.

The Spaniards, however, it is said, received the news with loud manifestations of delight.

In General Brook's division, a battery had just been advanced to position and the order to fire was about to be given, when a courier, his steed panting and covered with foam, dashed upon the field and informed the general that an armistice had been concluded.

General Brooke's sole reply was:

"Lieutenant, you arrived five minutes too soon. You should have been more considerate of your horse."

While our army did not have a chance to show all that it was capable of accomplishing, it was proven conclusively that the Yankees are good and brave fighters.

The sight of an army springing up out of nothing, the spectacle of the monumental work of military organization being pushed on to success in spite of mistakes, arrested the attention of all European nations.

One thing is certain—a noble victory has been nobly won; and won, happily at a cost, which, deplorable though it actually was, was relatively small, as must be acknowledged by every student of the warfare of the past.

CHAPTER X.

HOW THE PORTO RICANS RECEIVED US.

Whatever may have been the attitude and feelings of the Spanish officials and Spanish troops, there can be no doubt that the Porto Ricans themselves welcomed most enthusiastically the advent of the Americans and the dawn of a new era. The joy manifested at the sight of invaders in a conquered country was most extraordinary, and we can affirm with truth that it has no parallel in history.

It was most fortunate that little or no fighting took place, as thus many valuable lives were saved. There was no question whatever as to the result.

The number and location of the Spanish troops on the island just before the armistice was declared were as follows:

Aibonito, 1,800 men, and two 4-inch field cannon; Cavey, 700 men; Caguas, 600; Rio Piedras, 180; Carolite, 320; Arecibo, 320, and two 4-inch field cannon; Aguadilla, 320; Crab Island, 100; Bayamon, 395; San Juan, 1,706, making a total of 5,441, to which may be added approximately 500 of the Guardia Civil, doing duty in their own villages all over the island, and 200 of the Orden Publico, doing similar police duty in San Juan. Many members of the Guardia Civil in or near the territory held by the American troops joined the Americans.

It cannot be told with any certainty how much resistance the Spaniards would have offered had hostilities continued, but most of the fighting would have undoubtedly taken place within sight of San Juan. The Spaniards themselves believed this, as the preparations they made sufficiently indicated.

The native people generally were thoroughly delighted with the news that the island was likely to be ceded to the United States. Wherever the American flag went up, it was cheered with a vigor that probably was never given to the Spanish flag during all the centuries it has been in evidence.

Everywhere, the people rushed forward to welcome the invaders, and showered them with hospitable attentions. Pretty women dressed themselves in their richest garments and smiled their sweetest smiles to charm the conquerors.

Food, cigars and wines were pressed upon the soldiers; the civil authorities issued florid proclamations over the glad event of becoming ''Americanos,'' and the whole country blossomed with Star-Spangled banners. The only reason why even more of them were not displayed was because more of them could not be obtained.

It was one of the most unlooked-for and surprising things of this most surprising war, as a writer in the National Tribune of Washington observes.

The same writer goes on to say that really there is good reason for all this.

''The substantial people of Puerto Rico know that it is immensely to their interest to cut loose from Spain, and be grafted on to the United States. The greater part of their trade is with this country, and Spain has been bleeding them for the privilege of carrying it on. Now they can send their coffee, sugar, tobacco, tropical fruits, etc., directly to this market, get American prices for them, and buy American goods in return at regular American prices.

"They ought to be mighty glad to get into this country, but, being Spaniards, we hardly expected them to have so much sense."

Guanica was the first town taken by our soldiers.

The enthusiasm was unbounded, and numbers of the citizens called to pay their respects to the leading officers.

At Guanica the following proclamation was issued to the people of the island under the signature of General Miles:

"Guanica, Porto Rico, July 27, 1898.
"To the Inhabitants of Porto Rico:

"In the prosecution of the war against the Kingdom of Spain by the people of the United States, in the cause of liberty, justice and humanity, its military forces have come to occupy the islands of Porto Rico. They come bearing the banners of freedom, inspired by noble purposes, to seek the enemies of our government and of yours, and to destroy or capture all in armed resistance.

"They bring you the fostering arms of a free people, whose greatest power is justice and humanity to all living within their fold. Hence they release you from your former political relations, and it is hoped this will be followed by the cheerful acceptance of the government of the United States.

"The chief object of the American military forces will be to overthrow the armed authority of Spain and give the people of your beautiful island the largest measure of liberty consistent with this military occupation.

"They have not come to make war on the people of the country, who for centuries have been oppressed; but, on the contrary, they bring protection, not only to yourselves, but to your property, promote your prosperity and bestow the immunities and blessings of our enlightenment and liberal institutions and government. It is not their purpose to interfere with the existing laws and customs, which are wholesome and beneficial to the people, so long as they conform to the rules of the military administration, order and justice. This is not a war of devastation and dissolution, but one to give all within the control of the military and naval forces the advantages and blessings of enlightened civilization."

The mayor of Guanica also issued a proclamation, which was thus worded:

"Citizens: God, who rules the destinies of nations, has decreed that the Eagle of the North, coming from the waters of a land where liberty first sprang forth to life, should extend to us his protecting wings. Under his plumage, sweetly reposing, the Pearl of the Antilles, called Porto Rico, will remain from July 25.

"The starry banner has floated gayly in the valleys of

Guanica, the most beautiful port of this downtrodden land. This city was selected by General Miles as the place in which to officially plant his flag in the name of his government, the United States of America. It is the ensign of grandeur and the guarantee of order, morality and justice. Let us join together to strengthen, to support and to further a great work. Let us clasp to our bosoms the great treasure which is generously offered to us while saluting with all our hearts the name of the great Washington.

"Augustin Barrenecha, Alcalde.
"Guanica, Porto Rico, U. S. A., July 26, 1898."

Yauco was the next to surrender.

When the troops took possession of the town the mayor promptly issued this proclamation:

"Citizens:

"To-day the citizens of Porto Rico assist in one of her most beautiful festivals. The sun of America shines upon our mountains and valleys this day of July, 1898. It is a day of glorious remembrance for each son of this beloved isle, because for the first time there waves over it the flag of the Stars, planted in the name of the Government of the United States of America by the major-general of the American Army, General Miles.

"Porto Ricans, we are by the miraculous intervention of the God of the just given back to the bosom of our mother America, in whose waters Nature placed us as people of America. To her we are given back in the name of her government by General Miles, and we must send her our most expressive salutation of generous affection through our conduct toward the valiant troops represented by distinguished officers and commanded by the illustrious General Miles.

"Citizens: Long live the Government of the United States of America! Hail to their valiant troops! Hail Porto Rico, always American!

"Yauco, Porto Rico, United States of America.

"El Alcalde, Francisco Megia."

The alcalde is the judge who administers justice, and he also presides as mayor over the City Council.

The citizens of the town hugged the Americans, and some fell upon their knees and embraced the legs of the soldiers. It was a most remarkable spectacle.

On July 29, Ponce was formally given over to the Americans, without the firing of a single shot. The populace received the troops and saluted the flag with enthusiasm. When General Miles entered the city he was welcomed by the mayor, cheered to the echo by the citizens and serenaded by a band of music.

The mayor of Ponce issued a proclamation of the same tenor as that of the mayor of Yauco, although not quite so enthusiastic.

General Wilson was made military governor of Ponce.

A day or two after the taking of Ponce several local judges were sworn into office. This was the first time in the history of the United States that the judges of a foreign, hostile but conquered country, swore to support the Constitution of the United States.

The following was the form sworn to by the various officials:

"I declare under oath that, during the occupation of the island of Porto Rico by the United States, I will renounce and abjure all allegiance and fidelity to every foreign prince, potentate, state or sovereignty, particularly the Queen Regent and the King of Spain, and will support the constitution of the United States against all enemies, foreign or domestic, and will bear true faith and allegiance to the same.

"Further, I will faithfully support the Government of the United States, established by the military authorities in the island of Porto Rico, will yield obedience to the same and take the obligation freely, without mental reservation or with the purpose of evasion, so help me God."

On July 31, the commanding general sent a message to the War Department, the first official one received from Ponce. It read as follows:

"Secretary of War, Washington, D. C.:

"Your telegrams 27th received and answered by letter. Volunteers are surrendering themselves with arms and ammunition; four-fifths of the people are overjoyed at the arrival of the army. Two thousand from one place have volunteered to serve with it. They are bringing in transportation, beef, cattle and other needed supplies.

"The Custom House has already yielded $14,000.

"As soon as all the troops are disembarked they will be in readiness to move.

'' Please send any national colors that can be spared, to be given to the different municipalities.

"I request that the question of the tariff rates to be charged in the parts of Porto Rico occupied by our forces be submitted to the President for his action, the previously existing tariff remaining meanwhile in force. As to the government under military occupation, I have already given instructions based upon the instructions issued by the President in the case of the Philippine Islands, and similar to those issued at Santiago de Cuba.

"Miles."

When the soldiers entered Ponce the people sang the "Star-Spangled Banner" in a mixture of Spanish and English, and every time this tune was heard the police forced everybody to remove his hat!

"The natives are, upon the whole, exceedingly friendly," says a correspondent of the New York Sun, "and almost all of them welcome the American army. The flag is voluntarily displayed from many of the principal stores. If there are any Spanish flags in the city they are kept carefully concealed. In the stores American goods are sometimes to be found, particularly in hardware stores. All fabrics, foods, and luxuries, however, have been imported from Europe, mostly from Spain. The Spanish Government forces its colonies to import from home by levying a heavy discriminating duty upon all goods not Spanish. Prices are very high, notwithstanding which fact business is brisk.

The soldiers are good customers and buy all sorts of

curios as souvenirs for friends at home. The officers, too, buy considerable quantities of light underclothing. It is safe to say that there has never before been as much money in circulation here. All the merchants favor annexation.''

In an article in the National Magazine the following is said:

''The Porto Ricans have taken very quickly and kindly to American occupation. Some have been so quick in changing that their conversion may be doubted. For instance, the editor of La Nueva Era, a daily which in two scraggy leaves purports to be a 'journal of news, travel, science, literature and freedom,' was only a few weeks ago raving at the 'American Pigs'; while now he luxuriates under the eagle's ægis and writes eulogies upon Benjamin Franklin, George Washington and William McKinley.   Nor is he alone in his devotion to the American idea. The small boy curses his neighbor by calling him 'un Espanol,' and treats you with disdain if you suggest that he is simply a poor Porto Rican. 'No, no,' he says, pointing at himself. 'No, Espanol, Porto-Rican Americano.' His motives are not, however, always of the sincerest, for the boys have learned a trick of saying to the passing Yankee, 'Viva America,' and then putting up the forefinger with this half-asked question, 'one cent?' ''

A brilliant writer in one of the magazines says that in speaking with a leading merchant of Ponce, he asked him if the people were really so delighted with the new regime.

" 'Well, frankly, no,' he replied, 'the mass will welcome any change, but it is quite a question whether we shall gain by annexation to the United States. I have lived in America. Now the Spaniards taxed us heavily, but when they got their money they went off and let us alone. The custom-house officers stole nearly everything from the government. But then we have yet to see how the American custom-house officers will act. Spain knew us and we knew Spain; there were few complaints. The church tax was not heavy, and I never went to service. We do not want the negroes enfranchised till they are better educated. Then the money question is going to be bad for many of us here. We shall suffer dreadfully if the American government makes our dollar worth only fifty cents.'

"The man who uttered these words is a highly respected citizen, speaks English well, and understands America as well as Spain.

"While we were looking over the town we came upon the jail where there are about one hundred and sixty Spanish prisoners," the same writer goes on to say. "Many of these men were selling their chevrons and buttons and other marks of rank with an alacrity worthy of a better cause. One of our party, however, experienced a chill when upon asking one of the prisoners how much he would sell his chevrons for he got this reply, 'No, por el dinero en globo.' 'Not for all the money on earth.''

"There spoke the true spirit of Spain. The Spain which sent armies to Jerusalem, patronized Columbus,

conquered the half of America with a handful of men—
that Spain, with all her black tragedies, never sold her
chevrons. Let us be merciful to a fallen foe; at least, let
us be truthful. Thank God Spain's power in this hemisphere is crushed. Yet there was chivalry in the old
regime. We can afford to be magnanimous now; he who
bends above the fallen forever stands erect."

On August 4, when rumors of Spain's submission
reached Porto Rico, the editor of La Nueva Era wound
up his leading editorial with these words:

"Hurra por la anexion a los Estados Unidos!"

He also gave this excellent sanitary advice to the invading army:

"TO THE BOYS!

"Keep away from fruit of every description and Rum,
if you wish to keep your health in this climate."

Moreover, he published this:

"It is an undeniable fact that wherever the American
forces have landed they have been welcomed by the people as liberators amid the greatest enthusiasm.

"A new era has dawned for this country and is the
advent of happier times.

"The spectre of suspicion with which we were menaced has disappeared forever. We are now sure that the
air we breathe is ours and we can breathe it to our fill.

"The labor accomplished by the people of the United
States in taking this island, and we say accomplished,
as nothing can oppose their arms, is truly a labor of
humanity and redemption, and will be one of the greatest glories of the great republic.

"Let us render thanks to the Almighty for the blessing, and let us be well assured that Porto Rico has before it a future of unlimited progress and well-being."

The most rabid Spanish publication of all, La Democracia, issued an address to the public announcing the demise of the paper under its former name, and giving notice that it would reappear under the name of the Courier with a portion printed in English.

In making this announcement the editor promised in the new edition:

"To explain our ideas of brothership and harmony, answering to the ideas proclaimed to the press by our new military authority, such as that the American army has not come as our enemies, but with the purpose of harmonizing with the citizens of Porto Rico. We are pleased to make known that these ideas have been respected, and that all the acts of the forces occupying our city have been characterized by the most exquisite correctness, and that the American troops fraternize with our people."

At all events, these extracts serve to show the trend of public opinion.

"Mr. Morrisey in speaking of the Ponce of to-day says that 'the city is in a horrible sanitary condition, and I wondered how the United States troops stood it. I learned there had been an improvement since the soldiers' arrival, but there is room for considerable more, I think. I went to the Hotel Ingleterra, which is considered the best one in Ponce, and engaged a room. My first meal there was breakfast, which was served at 11 o'clock. My meal consisted of rice, black beans and coffee, all of which was fair. At dinner, which is always served at 6 o'clock, I had the same fare. I tried to get eggs after the first day, but was successful on only two occasions, and then had to pay 7 cents each for them. I learned that the soldiers had made a corner in eggs and had bought nearly all of them, which, of course, made them scarce at the hotels and eating places. All the water used in the hotel is filtered through a huge block of brownstone and even then it is pretty poor.'

"'Mr. Morrisey visited the place known as the market in the heart of the city of Ponce, and saw some very interesting scenes. A few of the better class of the natives visited the market several times during the day and made their purchases. There are no butchers in the city, and it is a queer sight, Mr. Morrisey said, to see the way the merchants deliver meat to the purchasers. This article is bought by the penny and a piece about as long as one's finger is sold for 2 cents. The meat is not cut into steaks but in huge lumps. Another thing in reference to the meat is that it is all killed the day before used, which, of course, makes it very tough. The beer on the island is kept in a warm place without any ice and is served in that state. Most of the beer is imported from Germany, and it is only recently that American beer has found its way in the country. This is kept in bottles and when it is served to a customer a small piece of ice is dropped into it. The beer drinker may imagine the rest. The natives do not use much of the beer, but are satisfied with the black coffee and wine.

"The money question has not assumed any large proportions in Porto Rico. Very little money is in circulation on the island. The better class of the natives who are supposed to have some money, spend most of their time and money in Spain, and the stores and merchants, as a result, do not get much of their money. These stores are plentifully supplied with goods, but there is no one to buy them. As soon as the United States soldiers arrived on the island the shopkeepers saw visions of money rolling into their pockets. The price on every article in the stores was increased, and what a native would buy for ten cents the American would be compelled to pay one dollar for the same article. The fare on the railroad running from Ponce to Playo, a distance of about three miles, is one dollar for an excursion trip. The natives make the same trip for twelve cents. Every scheme that can be thought of is practiced by the natives in order to get money from the Americans. In the street and at the entrances to the hotels numerous beggars can be found, all asking for money. Nearly all the inhabitants seemed to be engaged in this sort of work, and the sight of them lounging around, even inside the hotels, is disgusting, says Mr. Morrisey. It is a hard matter to get them to work, and their appearance in scarcely any clothes on the streets is a sight.

"The women go about the roads and plantations smoking large cigars, and are not affected in any manner by the weed. Children of both sexes up to the age of twelve years are permitted to roam about the streets naked, while their parents are not much better off. Nothing but a skirt is worn by the women and the men wear ragged shirts and trousers. Shoes are rarely seen in Porto Rico and a native who is lucky enough to have them is the cynosure of all eyes. The women do not know what silks and satins are, and, it seems, are not desirous of knowing. When night comes the men pre pare themselves for bed. This is not hard work, and takes very little time. They tie their heads up in large towels to protect them from the sting of the mosquito, and then lie down in the streets or roads and sleep. These people live mainly on the milk from the cocoanut. Bread is a stranger to them, and very little food is con-sumed by them, except the wild fruits and vegetables which abound in the outskirts of the cities.

"Mr. Morrisey said the soldiers at Ponce were in a fairly good condition, but it is his opinion that it is no fit place for them under the present condition of the country. He said when the soldier is taken down with typhoid malaria or dysentery he loses flesh rapidly, and he can never regain it as long as he stays in that climate."

All this, although it is in some respects different from some of the opinions we have quoted, is very interesting as it is from a recent eye witness, and shows how Porto Rico of the present impressed a very intelligent man.

The fourth town to surrender, previous to the news of the armistice and therefore the general capitulation of the island, was Juan Diaz. There was a report that there were some Spanish soldiers there, and four com-panies of the Sixteenth Pennsylvania were sent to find them. Couriers announced the coming of the Americans to the people of the town, and a brass band came out to meet them. The vast majority of the citizens assembled on the outskirts of the town and as the American volunteers appeared the band played "Yankee Doodle" and other patriotic American airs, while the people cried: "Vivan los Americanos."

A large number had presents of cigars, cigarettes, tobacco and various fruits which they loaded upon the soldiers, and many insisted upon taking the visitors to their homes. Everywhere, the American flag was waving. In the public square the mayor made a speech, in which he said that all the people of Juan Diaz were Americans now, and the crowd shouted:

"Death to the Spaniards!"

While speaking of Juan Diaz, perhaps it will prove of interest to insert the opinion of a correspondent of one of the New York papers as to the women of that town and of Porto Rico in general. He says:

"No one ever walks in Porto Rico. The mule's the thing here. The women ride a great deal. The better class use the English side saddle, although a few prefer the more picturesque and safer, but less graceful, Spanish saddle. In the country districts the pillion is occasionally employed, while among the lower classes many women ride astride without exciting comment. When the natives are both pretty and good riders they display considerable coquetry in the saddle.

"I noticed one rider near Juan Diaz who took my mind back to the old days of chivalry. She was a lovely girl of about fifteen or sixteen, with a face like a Madonna and a figure like an artist's model. One little foot crept out beneath her silk riding skirt, and to my surprise it was devoid of hosiery. The skin was like polished velvet, and was of a pinkish gold of an exquisite tint. It was shod with a slipper of satin or silk, embroidered in color and had an arched instep which made the foot all the more charming by its setting.

"The time to see the women at their best is on Sunday morning, when they ride from their homes to mass in the nearest church or cathedral. On one Sunday morning, while riding leisurely into a small village on my way to this town, I met a crowd of worshippers on their way to mass. Nearly all the women were on mule back, and sat or lolled as if they were in an easy chair in their own homes. A few, probably wealthier than the others, or else delicate in health, were accompanied by little darky boys, who held over them a parasol or an umbrella.

"On Sunday each woman wears a huge rosary, sometimes so large as to be uncomfortable. I saw several that were so unwieldy that they went over the shoulders and formed a huge line, larger indeed than a string of sleigh bells. These are ornamental rosaries and are not used for prayer. The praying rosary is as small and dainty as those used by fashionable women in our own Roman Catholic churches. Besides the fan and the rosary every woman was provided with a neat and often handsomely-bound prayer book and a huge lighted cigar or cigarette.

"This is indeed the land for women who love the weed. A few smoke cigarettes and pipes, but the majority like partajas, perfectos, Napoleons and other rolls of the weed larger than those usually seen in our own land. They smoke them at home and in the streets, at the table or on the balcony, lying in hammocks, or lolling on their steeds, and only desist when within the sacred walls of the church. The moment mass is over and they emerge into the sunlight the first thing the women do is to light a fresh cigar and then climb into the saddle.

"They make a beautiful picture upon the roads.   Imagine an intensely blue sky above, with below rich green vegetables and startling dashes of scarlet, crimson, vermillion, orange and white from the flowers which seem to bloom the year through, setting off the bright hues of the costumes.   It combines the picturesque side of New Orleans life, of Florida scenery, of the Maine lake country, and of the New Hampshire hills."

At Guayama there was even a greater reception than at Juan Diaz. In fact, everywhere, as soon as the people heard of the landing of our soldiers, the American flag was hoisted and kept hoisted, while the Spaniards were driven from the towns where soldiers were stationed.

A large number of Porto-Rican refugees now began to return to the island. These were men who had been engaged in revolution, and had been deported by the Spanish Government. Their progress to their homes was a continual ovation.

The returned refugees had a conference with the leading citizens and there was no doubt in any one's mind but that ninety per cent. of the people was in favor of annexation. They felt that the United States was their deliverer, and they would rather join the American Republic than have self-government.

There was also a conference between the most prominent citizens of Ponce, and Mr. Hanna, the American consul at San Juan.

The Porto Ricans had views which they wished to have presented to the United States, and were anxious to play some part in the new order of things and to hold some of the offices themselves. They were particularly desirous to know about the American school system and as to the possibility of introducing it into the island. They wished that their children should learn to speak English. Mr. Hanna explained the public school system of the United States, and the Porto Ricans were greatly pleased at what they heard. Then they again brought up the question of how they could participate in the reorganization of the island.

"Gentlemen," said Mr. Hanna, "the best thing you can do is to get together and find out just what you want. You have, of course, very good ideas as to what the American system of government is. You no doubt by this time know whether you desire to be attached to the United States as a territory, with a representative in our Congress. You may differ on the point of having Americans for your own officials here during the time that the government that is to prevail here is being put into shape. But you can safely leave your wishes in the hands of President McKinley."

A New York Herald correspondent has some interesting things to say as to the new Ponce, a town which is representative of the entire island:

"Ponce, only yesterday the base for our military invasion, is to-day the American capital in the West Indies. Ponce is deep in the second stage of political evolution.

"Ponce is learning the English language. Ponce is mastering the mysteries of American money. Ponce is inquiring into the methods of American politics. Ponce is preparing to abandon the church schools and adopt our system of education. Papeti, the chambermaid in the Hotel Francais, has already been taught to say, "Vive l'Americano!" Papeti's brother was shot by the Spanish a few years ago.

"El Capitan," the head waiter at the Hotel Inglaterra, has already mastered one hundred words of English, and his fortune is made. Passing down the street just now I heard a Porto Rican mother crooning her naked babe to sleep to the tune of 'Marching Through Georgia.' The Porto Ricans think that 'Marching Through Georgia' is a national anthem.

"As I write the advance guard of the American prospector to this tropical Klondike of ours are pouring up the broad highway from the playa to the town. They came on the Sylvia, the first merchant ship to reach Ponce from the United States since the town surrendered. They seem to have come literally by hundreds.

"I saw many familiar faces among the newcomers.

"Nearly all these men have come here on commercial

enterprises. Porto Rico is a fruitful field. Her agricultural resources, taking the American standard, are as little developed as those of Ohio seventy-five years ago. I imagine the coffee production of the island will be doubled in two years.

''Much American capital will be put into sugar, tobacco and fruits. Many of these men are inquiring about estates in the interior that can be purchased or leased, and about facilities for transportation to the seaboard. This means the building of railroads. Banks are also to be opened in Ponce under our national banking law, and I fancy there will be the liveliest sort of race between rival capitalists as to who shall get the electric railway franchise for the city of Ponce.

''The leading citizens of the island are as wideawake to American enterprise as are these eager gentlemen of the pocketbook who came on the Sylvia.''

Colonel Hill of General Wilson's staff was appointed Collector of the Port of Ponce, and he went very carefully into the subject of the probable resources of the island and what the new tariff should be.

In an interview with the Herald, he said:

''Most of my statistics are still incomplete, but I can give you a few facts, which will unquestionably be of great interest to the business men of the States. In Porto Rico everything is taxed, and most articles are taxed in several different ways. There is an impost duty on flour of $4 a barrel. I think that will be knocked off at once. As you know, this island paid no direct money to the former government of Spain. Everything in the way of salaries, pensions, etc., is paid directly out of the Custom House. The commander of the military forces on the island is a lieutenant-general, sent here from Spain. He gets an enormous salary. Many Spanish pensioners of prominence and rank have been sent to the island, and these pensions are paid by the island. Dignitaries of the church and priests are sent here in large numbers. They are paid out of the Custom House.

"Only yesterday I had an application from the widow of a Spanish general, who is pensioned, for the payment of her usual stipend. I had to take that matter under advisement. The priests here in Ponce applied for their usual salary for July. This, under the Spanish law, is a fixed charge. The matter came before me iu my capacity of judge-advocate on General Wilson's staff. I had to report that inasmuch as we were operating under the Spanish civil law, which made the salaries of the padres a proper payment from the customs funds, the money was due and should be paid or else the Spanish civil law in that respect should be annulled or suspended.

"General Wilson refused to authorize the payment of the priests' salaries, and the matter went to General Miles, who sustained General Wilson. Now here is a very interesting and unprecedented question. As a matter of policy it might be well to pay these salaries for the present. The padres, of course, the next time they address the congregation will say: 'Here is this new American Government which you welcomed with such pleasure refusing to pay your priests. You thought you were going to be relieved of taxation. We must ask you to go into your pockets and pay us yourselves. Thus you have an additional tax placed upon you.' "

But still the clergy, as a rule, were in favor of the United States.

Father Janices, a well-known and most intelligent priest, had this to say in regard to the attitude of the Catholic Church in Porto Rico toward the United States:

"We are neither cowards nor liars. We do not deny that we have always been loyal Spanish subjects, but it is the duty of the Church to save souls and not to mingle in international quarrels.

"With all our hearts we welcome the Americans. Your constitution protects all religions. We ask only for the protection of our Church. The Archbishop of Porto Rico is now in Spain, and the Vicar General of San Juan is acting head of the Church in the island. But we no longer look to him as our ecclesiastical head; but as soon as possible we shall communicate with Cardinal Gibbons and we await his wishes.

"Should any American soldier desire the administrations of a priest, they always shall be at his service. We have determined to become loyal Americans."

Moreover, on September 23, Captain Gardner, in company of General Wilson, called upon the President and made a report in which he elaborated upon the relation of the Church to the government. He stated that while a large majority of the Porto Ricans were Catholics, by profession, they were not offensively zealous. He placed the number of priests at 240, and the annual cost to the public treasury of their support at about $120,000 in American money.

Colonel Gardner, in addition to his report, also presented to President McKinley, an address signed by many of the leading Porto Ricans. The signers expressed their pleasure at the prospect of becoming citizens of the United States, and announced their hope that the Porto Rican people might some day become worthy to organize a State of the Union.

In this hope we are sure all Americans will most heartily join.

CHAPTER XI.

OUR CLAIM TO PORTO RICO.

One great question raised by the recent war was that of territorial expansion, and this question called forth many expressions of opinion both for and against.

There is no doubt, however, but that Porto Rico is ours by the right of conquest, and that it would be a crime from every point of view for us not to retain it.

That we shall retain it, too, now seems certain.

Let us now, in the first place, look back and see what two of our most prominent statesmen have said in the past. They may be looked upon almost as prophets.

The idea of territorial expansion is not a new one. In fact, it dates back half a century, and the thought of this expansion has been silently hatched ever since.

In 1846, William H. Seward, afterward Secretary of State under the administration of Abraham Lincoln, published an open letter under the title, ''We Should Carry Out Our Destiny.''

To carry out that destiny, said Mr. Seward in this letter, the United States should prepare themselves for their mission by getting rid of the Old World which still continued with ideas of another age upon portions of the American soil.

In the same letter Mr. Seward also said that the monarchies of Europe could have neither peace nor truce as long as there remained to them one colony upon this continent.

This Mr. Seward called buying out the foreigners. In 1846 he counted the ruler of Cuba and Porto Rico among the foreigners which should sell out their possessions to the United States.

It was he who during his term of office purchased Alaska from the Czar of Russia for the sum of $7,200,-000. He also negotiated for the acquisition of the Danish Antilles, but this project fell through, chiefly for the reason that at that time the President was opposed to it.

In politics Mr. Seward favored a system which he compared to the ripe pear that detaches itself and falls into your hand.

One thing seemed to him certain, and that was that the United States could not help annexing by force the people who would be too slow to come to them of their own free will.

"I abhor war," he wrote. "I would not give one single human life for any portion of the continent which remains to be annexed; but I cannot get rid of the conviction that popular passion for territorial aggrandizement is irresistible. Prudence, justice and even timidity may restrain it for a time, but its force will be augmented by compression."

It was a half century before the explosion occurred, but when it came its echoes resounded all over the world, carrying joy to some and fear to others, fear of this young giant of the New World.

Again in 1852, in a speech made before the Senate

upon the question of American commerce in the Pacific, Mr. Seward thus addressed his colleagues:

"The discovery of this continent and of those islands and the organization upon their soil of societies and governments have been great and important events. After all, they are merely preliminaries, a preparation by secondary incidents, in comparison with the sublime result which is about to be consummated—the junction of the two civilizations upon the coast and in the islands of the Pacific. There certainly never happened upon this earth any purely human event which is comparable to that in grandeur and in importance. It will be followed by the levelling of social conditions and by the re-establishment of the unity of the human family. We now see clearly why it did not come about sooner and why it is coming now."

At a reception given to his honor in Paris, just after the close of the Franco-Prussian war, Mr. Seward found himself the centre of a group, mostly composed of young Americans.

He had just almost completed a tour around the world, and in answer to a question as to what had impressed him most during his travels, he answered practically as follows:

"Boys, the fact is the Americans are the only nation that has and understands liberty. With us a man is a man, absolutely free and politically equal with all, with special privileges for none. Every one has a chance, whereas, wherever I have been I was impressed with the subjugation and oppression of the people. I had all my life talked in public and private of the greatness of our mission of civilization and progress, of the ideas we represented, and the lessons we were teaching the world, but I never realized how true it was that we were of all others the representatives of human progress. Now I know it. I am sure now, from what I have myself seen, that nothing I have ever said or others have said, as to the destiny of our country was exaggerated. I am an old man now and may not see it, but some of you boys may live to see American ideas and principles and civilization spread around the world, and lift up and regenerate mankind.''

The opinion of another old-time statesman, given some quarter of a century ago, is of vivid interest to-day.

In 1872, when the Geneva Convention was holding its deliberations, Mr. William M. Evarts spoke words of wisdom to a company of distinguished guests at a luncheon given by him at the house in which he was then living.

Among others present were Charles Francis Adams, Caleb Cushing, Morrison R. Waite, afterward Chief Justice; J. Bancroft Davis, Charles C. Beaman, and others of the American Commission.

What Mr. Evarts said was in substance as follows:

''Gentlemen, God has America in his direct keeping, and lets it work out its destinies in accordance with His own wishes and for His own purpose. When the time came and Europe needed an outlet for its surplus energy, God let down the bars and America was discovered. Then little colonies of enterprising and progressive men, seeking freedom from troubles and oppressions of their native land, founded homes along the Atlantic coast. He had let down the bars again for his own purposes. These men struggled and fought and progressed in civilization and liberty until the time came when again the bars were let down and we had the Revolution, and the colonies became a nation. Again the bars went down, and then came the Mexican war, giving the nation the room necessary for its expansion, the space necessary for the homes of the millions from the Old World who sought the freedom of the New. From Atlantic to Pacific that little fringe of people of the colonial times had evolved until they were a great nation. We needed the precious metals, and gold and silver were found sufficient for our purposes. God had let down the bars. But one thing remained, one canker and sore, one great evil which threatened and worried and troubled, but God in His own good time again let down the bars and it was forever swept away, for He allowed the rebellion. He gave humanity and justice and right the victory. He restored the Union, He will heal the sores, He will lead the people to its final destiny as the advance guard of civilization, progress and the upbuilding and elevation of mankind, and in good time the bars will be again let down for the benefit of humanity—when or why we know not, but He knows.''

In the light of recent events, the utterances of these two great men are certainly deserving of the utmost consideration. Both of them really seem to be seers, who, from their observations of the past, saw visions of the future for the native land they loved so well.

The Paris Figaro, in a remarkable article, says that, willingly or forcibly, America must belong to the Americans. The New World must gird up its loins and be ready to fulfill its mission. And this must be done by force when persuasion is not sufficient. And when the Americans shall have rejoined Europe in some portion of Asia, concludes the Figaro, and closed the ring of white civilization around the globe, will they stop or can they stop? That is the secret of the future. Its solution will depend upon what they will find before them— a Europe torn and divided, or, as it has been said, the United States of Europe. At all events, they will have the right to be proud, because they will have carried out their destiny.

Now to turn to an opinion by an Englishman, and be it remembered that England stood by us in a remarkable way from the very beginning of the Spanish-American war and undoubtedly prevented the other European nations from interfering.

The opinion we are about to give is from the pen of Mr. Henry Norman, the special commissioner of the London Chronicle.

Among other things, Mr. Norman says in an article entitled "A War-Made New America":

"The vision of a new Heaven and a new earth is still unfulfilled, but there is a new America. The second American Revolution has occurred, and its consequences may be as great as those of the first. The American people are as sensitive to emotional or intellectual stimulus as a photographic film is to light, but they are also to a remarkable degree, a people of second thoughts. Their nerves are quick, but their convictions are slow. The apparent change was so great and so unexpected that at first I could not bring myself to believe in its reality or its endurance. Unless all signs fail, however, or I fail to interpret them, the old America, the America obedient to the traditions of the founders of the republic, is passing away, and a new America, an America standing armed, alert and exigent in the arena of the world-struggle, is taking its place.

"The change is three-fold:

"I. The United States is about to take its place among the great armed powers of the world.

"II. By the seizure and retention of territory not only not contiguous to the borders of the republic, but remote from them, the United States becomes a colonizing nation, and enters the field of international rivalries.

"III. The growth of good will and mutual understanding between Great Britain and the United States and the settlement of all pending disputes between Canada and America, now virtually assured, constitute a working union of the English-speaking people against the rest of the world for common ends, whether any formal agreement is reached or not."

Mr. Norman goes on to say, after speaking of the possible American army and navy of the present and the future:

"And look at the display of American patriotism.

When the volunteers were summoned by the President they walked on the scene as if they had been waiting in the wings. They were subjected to a physical examination as searching as that of a life insurance company. A man was rejected for two or three filled teeth. They came from all ranks of life. Young lawyers, doctors, bankers, well-paid clerks are marching by thousands in the ranks. The first surgeon to be killed at Guantanamo left a New York practice of $10,000 a year to volunteer. As I was standing on the steps of the Arlington Hotel one evening a tall, thin man, carrying a large suitcase, walked out and got on the street car for the railway station on his way to Tampa. It was John Jacob Astor, the possessor of a hundred millions of dollars. Theodore Roosevelt's rough riders contain a number of the smartest young men in New York society. A Harvard classmate of mine, a rising young lawyer, is working like a laborer at the Brooklyn Navy Yard, not knowing when he may be ordered to Cuba or Manila. He is a naval reserve man and sent in his application for any post 'from the stoke hole upward.' The same is true of women. When I called to say good-by to Mrs. John Addison Porter, the wife of the Secretary to the President, whose charming hospitality I had enjoyed, she had gone to Tampa to ship as a nurse on the Red Cross steamer for the coast of Cuba. And all this, be it remembered, is for a war in which the country is not in the remotest danger, and when the ultimate summons of patriotism is unspoken. Finally, consider the reference to the war loan. A New York syndicate offered to take half of it at a premium which would have given the Government a clear profit of $1,000,000. But the loan was wisely offered to the people and the small investor gets all he can buy before the capitalist is even permitted to invest. And from Canada to the Gulf, from Long Island to Seattle, the money of the people is pouring in."

Mr. Norman concludes his article with these pregnant words, words which will force every man of any brains whatever to pause and think:

"Here, then, is the new America in one aspect— armed for a wider influence and a harder fight than any she has envisaged before. And what a fight she will make! Dewey, with his dash upon Manila; Hobson and his companions, going quietly to apparently certain death, and ships offering the whole muster roll as volunteers to accompany him; Rowan, with his life in his hand at every minute of his journey to Gomez and back, worse than death awaiting him if caught; Blue, making his 70-mile reconnoissance about Santiago; Whitney, with compass and notebook in pocket, dishwashing his perilous way round to Porto Rico—this is the old daring of our common race. If the old lion and the young lion should ever go hunting side by side——!"

Mr. Norman wisely leaves his last sentence unfinished. For no man can predict what the result would be. Would it be the subjugation of the entire world to the Anglo-Saxon race?

After considering what the French and the English have to say, now let us turn to the utterances of the Hon. Andrew H. Green, who spoke purely in the interests of a private citizen, one who desired the retention of the territory acquired by the American Government solely because he wished that the people of the United States should not underestimate the value of their grand opportunities for national enrichment.

"War with Spain," said Mr. Green, in the beginning of his interview in the Sun, "was declared by the authorized authorities, whether wisely or otherwise, it is not now of much profit to discuss. It has been prosecuted with vigor and brought to a successful issue with a dispatch unprecedented in conflicts of equal magnitude. What shall be done with its results? What, in this age of enlightenment and progress, shall we do with the territories and with their peoples and property that the fate of war has placed under our control and guardianship?"

Mr. Green concludes his interview as follows:

"As occasion offered heretofore the American people have insisted upon acquiring and holding territory when the interests of the country required it. Looking at all the precedents, at the present situation, at the signs and needs of the times, there is but little room to doubt that the permanent retention of all territory acquired from Spain will, in the interest of humanity and duty, be demanded with equal firmness. We shall go on in the same course of expansion which we have pursued from our earliest history as an independent nation. We have 'hoisted the mainsail' of the ship of state and started her about the world. While heeding Washington's warnings and the popular interpretation of the Monroe doctrine to keep the people of other nations from getting a foothold on this continent, we shall not pervert their spirit by stubbornly refusing to improve an opportunity to extend and increase our power and our commerce. Every extension of our territory hitherto made has been resisted by a spirit the same in essence as that which now timidly opposes our improving the wonderful opportunities put in our hands by the happy fortune of war; but such opposition has failed of its purpose invariably hitherto, and it will fail now with the American people. The sacrifices of the war will not have been in vain and the victories won by the valor of our navy and army will not fail of their legitimate and well-earned points."

We are a practical people. There can be no doubt about that, but still we are occasionally moved by sentiment, as when we undertook to free Cuba from oppression, but at the bottom of every national action there is a sound practical idea.

It was a pure and unselfish sentiment, however, that impelled us to prevent the extermination of the people of Cuba, a country so near to our own doors, and to demand for them by force of arms, the freedom and independence which was and is most unquestionably their right.

With Cuba freed, the rule of Spaniards in Porto Rico would be both absurd and dangerous. It would be a menace to the perpetual peace between Spain and the United States, which the latter are determined on for the future.

Moreover, as we have seen, Porto Rico wishes most strongly to become an integral portion of the Union, and we desire to receive her as such.

The rule of common sense should be applied, and both sentiment and practicality are united in calling for the conditions which the American Government has demanded as to the former Spanish possessions in the Western Hemisphere.

The war against Spain was inevitable, was just and necessary for the sake of humanity and the progress of the world.   Both our army and navy have shown glorious bravery and heroism, and their marvelous achievements must not be allowed to bring forth no results.

By the fortunes of war a great responsibility has been placed in the hands of the United States, and it would be criminal to shirk in any respect this responsibility.   We must not give back to Spain any portion of the earth in which to continue her abominable misrule. Let the United States move forward to its manifest destiny.

In a powerful editorial the New York Sun declares that our success will make for the world's peace.   We alone were the nation to free Cuba and the other Spanish colonies. No one of the European powers could have come forward to the rescue of the colonies without provoking the enmity and jealousy of the other powers. If we had neglected to discharge our duty, then that duty would probably have fallen to a commission of the European nations. The consequence would have been that Spain would have been superseded in the Spanish

Antilles by a strong European power, which would have led sooner or later to a partition of Spanish America. The United States alone could upset Spanish colonial rule without exciting an uncontrollable outburst of envy and greed in Europe, and occasion a general scramble for the spoils of the New World.

Neither Cuba nor Porto Rico could have been kept by Spain with any assurance of the general safety of nations. So long as the so-called mother country exercised any power there, both the islands would have been firebrands, which, if not aflame, would surely have been smouldering.

The Sun concludes its editorial with these words:

"It is, in a word, for the interest of the whole civilized world that all of Spain's colonies, with the possible exception of the Canaries, should be turned over to us. It is for the world's interests because, in her hands, they always have been, and always would be, a menace to the general peace. If this be true, and that it is cannot be gainsaid, the sooner the transfer is made the better. The fire, which now is localized, should be put out quickly, lest it spread. A thousand accidents, contingencies, inadvertencies, may lead to the very complications which all of the European powers, except Spain, are anxious to avoid. We except Spain because, in putting off the evil day and in postponing submission to the terms which our duty to mankind compels us to impose, she can have no other hope, no other purpose, than to bring about such international entanglements as may cause a general war. Spain alone has anything to gain from such a contest; in it she would at least have allies, and would expect to see her thirst for revenge upon us gratified. The great powers of Europe, however, do not mean to risk an œcumenical convulsion for the sake of a decadent monarchy, which, considered as the trustee of colonies, has been tried in the balance and found wanting. They recognize that, in seeking to evade the sentence of rigorous isolation which the conscience of mankind has passed upon her, she is jeopardizing the peace of the world. For that reason they are exerting and will continue to exert all the means of moral pressure at their command to induce the Spaniards to accept promptly such terms as our Government may offer.''

The people of the United States, after the armistice was declared, were united in one thing, and that was, that apart from the question of indemnity, the one condition of peace, final and unvariable, would in the nature of the case be this:

The surrender and cession to the United States, now and forever, of all Spain's possessions in the western waters of both Atlantic and Pacific.

The fortune of a war begun for the liberation of one people has put it into the power of the United States to liberate several peoples. All this territory, which is ours by right, must henceforth be consecrated to freedom.

Colonel Alexander McClure, in an address at the laying of the cornerstone of the new State Capitol of Pennsylvania, expressed most eloquently the true American feeling in regard to the possessions which our naval and military prowess won from Spain:

"The same supreme power that demanded this war will demand the complete fulfillment of its purpose. It will demand, in tones which none can misunderstand and which no power or party can be strong enough to disregard, that the United States' flag shall never be furled in any Spanish province where it has been planted by the heroism of our army and navy.

"Call it imperialism if you will; but it is not the imperialism that is inspired by the lust of conquest. It is the higher and nobler imperialism that voices the sovereign power of this nation and demands the extension of our flag and authority over the provinces of Spain, solely that 'government of the people by the people, and for the people shall not perish from the earth.'

"Such is the imperialism that has become interwoven with the destiny of our great free Government, and it will be welcomed by our people regardless of party lines, and will command the commendation of the enlightened powers of the Old World, as it rears, for the guidance of all, the grandest monuments of freedom as the proclaimed policy and purpose of the noblest Government ever reared by a man or blessed by Heaven.''

CHAPTER XII.

WHAT THE POSSESSION OF PORTO RICO WILL MEAN.

The heading of this chapter presents a most difficult problem at this time. It would require an inspired prophet to answer the question, and all that we can do is to look at it as dispassionately as possible, and to show the opinions of those who are more or less informed upon the subject. From these opinions the reader must of necessity draw his own conjectures.

Of course, from the very nature of conditions the land is at the present time of writing in a most unsettled state, from a political, commercial and social point of view.

A new element has entered into the lives of the Porto Ricans, and this new element naturally brings with it an unknown future.

The Spaniards and Porto Ricans have but little idea of political tolerance. They are enemies, now, and both seem to think that the opposite party is to be abused, persecuted and even tortured.

Many of the Porto Ricans, on the word of a competent authority, believe that violence to the persons or property of the Spaniards will be acceptable to the Americans. The Spaniards, sharing this belief, live in a constant state of terror, fearing for their possessions and even for their lives.

The withdrawal to an extent of the Spanish troops gave the guerillas full license, and they burned a number of plantations before our forces were put in charge.

Both natives and Spanish, it might be said, were busy in cutting each other's throats. The people became more or less terrorized, and begged for American protection.

About the first of September, Major-General Wilson met at dinner a large number of prominent islanders, and in response to a toast, he made a rather long speech. As this speech was and is of great interest, we make no apology for reproducing almost in full here.

General Wilson said:

"The great Republic, unlike the governments of Europe, has no subjects. It extends its rights and privileges freely and equally to all men, regardless of race or color or previous condition, who reside within its far-reaching dominions. It makes citizens of all who forswear their allegiance to foreign Powers, princes and potentates, and promise henceforth to bear true faith and allegiance to the United States.

"The expulsion of the Spanish power from your beautiful and long-suffering island and the hoisting of the American flag will be followed shortly, let us hope, by the establishment of a stable civil administration, based on the American principle of local self-government.

"The government now exercising supreme authority in the island, you will understand, is a government of conquest, in which the will of the military commander is substituted for that of the Spanish king and Cortes. It does not pretend to interfere with the local laws, except in so far as may be necessary to protect the army of the United States and maintain peace and good order among the people of the island. It looks to the local courts to do justice as between man and man, and to the moderation and good sense of the people themselves for the maintenance of public tranquility, and for the cultivation of that perfect respect for the rights of persons and property which constitutes the foundation of the American system of government.

"It has been wisely said by one of the fathers of the republic that 'That government is best which governs least,' and this is the principle which Porto Rico should keep constantly in view. Government interference is necessary only when the people, instead of confining themselves exclusively to their own particular affairs, presume to interfere with the affairs of their neighbors.

"If every one, high and low, rich and poor, Porto Rican and Spaniard, devotes himself strictly and exclusvely to his own private or official business, eschewing politics and public affairs, for the next year, everybody will find at the end of that time that the island has been well governed and prosperous, and your American fellow citizens will proclaim you worthy of the good fortune which has united your destinies to those of the great Republic.

"Permit me to add that as soon as the Spaniards have evacuated the island, and the sovereignty of the United States is fully established, a military governor will be appointed by the President, and he will govern in the main in accordance with the principles I have indicated.

How long this military government will last must depend largely upon the people of Porto Rico themselves.

"In the natural and regular course of events the military government should be followed by a territorial government established by act of Congress, and this in time should be followed in a few years by a government which shall make Porto Rico a sovereign State of the great Republic, and give it all the rights guaranteed by the constitution of the United States.

"Permit me to add, before concluding, that you are likely to meet with delay in the realization of your hopes from two principal causes.

"It is well known in the United States that Porto Rico is a Roman Catholic country, and there is grave objection on the part of many good people against the admission of a purely Roman Catholic State into the Union. This is based not so much on opposition to that particular religion as on the feeling that the domination of any sect would be prejudicial to our principles of government. We have, perhaps, ten millions of Roman Catholics in the United States, but they are scattered throughout the various States, and intermingled everywhere with the Protestant sects, so that no one has a majority. We have no established Church, and under our policy Congress can pass no act concerning religion or limiting the right of any citizen to worship God as he pleases.

"The result is that all the churches are absolutely free, and none concerns itself with politics. Each watches to see that the other does not get control of the State.

"Now that the Spanish government has been expelled, it can no longer support the Church in this island, hence the Church will necessarily have a hard struggle till it can establish itself on the basis of voluntary parochial support. Meanwhile the Protestant denominations in the United States will have the right to send their missionaries into this inviting field, where they will doubtless receive a hearty welcome, but still the advantage will remain with the Roman Catholic Church, in which the people have been born, married and buried for the last four hundred years.

"Besides, it must not be forgotten that the Church, like every other institution of the island, will surely realize its full share of the benefits arising from the union of the island with the great Republic. It will, therefore, become more liberal and independent, as well as more powerful than it has ever been.

"Fortunately for you, however, every other Christian denomination will from this time forth be free to make converts, establish churches, open schools and circulate religious books and newspapers, and generally to show that it is a worthy teacher and guide to a higher and better civilization than ever prevails where one Church holds undisputed sway.

"The second great menace to the future of the Porto Rican people is the danger of an outbreak of violence and intolerance on the part of one section of your people against another; the danger of insular turning against penisular; of Porto Rican turning against Spaniard, with the torch and dagger, to avenge himself for the wrongs and oppressions, real or imaginary, which have so long characterized the Spanish domination in this beautiful island.

"It needs no argument to show that such an outbreak if it becomes general, cannot fail to bring discredit on your countrymen as a turbulent and law-breaking people who cannot be intrusted with the precious privilege of self-government, and must therefore be ruled by a military commander.

"I firmly believe that the Porto Ricans are a docile, orderly and kindly people, well prepared for a better government than they have ever enjoyed, but you must lose no opportunity to impress upon the United States that you are tolerant and magnanimous as well.

"Your wrongs, whatever they were, have been avenged by the expulsion of the Spanish flag and the Spanish dominion, without exertion or cost on your part, and the least you can do in return is to repress the spirit of revenge and resolve to live in peace and quietude with your Spanish neighbors, respecting their rights of persons and property, as you desire to have your own respected.

"In this way, and in this way only, can you show yourselves to be worthy of the great destiny which has overtaken you, and which, let us hope, is to speedily clothe your island with sovereignty as a member of the great continental Republic.

"Thus, and thus only, can we become fellow citizens

indeed in perpetual enjoyment of our common and inesti-
mable heritage as citizens of the freest, richest and most
powerful nation in the world.'' The Hon. A. H. Green
speaks as follows of the present condition of Porto Rico:

''The problems that force themselves upon the attention at the outset are those of government and of finance.
The first question that naturally arises is, what shall be
done with these possessions? How shall they, with
their unassimilated populations, be cared for? The presence of a military force will doubtless be an immediate
necessity. It should be administered in the mildest
form, unless riot and disorder otherwise require, and be
controlled by officers humane and intelligent, inclined
to encourage at the earliest practical time the inauguration of a civil rule which shall gradually and as rapidly
as may be found wise invite an official participation of
representatives of the indigenous populations. Can this
be done? Let the doubting and the timid recall what
has been done, and is now doing toward improving the
conditions of the peoples of the East and ask themselves
whether America is not likely to be equally successful
in caring for those whose destinies she has assumed to
direct; whether it is not her duty to enforce order and
to keep the peace among peoples who by her acts have
been left disorganized and defenseless, a prey to the internecine strifes of barbarous chiefs and to the intrigues
of roaming banditti? And have not experiences in as-
similating Spanish territories hitherto successfully annexed or conquered proved abundantly our ability to
do all this?

"It is natural enough that conservative minds should adhere to the traditions of the past, but times are changed, and the wisest of our forefathers were not able to foresee what the workings of centuries might effect. The atrocities to which the inhabitants of Cuba have been subjected in the past two or more years aroused the indignation of the civilized world.

" 'Their moans, the vales redoubled to the hills,
   And they to Heav'n.'

"The financial problem, which is already command ing the serious attention of the Government, is next in order. How are the great expenditures of the war to be recouped? Shall we, in addition to territory acquired, demand cash indemnity? If the care of these acquisitions is to be as costly as some suppose, it would not be an unreasonable requirement. While we shall lose the revenues derived from imposts upon importations into the United States from these possessions, which were not large, this will be more than compensated by the duties which we can impose upon importations from other nations into them. In making up the estimates of the whole financial situation it will be safe to assume that at first our Government outlays will exceed income; our people, however, will have the profit of furnishing products of the United States to an added population of 10,000,000 to 12,000,000, freed from the duty that we can impose upon the imports of other nations. Of the $10,000,000 in value of imports into the Philippines from all countries, we supplied less than $200,-000, while we took from them nearly $5,000,000.

"The interests of the people who gain their living and manual labor are among the first to be considered and jealously guarded. Fortunately the far greater part of these in America are engaged in employments, which will be benefited by annexation. A fresh and unrestrained market is to be opened for our products, and the indigenous products of these regions are to be brought here free of duty to give added employment to our factories. No competitions of labor are to arise."

As to our new acquisition of new colonies by the United States, Theodore S. Wolsey, Professor of International Law at Yale University, has this to say, and every word he utters is pregnant with meaning, for no one could be a more capable judge:

"It has already been said that England learned the lesson of the American Revolution, while Spain has never heeded it nor the loss of her own colonies. Yet it really was not until fifty years ago that their methods sharply diverged. As early as 1778 Spain had begun to open her dependencies to foreign trade, and early in this century they were allowed to trade with one another. So, likewise, although great changes had been earlier made in the English colonies, the spirit of monopoly and of a restrictive policy was in force until about 1815. So far as relates to the evils of the colonial system, then, the two were not very unlike. But into the field of administrative reform and the grant of autonomous powers to her colonies, Spain never has entered. The abuses of the early part of the century characterize also its later years. Discrimination against the native-born, even of the purest Spanish stock; officials who regard the colony as a mine to be worked, not a trust to be administered; forced dependence upon the mother country for manufactures, even for produce, so far as duties can effect it; self-government stifled; representation in the Cortes denied or a nullity; a civil service unprogressive, ignorant, sometimes corrupt—compare these handicaps with the growth, the prosperity, the independence, above all, the decent and orderly administration, of the colonies of England. One of the wonderful things in this half century is that army of British youth, with but little special training or genius, or even, perhaps, conscious sympathy for the work, learning to administer the great and growing Indian and colonial empire honestly and wisely and well, with courage and judgment equal to emergencies, animated by an every-day working sense of duty and honor, but not very often making any fuss or phrases about it. It is not that Spanish colonial government is worse than formerly, which is costing it now so dear, but that it is no better, while the world's standard has advanced and condemns it. Never yet has Spain looked at her colonies with their own welfare uppermost in her mind. She has never outgrown the old mistaken theories. Her fault is medievalism, alias ignorance.

"It is not a cause for wonder, therefore, quite apart from special sources of discontent, that Cuba, which, by position is thrown into contact with progressive peoples, should chafe at her leading strings. Without reference to the corruption and cruelty, arrogance, injustice and repression which are alleged against the mother country, without rhetoric and without animosity, we may fairly say that Spain is losing Cuba, perhaps all her colonies, simply because she has not conformed to the standard of the time in the matter of colonial government. If England had not altered her own methods, her colonies would long since have abandoned her as opportunity offered. The wonder really is that Spain has held hers so long; for Cuba, at least, owing to its exceptional fertility and position, has relatively outstripped its declining mother.

"There remains the moral of the story.

"If we are not mistaken as to the fundamental causes of Spain's colonial weakness, other colonial powers must take warning also, and the United States in particular, if it yields to the temptations, or, as many say, assumes the divinely-ordered responsibilities, of the situation. For its protective system is a derivative of the mercantile system, as the colonial system was. If it becomes a colonial power, but attempts by heavy duties to limit the foreign trade of its colonies, if it administers those colonies through officials of the spoils type, if it fails to enlarge the local liberties and privileges of its dependencies up to the limit of their receptive powers— if, in short, it holds colonies for its own aggrandizement, instead of their well-being—it will be but repeating the blunders of Spain, and the end will be disaster."

Colonel Hill has declared that the heavy burdens under which the business world of Porto Rico has been staggering in the past have been almost inconceivable.

Something of this has already been said, but it may be well to give Colonel Hill's views, as he is certainly a most competent judge. The colonel says that in the first place there has been a tax on every ship that comes in and goes out. There has been a heavy tax on all articles of impost and a special tax on all articles not enumerated in the tariff. In addition to that, an additional tax of ten per cent. on the bill was added. Each hackman who plied between the port and the town of Ponce had to pay a tax of eight dollars a month. No person could write a letter to an official without first going to the collector and purchasing a certain kind of official paper, for which he must pay fifty cents to one dollar a sheet. The price was regulated by the rank of the official who had to be written to.

The effect of all this was rather to increase the number of complaints from citizens than to increase the revenues of the island.

To General Ernst, who was the officer in command of the territory of Coamo, a large number of protests were made. In especial, a delegation of twelve to fifteen citizens called upon the general to request the removal of the alcalde, on the ground that he had been an officer in the Spanish volunteer army, and was unsatisfactory because of his former connections. The gentleman, however, had gracefully accepted the new condition of affairs and was performing the duties of his office earnestly and faithfully. These facts General Ernst was in possession of and he was forced in consequence to deny the request of the delegation.

For his own protection and to remove any false impression there might be in the public mind, General Ernst issued the following proclamation, which was printed in both English and Spanish:

"Headquarters 1st Brigade, 1st Div.,
   1st Army Corps, Camp Near Coamo,
      Porto Rico, September 3, 1898.
To the People of Coamo and Neighboring Districts:

"To prevent misunderstanding as to the rights and duties of the various members of this community, you are respectfully informed:

"1. That no change has been made in the civil laws of Porto Rico, and that none can be made except by the Congress of the United States. The present civil authorities are to be obeyed and respected.

"2. That no prejudice rests against any citizen, whether in office or not, for having served as a volunteer, if he now frankly accepts the authority of the United States.

"3. That the persecution of persons simply because they are Spaniards, or Spanish sympathizers, will not be tolerated. They, as well as the Porto Ricans, are all expected to become good American citizens, and, in any event, they are entitled to the protection of the law until they violate it.   O. H. Ernst,

"Brigadier-General Commanding."

About this time President McKinley promulgated through the War Department the revised customs tariff and regulations to be enforced by the military authorities in the ports of Porto Rico.

In general, the regulations for Porto Rico were practically the same as those promulgated for Cuba and the Philippines. The one important difference was that trade between ports in the United States and ports and places in the possession of the United States in Porto Rico be restricted to registered vessels of the United States and prohibited to all others. It was provided that any merchandise transported in violation of this regulation should be subject to forfeiture, and that for every passenger transported and landed in violation of this regulation the transporting vessel should be subject to a penalty of $200.

This regulation should not be construed to forbid the sailing of other than registered vessels of the United States with cargo and passengers between the United States and Porto Rico, provided that they were not landed, but were destined for some foreign port or place.

It was further provided that this regulation should not be construed to authorize lower tonnage taxes or other navigation charges on American vessels entering the ports of Porto Rico from the United States than were paid by foreign vessels from foreign countries, nor to authorize any lower customs charges or tariff charges on the cargoes of American vessels entering from the United States than were paid on the cargoes of foreign vessels entering from foreign ports.

The regulations as to entering and clearing vessels and the penalties for the violation were the same as those fixed for Cuban ports in the possession of the United States. The tonnage dues were reduced, as in Cuba, to twenty cents per ton on vessels entering from ports other than Porto Rican ports in the possession of the United States, and two cents a ton on vessels from other ports in Porto Rico. The landing charge of $1 per ton was abolished, and the special tax of fifty cents on each ton of merchandise landed at San Juan and Maya-guez for harbor improvement was continued.

As in Cuba, the Spanish minimum tariff was to be collected. On most articles, however, this was much higher than the minimum tariff which was imposed by Spain in Cuba. The differential in Porto Rico imposed on goods imported from countries other than Spain was much smaller than in Cuba, so that under Spanish rule there was not a wide difference between duties on goods from countries other than Spain imported into the two islands. Under the operation of the President's orders imposing the minimum tariffs in both islands the effect wouldbe to tax most articles much higher in Porto Rico than in Cuba. As in Cuba, a tariff was imposed on to-bacco, manufactured tobacco, cigars and cigarettes equivalent to the internal revenue taxes imposed in the United States.

Richard Harding Davis says that there will be no such complications in Porto Rico as those which exist in Cuba for the United States troops there were not allies. They were men who came, were seen and con-quered. The revolutionary leaders had no share or credit in their triumphal progress.

Now to examine into what Porto Rico offers for American enterprise and capital.

In the first place, United States Consul Hanna has been flooded with letters from fortune hunters. He strongly advised all of them to remain at home until the Americans were in complete control. Now, let us examine what one or two competent authorities have to say of Porto Rico, so far as American enterprise is concerned.

Here is the opinion of a man who has lived in Porto Rico for several years and who knows of what he is speaking:

"We take Porto Rico, too, at a time when everything favors increased prosperity. It has not been ravaged and wrecked, like Cuba, by war. Its foreign trade in 1896, amounting to $36,624,120, was the largest in its history, the value of the exports then, for the first time in over ten years, exceeding that of the imports. Of course the main trade has always been with Spain, but the trade with us stands next, and during the year in question was over two-thirds of that with Spain. Of late, it is true, our trade with Porto Rico has been relatively declining, being far less than it was a quarter of a century ago. During the reciprocity period of a few years since it increased somewhat, but after that it fell off again. It is important to note, however, that our exports to Porto Rico have kept well up of late years, the falling off in total trade being due to the decline of our imports, so that now the exports are not far from equal to the imports, instead of being much inferior as formerly. It is a noteworthy fact that the exchange from both countries is mostly of products of the soil. That is the case with ninety-nine hundredths of Porto Rico's exports to us, sugar and molasses comprising 85 per cent., with coffee coming next, and it is also true of over three-fifths of our exports to Porto Rico, among which breadstuffs and meat foods are prominent.

"But with Porto Rico fully ours, and the discriminations enforced by past laws in favor of Spanish trade wiped out, there must be a change in the currents of her commerce. We shall expect to furnish the chief markets for her products, and on the other hand to send to the island more food products than ever, more machinery, textile fabrics, iron and steel. Her capabilities will be developed, perhaps notably in coffee cultivation. Her peaceful and industrious people will welcome American enterprise and capital, American progressive methods, and free institutions. Indeed one of the most striking events of this year was the extraordinary enthusiasm with which American troops were greeted all along the southern shores of the island. It was as if the people could already forecast the great future in store for them, under American laws and the American flag."

A correspondent of the New York Evening Post, who signs himself by the initials A. G. R., speaks with authority as follows:

"The prominence given to the island by the events of recent months has led many of our people to think it of vastly greater importance, commercially, than it really is. Consul Hanna, who is back in his old quarters in

San Juan, has a small wheelbarrow load of letters from all parts of the United States, asking detailed information upon all conceivable lines of trade, manufacture and profession. To answer them according to the terms of their requests would be the work of a short lifetime. But they indicate the widespread interest of American business men in Porto Rican mercantile affairs. Every steamer arriving here brings its group of American passengers. Some are visitors who make the trip only through curiosity. The majority come with an idea of some form of business, either in the shape of a speculative flyer, permanent investment, or a commercial or industrial establishment.

"A large percentage of those who come are young men, who have just about enough money to get them here, to keep them here for a week or two, and then get them home again. These come in the hope of finding immediate employment, of catching on to something which will maintain them. They invariably go home again. The island is no place for such. None but the capitalist, the investor, or the business man with money for his business, should come to Porto Rico with anything more in view than an outing or a vacation. As things are at present, there is little enough to interest the capitalist or the investor. The man who is looking for a job should look for it at home; his chances are infinitely better than they are here. There is absolutely nothing for the position hunter, for the clerk, or for the workman. In time there may be something, but it will be, at the least, many months before such opportunities are open, and even then they will be few. Until then the case is hopeless, and those who come will but do as their predecessors have done—go home again, poorer and wiser men. If a young man can afford to spend a couple of hundred dollars in the purchase of that particular form of wisdom, the opportunity is open to him here on this island. If he cannot afford it, he will do better not to risk it.

"Merchants will find nothing to do here, except to glean a certain amount of information of rather doubtful accuracy, until the question of tariff rates shall have been definitely settled. There is now nothing on which to base any plans or calculations for business operations. The native merchants are complaining seriously. They are waiting to place orders for hundreds of thousands of dollars' worth of goods to replenish stocks which have been depleted through many months of uncertain trade conditions, and are losing business which they have been led to expect would be open to them almost immediately after the American occupation of the different cities in which they are located. Nor is it at all easy for an American to obtain any definite information or accurate details regarding any particular line of business and its possibilities. Local commercial methods are not reduced to the system which prevails among American business men. The Porto Rican merchant buys and sells, but I fail to find evidence of that close study of business and business methods by which the American merchant increases his trade and his profits.

"The entire trade of the island is of no very great

magnitude. The local trade in local products is chiefly confined to the morning market for table supplies, which is held in all the cities and larger towns. The total imports and exports hardly reach a gross amount of thirty millions of dollars a year, and the imports exceed the exports by a couple of millions. I have been unable to find any statistics which I was willing to accept as wholly reliable. So far as I can learn, no complete report has been submitted by the United States Consul, and there are discrepancies which I cannot reconcile in the published reports of the English Consul and those of the Dutch Consul. I can, therefore, only give figures which are approximate, though they are sufficiently close for general purposes.

"Cotton goods appear to be the largest item among the imports, and they represent a trade of two or three millions of dollars, varying from year to year, according to the prices and the success or failure of the crop products of the island. Rice is imported to the value of one and a half to two millions of dollars. Flour, chiefly from the United States, approximates three-quarters of a million dollars. Dried, salt and pickled fish, of which Canada seems to obtain the lion's share of the trade, represents a million to a million and a quarter. The United States has the major portion of a trade in pork and pork products which about equals the fish business.

"Woollen goods are, naturally, of but limited consumption in so warm a climate, and the trade is probably less than $150,000 in amount. Agricultural implements represent a business of three to four hundred thousand dollars. Boots and shoes, almost exclusively from Spain, represent some five or six hundred thousand. Chinaware, glassware, lumber, coal, soap, furniture and other articles of general use and consumption represent amounts varying from one to three or four hundred thousand dollars.

"The most astonishing thing in the whole list of importations is the item of vegetable and garden products. These are imported into this country, which is in itself but a natural garden in which can and should be raised every form of vegetable necessary or desirable for consumption, and the annual value of the imports approximates $400,000 and the weight 7,000 tons. The island uses $150,000 worth of imported candles and $50,000 worth of imported butter yearly. It uses two to three hundred thousand dollars' worth of cheese, of which the Netherlands have, for the last few years, furnished much the greater part. Uruguay and the Argentine supply it with one to three thousand tons of jerked beef annually. Wines, beers, and liquors take something more than a half a million a year out of the country.

"Among Porto Rican exports coffee is the heaviest item. This reaches an average valuation of some $10,-000,000 a year. Sugar ranks next, and approximates three to four million dollars. Tobacco goes to the extent of some half a million, and molasses touches about the same figure. Hides, cattle, timber and fruit are represented in the list, but their value is comparatively inconsiderable. Guano to the extent of half a million a year appears in the reports for some years, but I am unable to account for either the article or the amount. Some corn has been sent to Cuba, some native rum to Spain, and some bay rum to France and to the United States.

"It will thus be seen that, as yet, the island offers but a comparatively limited amount of business, either in buying or selling. Under wise laws, and a just and equitable system of taxation, with a suitable railway system and improved highways, and with the ports of the United States and of the islands open to the exchange of commodities, free of duty, a very material increase of the business of the island will inevitably follow. It is quite possible to double the trade within the next ten or fifteen years. There will be some wild-cat speculation, some unwise investment and some loss to investors. The schemer and the promoter will find victims who will put their money into companies whose future is wholly hopeless. But along with that there may reasonably be expected a steady growth and improvement. But it will come by gradual increase and development, and not by a sudden bound."

According to Mr. William J. Morrisey, a prominent real estate dealer of Brooklyn, who spent some time in Porto Rico, the island is no place for an American to invest any money at present. He says that the place can be made to pay, provided the United States Government clears the entire island of Spaniards and fills the towns and cities with the American people.

Mr. Morrisey also states that the natives of the cities are desirous of becoming American citizens, but that out in the country, it is far different. These people are constantly in fear of the Americans, and their sole desire is to dispose of their property as soon as possible and return to Spain. The more enlightened of them are of the opinion that the United States Government will banish all the Spaniards from the island and thereby make it more agreeable for the residents.

A dispatch of the Evening Post says that in view of representations made to the War Department that the municipal councils in Porto Rico were making hay while the sun shines, and granting business franchises right and left under the Spanish law empowering them to do so, orders were recently issued to General Brooke to put a stop to the practice forthwith, and the announcement was given out that on the evacuation by the Spaniards, and our assumption of military authority in the island, no more of these loose grants would be made. Meanwhile American shippers were in a state of mind over a lack of ships with which to conduct the normal commerce of this country with Porto Rico. The change of status for the island, from being a foreign possession to a port of the United States coast, had made the rigid regulations of our coasting trade applicable to it, and the purchase of so many of our coasting vessels by the government for use as transports, coalers, and the like, had embarrassed the progress of coast commerce not a little. The regulations had to be suspended on two or three occasions to let in ships which seemed absolutely necessary, and now the question came up whether it would be best to suspend the regulations altogether or to have each separate vessel which needed American papers apply to Congress for special legislation.

There was another question, and a very important one, which came up, and that was how far Louisiana and other sugar-producing States would be affected by the annexation of Porto Rico.

In no State in the Union does a single interest play so important and so peculiar a part as the sugar industry in Louisiana.   Fully two-fifths of the inhabitants of the State are more or less interested in sugar, and any great disaster to the crop would injure ninety per cent. of the population in southern Louisiana.

So far as Porto Rico goes, it is very doubtful if it will injure Louisiana in any way.   As has been said before, the island is densely populated, small in area, and with little additional land available for sugar.   It is by no means probable that it will increase materially in its sugar production.   American laws will militate against the importation of contract labor, and will therefore prevent any undue competition.   As the New York Sun very justly observes, the bugbear of the Louisiana sugar planter is not territorial expansion, but the war taxes and the possibility of their permanent adoption, bringing with it the reopening of the old tariff agitation, which they supposed was permanently closed.

Taking it all in all, territorial expansion has certainly no terrors for the Louisiana planters.

With the evidence we have given, it is easy to see what Porto Rico has to offer, or not to offer, to Americans.

With their usual manana, the Spaniards have been slow to evacuate the island, but a decisive stand has been taken by the President.

The chief intent of the administration is to clear the island of Spaniards, put at work American methods in sanitary, civic and economic administration, and, for the purpose of doing this without annoyance, to have forces enough for police duty.

The day fixed for the hoisting of the American flag over San Juan and the complete and permanent occupation of Porto Rico by the military forces of the United States was October 18.

It was possible for the Administration of the United States to take this step by virtue of war powers and of the establishment of the fact that Porto Rico is to be wholly and permanently American.

At the present time of writing Porto Rico is still a foreign country, so far as the laws of the United States are concerned, and until changed by Congress, customs duties will be collected on imports from the island. So, too, with the navigation laws, and American ship-owners are warned to secure registers for foreign commerce before entering the Porto Rico trade, as vessels with only coasting enrollments and licenses will be subject to penalty on their return to the United States.

On the 18th of October, promptly at noon, the flag was raised over San Juan.

An excellent description of the proceedings has been given in the Boston Herald, and reads as follows:

"The ceremony was quiet and dignified, unmarred by disorder of any kind.

"The 11th regular infantry, with two batteries of the 5th artillery, landed. The latter proceeded to the fort, while the infantry lined up on the docks. It was a holiday for San Juan, and there were many people in the streets.

"Rear Admiral Schley and General Gordon, accompanied by their staffs, proceeded to the palace in carriages. The 11th infantry regiment and band, with troop H of the 6th U. S. cavalry, then marched through the streets, and formed in the square opposite the palace. At 11.40 A. M. General Brooke, Admiral Schley and General Gordon, the United States evacuation commissioners, came out of the palace with many naval officers, and formed on the right side of the square. The street behind the soldiers was thronged with townspeople, who stood waiting in dead silence.

"At last the city clock struck the hour of 12, and the crowds, almost breathless, and with eyes fixed upon the flag pole, watched for developments. At the sound of the first gun from Fort Morro, Major Dean and Lieutenant Castle of General Brooke's staff hoisted the stars and stripes, while the bland played the 'Star Spangled Banner.'

All heads were bared, and the crowds cheered. Fort Morro, Fort San Cristobal and the United States revenue cutter Manning, lying in the harbor, fired 21 guns each.

"Senor Munoz Rivera, who was president of the

recent autonomist council of secretaries, and other officials of the late insular government were present at the
proceedings

"Congratulations and handshaking among the American officers followed. Ensign King hoisted the stars and
stripes on the Intendencia, but all other flags on the
various public buildings were hoisted by military officers.
Simultaneously with the raising of the flag over the captain-general's palace many others were hoisted in different parts of the city.

"The work of the United States' evacuation commission was now over. The labors of both parties ter-
minated with honor for all concerned."

After the parade the bands and various trade organizations went to General Henry's headquarters. General
Henry in a speech said:

"Alcalde and Citizens: To-day the flag of the United
States floats as an emblem of undisputed authority over
the island of Porto Rico, giving promise of protection
to life, of liberty, prosperity and the right to worship
God in accordance with the dictates of conscience. The
forty five States represented by the stars emblazoned
on the blue field of that flag unite in vouchsafing to you
prosperity and protection as citizens of the American
Union.

"Your future destiny rests largely with yourselves.
Respect the rights of each other. Do not abuse the government which accords opportunities to the individual
for advancement. Political animosities must be forgotten in unity and in the recognition of common interests.

I congratulate you all on beginning your public life under new auspices, free from governmental oppression, and with liberty to advance your own country's interests by your united efforts."

General Henry then introduced Colonel John B. Castleman, who spoke with great effect as an old Confederate.

The alcalde replied in part:

"We hope soon to see another star symbolic of our prosperity and of our membership in the great republic of States. Porto Rico has not accepted American domination on account of force. She suffered for many years the evils of error, neglect and persecution, but she had men who studied the question of government, and who saw in America her redemption and a guarantee of life, liberty and justice.

"Then we came willingly and freely, hoping, hand in hand with the greatest of all republics, to advance in civilization and progress, and to become part of the republic to which we pledge our faith forever."

When the Spanish flag was hauled down all over the island and the Stars and Stripes raised in its place, General Brooke became the chief executive of Porto Rico. Actually, but not in name, he was the military governor of the island. The plan of a military governor for Porto Rico, to hold until the Washington authorities deem it wise to substitute a purely civil administration, has not been fully arranged. From October 18 until the plan of the Government has been put into effect, General Brooke, or the military officer who will succeed him if he asks for detachment, will be in supreme control of civil and military affairs. It is the intention, however, of the Government here to have as little of the military element as possible in the administration of affairs, and so to all intents and purposes a civil administration will be in operation from the time the Spaniards surrendered authority.

Still, when all has been said, it is perfectly sure that in the end Porto Rico will become one of the most important of our possessions. Superstition and tyranny will be driven from this most fertile island, and hope and peace, under the Stars and Stripes, will be brought to the thousands so long under foot.

Hail, therefore to Porto Rico! And some day may it become a bright star in the flag that brings protection and freedom to all!

(THE END.)

www.ingramcontent.com/pod-product-compliance
Lightning Source LLC
Chambersburg PA
CBHW021752110726
47902CB00006B/1494